THE VIPER'S NEST ROADHOUSE & CAFE

SEANA KELLY

The Viper's Nest Roadhouse & Cafe

Copyright © 2023 by Seana Kelly

Ebook ISBN: 9781641972468

KDP POD ISBN: 9798865839071

IS POD ISBN: 9781641972819

NYLA Publishing

121 W. 27th St., Suite 1201, NY 10001, New York.

http://www.nyliterary.com

Titles by Seana Kelly

The Sam Quinn Series

The Slaughtered Lamb Bookstore & Bar
The Dead Don't Drink at Lafitte's
The Wicche Glass Tavern
All I Want for Christmas is a Dragon (novelette)
The Hob & Hound Pub
Biergarten of the Damned
The Banshee & the Blade (novelette)
The Viper's Nest Roadhouse & Café
The Bloody Ruin Asylum & Taproom

The Sea Wicche Series

Bewicched: The Sea Wicche Chronicles
Wicche Hunt: The Sea Wicche Chronicles

For Roseann, Mary Beth, and Monica
We all need people in our corner to love
and support us. These woman are always
firmly in my corner.
I am so very lucky and grateful.

ONE

What Does One Wear to a Biker Bar?

I wasn't positive, but the closets in the new house seemed even larger than the ones at the nocturne. How was that possible? We'd moved into the Seal Rock house last week, and I couldn't love it more. We'd taken a three-story apartment building, gutted it, and then transformed it into a two-story Tudor masterpiece. *We,* of course, was Clive and the magical architect and construction crew. I had little to do with it, as I'd been working at The Slaughtered Lamb. And avoiding death. I did, however, insist on final approval of the library.

Clive had kept me updated on the progress of the remodel, and that had been enough. I'd told them I wanted lots of windows at the front of the house—tinted to cut down on UV rays that were deadly to vampires, of course. The second-floor windows had shutters installed that dropped ten minutes before sunrise. Would all those windows mess up the traditional Tudor design? Probably, but our architect has skills and was able to alter the plan just enough to give us amazing views of the green running from our home to The Slaughtered Lamb and the ocean beyond. He'd even given us extra windows looking out at our back garden, as well.

I'd requested a fenced backyard for Fergus, expecting a lawn and some shrubs. Clive, never one to half-ass it, called in an incredibly talented landscaping crew to transform the front and back yards into romantic English gardens, bursting with life and color. Giddiness bubbled up inside me every night as Fergus and I walked home after work to this idyll waiting for us.

Earlier today, Stheno had stopped by the bar to let me know her new place, The Viper's Nest Roadhouse and Café, was ready for a soft opening, and she expected me there. Apparently, she and her sisters Medusa and Euryale had been acquiring properties all over the world for centuries. Euryale loved the business end of things, loved envisioning what could be and then making it happen. The other two rarely got involved. They just appreciated there was always enough money to buy a case of wine with dinner. Each.

All of that is to explain why I was standing in my room-sized closet, staring at an embarrassing amount of clothing and accessories. My gaze kept snagging on the sundresses. I never wore those things. I'd been wearing jeans and long-sleeve tees to cover my scars for so long, I was having a hard time considering anything skimpier.

Dave's dad had recently agreed to erase the scars I'd accrued on his son's behalf while in Hell. With a wave of his hand, though, both old and new scars had disappeared. I was still getting used to it.

"What does one wear to a biker bar?" I asked, having heard Clive moving around the bedroom.

"Hmm?"

When I ducked my head out of the closet, I found him in the sitting area before huge windows showcasing a purpling sky over raging surf. Fergus sat beside him, his head resting on the arm of the chair, Clive's fingers absently scratching the top of our overlarge dog's head.

Clive's gaze was fixed on his phone before he looked up and smiled, body relaxed, legs shot out, and ankles crossed. Sometimes he just took my breath away. He had a face chiseled by the gods, with stormy gray eyes and burnished hair. He wore a black t-shirt that was molded to his broad chest, with black jeans and scuffed leather motorcycle boots.

"Sorry, darling. What did you say?"

"I'm just trying to figure out what to wear to a gorgon dive bar on the docks." How was this my life, and how did he look so sexy just sitting there doing nothing? It wasn't right.

"One of the things I enjoy about seedy establishments is the lack of a dress code. All are welcomed if you have a bit of the ready. Be it ballgown or bikini, you won't raise an eyebrow. It's quite freeing." His phone buzzed.

I turned back to the closet, exasperated. "You put more clothes in here. Every time I turn around, there are more clothes." Grumbling, I moved back into the closet. I could always do my usual jeans and a hoodie. That'd be comfortable.

Clive leaned against the doorframe. "I hate to break it to you, but as I said when you first moved into the nocturne, that wasn't me. I don't flip through catalogs, picking out clothes for you. I love you, darling, but couldn't care less what you wear." He moved in farther and began opening drawers. "Except the leather pants. I'm quite partial to those."

"Wait. If you aren't filling this closet, who is?" I mean, I guess Audrey would be okay, but the closet had been filling up before Audrey joined the cool kids.

"Godfrey," he said, pulling out the black leather pants and draping them over the bench in the middle of the closet.

"Godfrey?" I paused, considering. "What?"

"It's true. He's quite the clotheshorse and I believe he enjoys dressing you up." Clive sat on the bench and crooked his finger.

"No. I need to get dressed." I felt a clench low in my abdomen. Just looking at him was making me needy. Stupid sexy vampire.

"There's time. We're not expected to clock in." He crooked his finger again and I relented. Pulling apart my robe, he ran his hands up and down my body. "Exquisite," he murmured. He leaned forward, caught my nipple in his mouth, and dragged me onto his lap. Okay, fine. There wasn't much dragging involved. We did discover that it was a very sturdy bench, though.

Later—much later—I was back to the original question: What to wear? I had my leathers in one hand and jeans in the other. This was stupid. It was summer. Granted, San Francisco summers were often chilly, but not today. It had been hot today and was still quite warm out.

I stood, indecisive for a moment, and then internally slapped myself. No backsliding. No hiding. I was strong and capable, also it was too hot for a hoodie. Dropping both pairs of pants, I stomped across the closet floor, yanked a sundress off a hanger, punched my arms through, and wrenched it down as though the garment had insulted my whole family. It wasn't the damn dress's fault I still had a lot of anxiety surrounding my body. The stupid pretty dress hadn't done anything.

I sensed movement and turned to find Clive leaning and watching.

"You don't need to push yourself. If you aren't ready for a sleeveless dress, pick something else." He gestured to the huge closet. "Whatever you'd like."

"I'm being a baby." It was just a stupid dress.

He moved to me, ran his fingertips down my bare arms, and then pulled me into a tight hug. "You most certainly are not. For someone else, it might be just a dress. For you, it's baring a part of yourself that you've kept hidden for eight years. It's your decision when and if you ever decide to wear clothes like this. What I do know is that nothing needs to be decided tonight. You have your whole long life to mull it over."

I snuggled in and squeezed him tightly, my eyes falling on a light denim jacket. "Maybe I'll do both," I said, grabbing the jacket and sliding it on. "My arms are covered but I have the option of taking it off."

"Good. Now—" he said, looking around, "—where are your blades?"

While Clive buckled my sword's scabbard around my waist, I slung on the thin, flat leather sheath for my axe. The head of the axe lay in the center of my back, the handle sticking up over my left shoulder. Both blades and sheaths had been spelled to disappear when I put them on. I didn't want to scare people, walking down the street fully armed. I paused a moment at the mirror to make sure they were invisible. Clive slid his arms around my waist, holding me in place before resting his chin on my right shoulder.

"Beautiful."

I looked everywhere but in the mirror before elbowing him to let me go. Mirrors made me uncomfortable. The old reflection in my mind's eye was always too close to the surface: my red-eyed, brutalized face and savaged body.

Clive kissed my neck, spinning me away from the mirror and into his arms. "That's not you anymore, love." Lifting a hand, he wrapped his fingers around my jaw, his thumb brushing back and forth along my cheekbone. "I'd thought you so fragile when we'd first met." He shook his head. "Stupid of me. You're a warrior, a titan." Leaning in, he kissed me softly. "You never give up. No matter what's thrown at you, no matter what abuse you have to endure, you get back up and keep fighting."

I grinned, embarrassed. "It's just a dumb dress."

"It's a lovely dress, but that's not all it is, and you and I both know it." Kissing the tip of my nose, he asked, "Now, what are your thoughts on motorcycles?"

Fergus ran to the elevator door to ride down with us, but I stopped him. My poor ninety-pound baby didn't enjoy being left home alone. I gave him a hug and a scratch, promised we'd be home soon, and then went to the treat drawer. He followed me, plopping his butt down and looking up adoringly. His gaze wandered to the as-yet unopened drawer before snapping back to me.

"You can nap on your favorite couch while we're gone." I opened the drawer, pulled out a bully stick, and handed it over.

Our departure already forgotten, he flopped down in his bed and began to chew. "I love you, little man. Be good."

We took the elevator down to the garage, where all of Clive's cars were showcased. When the doors opened, a vintage motorcycle waited for us.

"I didn't know you rode these?" I circled the black and white two-toned beauty. "Pretty."

"It most certainly is not," he said, sounding put out. "This is a Harley Davidson 1965 Electra Glide. She has a seventy-four-inch, fifty-five horsepower, OHV V-twin engine that—" He stopped when he noticed me grinning.

"No," I teased. "Tell me more. What kind of transmission does it have?"

Rolling his eyes, he handed me a helmet and then put on his own. It felt weird and bulky, like I was a human bobblehead. Clive tapped something on his helmet, and I heard, "All right, darling?"

"Yes. This is so cool."

He got on the bike and then told me where to put my foot before I swung my leg over the seat. When he started it up, thunder echoed off the walls, making me jump.

He pulled my arms tightly around himself, saying, "Hold on."

All of his vehicles had a chip in them that communicated with the garage door. Clive barely had to pause as he drove us under the reinforced garage door and out onto the street. The door closed a moment later, our home locked up tight.

"I haven't driven this in a while. Do you mind if I take the scenic route?"

It was exhilarating and terrifying all at once. "Sure." Note to self: don't wear dresses on motorcycles. I had to hold on with one arm while I tucked the skirt tight around my legs. Turning my head to the side, I leaned into Clive's back and watched San Francisco fly by.

He took us through Sea Cliff—where the dragons lived—before meandering around the Presidio. He looped round the Palace of Fine Arts—where we were married—making me smile and squeeze him a little tighter. The Marina, through Fishermen's Wharf, and then down the Embarcadero, past the Ferry Building and finally to Pier 50. Stheno had said the Viper's Nest was right next to a big *Port of San Francisco* sign.

We found the joint easily enough. The dock was dark, the yellow streetlights not up to the task of illuminating anything beyond the streets. Flashing in the near dark was a neon sign. *The Viper's Nest Roadhouse & Café.* A coiled green snake blinked on and off, its head seeming to bob back and forth. Perfect.

Clive parked his motorcycle near the others. A couple of men standing outside took an interest without making it obvious.

Should we be worried about someone stealing your bike?

He smiled, giving me his hand to help me off. *They could try.*

Stheno had been talking with me about the new place, so I knew a lot of work had gone into remodeling the old tavern and getting it ready to open. To look at it, though, it appeared to be the shittiest of dive bars, the windows blacked out, the paint peeling, what appeared to be a sizeable bloodstain on the concrete near the front door.

"Clever," Clive murmured. "Give customers a safe walk on the wild side."

The guy on the door flexed his muscles as we approached. He was dressed all in black, like Clive, but his motorcycle boots were beat to shit. "IDs," he grunted.

I took a sniff as I flipped open my wallet, showing him my new license. He was full human, which told me the clientele must be human as well. This guy might have been taller than Clive and built like a truck, but he was no match for a supernatural.

Meager light from bare bulbs dimly illuminated the bar. Black vinyl booths lined three walls. The wood used for the booth frames and scattered tables was worn, with threats, offers, and physically impossible commands carved into surfaces. The bar lay opposite the door, a wall of bottles glowing behind the bartenders. Incongruously, a refrigerated pie display stand rotated baked goods at the far end. The light inside the display case was the brightest in the room. Unsurprisingly, I now craved a piece of lemon meringue pie.

Shouts nearby made me jump. Clive pulled me out of the way just as a large man almost barreled into us. He hit the doorframe and dropped instead. The bouncer was there a moment later, hauling the bleary-eyed man with blood dripping from his nose out the door. Stheno wiped down the bar, threw back a shot, and waved us forward. "What'll you have?"

TWO

No Poaching!

C live and I took two empty barstools on Stheno's side. Pounding my fist on the gleaming wood, I said, "Barkeep, give me your finest cherry cola! Pronto."

Stheno glared with one eye, her left hand rising threateningly to her eye patch. Stheno, one of three gorgon sisters, had been hired to be my bodyguard when Clive and I had traveled to New Orleans for vampire shenanigans. Stheno and I had been ambushed one evening. She'd already turned quite a few vampires into statues, so when they attacked, they were prepared and went for her eyes. Now one was on the fritz and the other—the one under the eye patch—was a perpetual death ray. It was why she wore the patch. She wasn't looking to lay waste to all of San Francisco. Unless we pissed her off, that is.

"All right, all right. Jeez. Cranky. Any soda of your choosing would be lovely. Thank you."

A very distinguished Black man with perfect posture and a commanding presence was sitting beside me. I had no idea who he was, but he was definitely a supernatural and an incredibly powerful one. My whole right side tingled.

Switch seats with me. I have no idea who he is either, but I'd be more comfortable sitting between you.

No. It's okay. Stheno wouldn't endanger me. It just feels weird, not bad or dangerous.

A tall glass of soda slid to a stop by my hand. Stheno hadn't moved. Glancing to the left, I saw a very familiar mountain of a man who bore a striking resemblance to Thor.

"What the heck are you doing here?" I'd just left Fyr at The Slaughtered Lamb an hour ago.

He shrugged one beefy shoulder. "I like to keep busy. Besides" —he gestured to the bar with his towel— "I'm more comfortable with this clientele." Fyr didn't like our fae customers. The fae had worked with a vampire to keep him imprisoned for far too many years.

I turned to Stheno, glaring right back. "You're poaching my people?"

Stheno smirked. "Only a couple."

"*Couple*? Who else?" This was bullshit. I needed all my people.

With a flourish of her hand, she directed our attention to the refrigerated case at the end of the bar. "Dave makes our pastries."

Dang. That was a really good idea. Dave had always been a great cook, but since meeting Arwyn, my newly found wicche cousin who was a magical baker, artist, and psychic, his baking had gone next level. She'd sent him tutorial videos as payment for some demon work he'd done for her and now he was kicking ass in the baking realm.

Catching Fyr's gaze, I asked, "You're not quitting The Slaughtered Lamb, are you?"

Shaking his head, he poured two beers from the tap and then walked them around the bar to a corner booth, placing the beers in front of two muscular dock workers whose shirts were sweat-stained and straining at their biceps. One was wearing a knit beanie over dark curly hair. The other had short reddish hair. Sitting between the men was Stheno's sister Medusa, an overlarge wine glass in front of her. Medusa, like Stheno, had beautiful olive skin with golden-brown eyes, and long black corkscrew curls— curls that occasionally lashed out when she was angry.

As Medusa's glass was empty, Fyr grabbed one of the bottles lined up on the wooden frame of the booth. Opening it, he poured the entire bottle's contents into her glass and brought the empty back behind the bar, dropping it into the recycle bin.

"Hey, she has a glass like the one I got you." With the way the sisters drank wine, it only made sense to have extra-large glasses around.

Stheno lifted a wine glass from a shelf under the bar, identical to her sister's. Winking her one good eye, she drank it down and then replaced the glass. "Euryale bought the company that makes those. We'll always have proper-sized glasses now."

I felt the man beside me chuckle.

"Oh, sorry." Stheno reached across the bar and patted the arm of the man. "Djehuty, these are the two I was telling you about. This is Sam and her husband Clive." She glanced at us while gesturing to the man. "And you two, this is Djehuty." Leaning in, she added in a whisper, "He's a god so don't be assholes."

No wonder my side was buzzing. I was sitting next to a god! Was I supposed to curtsey? He turned his head and met my gaze. It was like a punch to the solar plexus. I let out a sharp breath, my body buckling in on itself. Clive was suddenly between us, his arm around me, pulling me from the stool.

"Sir," I said, trying to catch my breath, "it's an honor to meet you." *I'm okay. Don't anger the god.* I didn't want him getting into a brawl with a deity.

"Apologies, child. I'm afraid I've become careless. Most aren't as sensitive to me as you seem to be. I've buttoned myself up. It's safe for you to look upon me now." His voice was deep, almost musical, with an accent I didn't recognize.

Hesitantly, I looked up and let out a breath. It was okay now. His hawkish features had softened, his gaze less intense. He had sharp cheekbones and a pointed chin, close-cropped hair and broad shoulders. I couldn't wait to get home so I could look him up and find out which god we had visiting.

"You may call me Thoth." He wore a loose white shirt over

loose black pants and seemed to be drinking some kind of tea. "Stheno was telling me a bit about you. Where I come from, there are no wolves, but we have hyenas who, like yourself, are tied to the moon and therefore me."

Clive held out his hand and shook Thoth's while my brain raced. Hyenas, not wolves. Africa? Moon god? *Shitshitshit.* Who were we dealing with?

Buzzing in Clive's pocket derailed my thoughts. He excused himself to go outside and take the call, leaving me with our new friend.

"So, what brings you to San Francisco?" I wasn't great with small talk in the best of circumstances. This guy exuded so much power and strength, I was shaking on my barstool.

"Stheno and I have known each other for a great many years. We enjoy dropping in on one another and catching up. When she told me about you, I was intrigued and decided to visit." He took a sip of tea before we both turned to the angry voices at the far end of the bar.

One of the bikers was getting into it with a longshoreman. Fyr leaned over the bar and slapped a hand on the aggressor's chest, pushing him back. "Knock it off." The men grumbled in an effort to save face but knocked it off.

"The tall young man you were speaking with earlier?" He paused.

"Fyr? George Fyr?" I sat up straight, wanting to make a good impression.

Thoth nodded. "Fyr. Yes. He's quite effective. Some of the men here tonight are exhibiting hyper masculine behaviors. The markings on their skin, the leather clothing, the roaring vehicles. And then this other group who work on the docks are short-tempered and seem to be quite territorial about this bar. I don't anticipate these two groups mixing well."

Stheno slid a bowl of nuts in front of us. "That's because this used to be a seedy hole-in-the-wall for dock workers. When we bought the place, we bought the whole building, including the two empty storefronts next door. We gutted the whole thing and built it back as the beautiful roadhouse you see today."

The sound system was loud for supernatural hearing, but the humans seemed to be digging it. When the song changed, a woman squealed and a biker dude picked her up and placed her on a tabletop to dance.

Stheno rolled her eyes. "No."

Fyr walked around the bar again, stood in front of the woman, and held out his hand to help her down. She pretended not to see him for as long as she could before laughing and stepping down. Fyr wiped off the tabletop and returned to the bar.

Some people were dancing, but most were standing around talking. The lucky few were sitting in booths, eating slices of pie.

I was studying the display case, trying to decide what to order and if three pieces were too many, when Stheno and Fyr raised their heads and stared in the direction of the front door.

A man staggered in. I would have assumed he was drunk, but I smelled it now too. Blood.

Clive followed the man in, his brow furrowed. When the man started to go down, Clive caught him and half carried him to a nearby booth. A few people noticed and moved out of the way.

"Is he okay?" a woman asked.

Clive shook his head. "I don't believe he is. He appears to have lost a great deal of blood. Stheno, you should call the authorities."

Thoth murmured to Stheno, "I smell vampire."

"Oh, my husband—" I began.

"Not him," Stheno said. "Fyr?"

He nodded and picked up the phone.

"I swear," Stheno grumbled under her breath, "if some rogue bloodsucker starts picking off my customers, there's going to be hell to pay." She pulled out her phone and swiped through screens before lifting it to her ear.

Lowering her voice even more, she said, "One of my customers just staggered in here with a bite on his neck and without the blood necessary to live." She paused. "Well, he didn't sell it."

Pause. "We smell your kind." Pause. "We've already called the human authorities," she said before disconnecting.

"Fuck," Medusa ground out.

Stheno shook her head. "There goes opening night."

And then the stench of death hit.

The vampires arrived before the cops, but just barely. They only had a moment to study the man and catalogue scents before the police were pushing through the front door. Music off, lights up, customers were questioned and released quickly.

Clive, on the other hand, was treated to a far more intense interrogation. He had been, after all, outside in the parking lot with the man, following him into the bar. He was also the one who'd caught him. From the cop's point of view, he must have seen something.

We all—the supernaturals, that is–listened in on the interrogation.

"Were there a lot of people in the parking lot?" A detective, who looked to be an Asian man in his thirties, with short dark hair and a goatee and who wore a navy suit, was crouched beside the dead man. Wearing a glove on one hand, he opened the man's jacket, searching his pockets.

Two uniformed officers stood by the door, talking in a whispered conversation.

"...second one this week," the one with dark curly hair said.

"I heard the coroner found a bite mark on the first one's neck," the guy with sandy-colored hair said.

"A bite? Like a cannibal was chewing on him? What the fuck?"

"No. Like"—Sandy curled two fingers and tapped his neck— "like a vampire bite."

"Shit. You idiot," Curly scoffed. "Your girlfriend reading those vampire romances again?"

Sandy laughed. "I love it when she does."

The detective stood and gestured to Curly. "Check on the ETA of the coroner." He then walked over to the booth where Clive was sitting and slid in across from him. The detective checked the small notebook in his hand. "Mr. Fitzwilliam, I'm Detective Lee. We appreciate your cooperation." He checked the notebook again. "Given your address, can I assume the vintage Harley out there is yours?"

"It is," Clive said.

"Nice. This seems like an unusual spot for a man like yourself." Clearly, he was on a fishing expedition.

Clive smiled. "Not at all. The Viper's Nest is owned by my wife's friend. We're helping to celebrate the opening."

"I see." He made a note. "And you were outside when this man arrived? What were you doing at the time?"

"Talking on the phone."

"Who with?" he asked.

Clive tipped his head to the side, studying the detective. "How is that pertinent?"

THREE

Just the Facts

The detective smiled without humor. "Everything is pertinent in an investigation."

"I see. I was speaking with a friend, Russell Jones."

More notes. "When did you first notice the victim?" The detective leaned back in his seat, his focus on Clive.

"As I was walking back in, I noticed him holding onto the wall, staggering toward the door."

"Had you ever seen him before?"

Clive shook his head. "No. I have no idea who he is."

Detective Lee nodded and made a note. "What did you think when you saw him hanging on to the wall?"

"I wondered if he'd had too much to drink and was perhaps ill with it." Clive slowly drummed one finger on the table.

Detective Lee stared at Clive's finger and then asked, "Did you see the victim in here drinking? At the bar or in one of these booths?"

"No. As I just said, I'd never seen him before."

"You're sure?" the detective asked again.

"Positive."

"Hmm. Odd." The detective flipped back through his notebook. "How about Elise Chabot? Do you know her?"

Shit. I saw it the minute the detective said her name. Clive recognized it.

"Elise? Of course I know her. She used to work for me. Has something happened to her?" Clive leaned forward, pinning the detective with a glare.

"What sort of work did she do for you?" he asked, his expression that of a cat playing with a mouse.

Clive shook his head, clearly annoyed. "My liaison. Executive assistant. Why? Has something happened to her?"

"This man, though—the one you followed in and grabbed when he fell—you don't know him?" Lee said again.

"No. Detective, as I've stated multiples times now, I do not know that man. I caught him when he fell because I didn't want anyone to hurt themselves in our friend's establishment. That's all." Clive was pissed, but he wasn't influencing the detective. He was keeping his powers in check. Good Master vamp.

"See, that's what seems so strange to me because if that was true, why would he be carrying your business card in his pocket?" The detective held up a clear evidence bag holding one of Clive's cards.

Clive shook his head slowly and then closed his eyes. "She's dead, isn't she? That's what you aren't telling me." Swearing, he rose from the table.

"Mr. Fitzwilliam, I'm not done." The detective stood as well.

Clive held up a finger. "A moment." He turned to me. "Darling, call our lawyer." He swiped through and placed another call. "Something's happened to Elise. Please see what you can find out. Someone's fucking with me and I think they've hurt her… Yes. Thank you." Disconnecting, he turned to me.

I told our lawyer what was going on and he said to tell Clive to stop talking and he'd be here shortly.

"I just have a few more questions," the detective began.

I hopped off the stool to stand beside Clive. "Leon says to wait for him."

Clive nodded. His phone buzzed and he swore, handing it to me.

> Godfrey: Elisa is dead. She was found exsanguinated in her apartment. A bite mark was visible on her neck.

"Is there a reason you need a lawyer, Mr. Fitzwilliam?" Detective Lee didn't appreciate being dismissed.

When Clive turned, rage clear on his face, the detective took a step back. "We both know the card means nothing. I can produce invoices that prove I've owned hundreds of those cards and have been giving them out for over a decade. One of them could have come into his possession in a myriad of ways. If you want to continue this discussion, it will need to be through my lawyer."

The look on the detective's face said he knew this was his last shot. He had nothing on Clive and we all knew it. "Do you know what that mark on the side of his neck is?"

"His neck?" Clive went to the body and leaned close, studying the wound, his brow furrowed as though trying to puzzle it out. If I didn't know my husband was a vampire, I would have totally bought it. "Precise punctures... syringe marks? Some kind of taser?" He shrugged. "This isn't my area of expertise. I assume your doctors would know better than myself."

It got chaotic after that. The coroner arrived, along with forensic techs. On their heels came our lawyer, who shut it all down.

Wouldn't it be better to get it all over with now? It's not like you and Leon can go to the station for more questions in the morning.

What I said was true. If I was too accommodating, it would have been suspicious. Am I one of those killers who likes to insert himself into the investigation? If I'd shut him down immediately, was it because I had something to hide? I helped with what I could and when he seemed to be overstepping, I called my lawyer. Even after that, though, I still answered one more question. I'll remain on his suspect list, but I'm hopefully not at the top.

I don't like this, Clive. Why are the bite marks still visible? Why your business card?

I have no idea, but we'll find out. Someone seems to want to implicate vampires in general and me in particular. They went out of their way to stop it from healing.

Is it even a vampire?

The scent is vampire, but not one I know.

And Elise?

He nodded at whatever Leon was telling him. *Elisa was Norma before Norma. She was my human liaison. She met a man, fell in love, and her desire to join my kind changed. They were married three years ago. They had an evening wedding so we could attend. Her family situation was fraught, so she asked me to give her away.*

Aww.

She was pregnant with their first child.

Oh, Clive, I'm so sorry.

He patted Leon on the shoulder in farewell before turning back to me and crossing the near empty barroom. *As am I.*

Stheno, Thoth, Fyr, Medusa, Clive, and I were the only people besides cops left in the bar. Fyr removed the bar towel he kept tucked in the waist of his jeans, dropping it into the soiled linens bucket behind the bar. Stheno freshened up Thoth's tea, shaking her head at the scrum of cops at the front door.

"Eh, look at it this way," Medusa said, keeping her voice low, "night one and we have a reputation. This place is killer."

The corner of Stheno's mouth quirked up. "Our ads can end with *Enter at your own risk.*"

"Anyone know who he is?" I asked.

A round of head shaking followed.

"Boss, if we're done, I'm going to take off," Fyr said.

It took me a minute to realize I wasn't the *boss* in question.

Stheno waved him off and he rounded the far end of the bar, disappearing down a dark hallway.

"Sam and I need to leave as well," Clive said. "It may not have ended well, but up until that man collapsed, you seemed to have a hit on your hands."

Stheno sighed and drained her large glass of wine. With a shrug of one shoulder, she said, "Fucking bloodsuckers. Do we know who got him and why they left him here?"

Clive shook his head. "We do not, but we plan to find out."

"Good. Let me know when you do," Stheno responded.

"Sorry," I said. "I love the place, though."

Her face softened. "Thanks, kid."

Overcome by my nearness to a god, I turned to Thoth. "It was an honor to meet you, sir." I held out my hand, but he shook his head.

"I hope we get to spend more time together while I'm visiting. I don't think it would be a good idea to touch you, though, given our issue earlier."

"Of course." I dropped my hand and hopped off the stool.

Clive shook for both of us. We skirted the officers and techs on the way out and were through the front door a moment later, Detective Lee's gaze never leaving us.

Unlike when we'd arrived, the parking lot was empty of all but cop cars and a big white van. Clive gunned the engine, and we were off. Through the microphone in the helmet, he said, "I was on the phone with Russell because he received a request from Garyn's people to visit the nocturne tonight."

I gripped his waist tighter. I'd known it was coming, but I'd really been hoping she'd forget for a century or two.

He patted my hand. "We don't have to go, if you'd prefer. We're no longer associated with the nocturne. I thought it would be better to see her tonight than wait for her to come looking."

It had turned cold while we'd been in the bar—or I was scared. Either way, I plastered myself to Clive's back, using him as a wind-break. "Plus, waiting for her to make the first move leaves us looking weak."

"Precisely." He turned left and we began our zigzagging ascent to Pacific Heights, where the nocturne was located. "We show her she doesn't scare us, try to find out why she's here, and go on our way."

"Okay." My stomach wobbled again, for a different reason. Garyn was Clive's maker. She was super old—older than Clive's thousand years—and scary powerful. Clive had sought the dark kiss after his sister had been brutally raped and murdered by three men. They had left her body in the woods, barely a quarter of a mile from Clive's family farm.

He'd been sure the men were the Atwoods, a father and two sons. When he'd confronted them, they'd almost beaten him to death. One of the sons had kicked him in the gut, saying how much Clive was like his sister, before they'd ridden off.

Clive's mother had died, grief-stricken, within three months. His father's heart had given out the previous harvest season, so with his sister and then mother's deaths, Clive had been left alone. In the silence of his cabin, the need for vengeance burned white hot in him. He couldn't allow those men to walk free.

The Atwoods were a wealthy and therefore powerful family. They employed most of the village, other than a few scattered family farms like Clive's. No one was going to hold them to account if it meant losing their jobs and being unable to feed their own families.

I didn't know how he'd met her, how he'd known what she was—

I didn't, he said mind to mind, picking up on my thoughts. *I'd been drinking heavily in a tavern, drowning my sorrows but also plotting how I would kill them. I was weaving on the dark road home, my brain sloshing in my skull, when she just appeared in my path.*

She led me off into the trees and then nothing. Now that I'm on this side of the fangs, I know she mesmerized me. The next morning, I woke up in my bed. The evening before was fuzzy and I assumed the lightheadedness was from drinking too much.

We were only a couple of blocks from the nocturne, so he pulled over to finish his story before we arrived.

I worked in the fields all day, still preoccupied with how to get at the

Atwoods. I'd started late and was therefore finishing up late. I'd intended to walk to the tavern for a hot meal but was still feeling off. At midday, I'd had some stew that had been simmering over the fire all day. I didn't have a hand for cooking, though, and it was dreadful.

I was contemplating just having more of that rather than walking to the village center, but then I saw the shutters were open and there was a silhouette in the window. Again, I don't remember anything more and again, I woke in my bed in the morning.

Isn't that unusual? I interrupted. *I thought you guys fed from different people because it was harder to wipe the minds of people you came back to again and again.*

It is. She didn't seem to care that I'd begun to remember her eyes, her face, her voice. She fed from me every night for over a week. During the day, sweating in the sun, I worried for my sanity.

She was stalking you.

Yes. I think she'd decided she wanted to collect me, so the next night when she came, she didn't blind me to her. She arrived on my doorstep and talked with me about unparalleled strength and speed, an eternal life that was nearly impossible to snuff out. I'd wanted that, wanted to have the power to destroy the men who'd taken Elswyth from us, who'd brutalized that kind, sweet, gentle girl.

I'd accept whatever came afterward. I'd assumed an eternity of damnation, but I didn't care. There needed to be justice for what they'd done to our Elswyth. I agreed and then I was on the floor, her mouth at my neck. Pain. Fiery thirst. Blood lust that consumed me for days, weeks.

Finally, my mind and body were back under my own control and there I was, in an earthen basement in a small, derelict cottage in the woods. Garyn was with me, and so our lessons began.

Why do you think she wanted you? That wasn't a spur-of-the-moment decision. She kept coming back night after night for you.

No idea. She did have a strange habit, now that I'm thinking about it, of petting me. It wasn't sexual. It was the way you sometimes pet Fergus, the way a mother pets the hair of a favorite child.

Huh. Do you think she's here now because she misses you?

Doubtful. I've been gone for quite some time. He fired up the engine. *I guess we'll find out soon enough.* He drove the remaining blocks to the nocturne.

Meeting this woman had me jumping out of my skin. If she was Clive's maker, did that mean she was more powerful than him?

FOUR

I've Missed Them

The vamps on the gate were already opening it as we came around the corner, their heads bowed. Clive may no longer have been the Master of the City, but he still commanded their respect. He drove through, accepting their deference as his due. Some habits were hard to shake.

He started to make the turn around the nocturne, heading for the garage, when he remembered himself. He was a guest now, not the Master. Spinning the bike, he cut the engine on the far side of the slate drive. He could play it off as leaving room for Garyn's cars, but I was sure he'd forgotten.

He held out an arm to help me balance, but I had this now, dismounting easily. I took the helmet off and put it in one of the two storage boxes at the rear of the motorcycle. Clive put his in the other.

"Can you teach me to drive one?" I was kinda loving this thing.

Grinning, he leaned in and gave me a kiss. "I can and will. And you're right. I did forget."

"Hey, stop it." I slapped a hand over my forehead.

"Not my fault. You're projecting rather loudly tonight." He wrapped an arm around my waist.

"I am?" Ugh. Garyn and the dead guy had me all worked up.

Are we sure Garyn doesn't have something to do with framing you for the dead guy?

I'm not sure of anything, but I can't imagine why she would. Flaunting our existence to authorities is verboten. I'm wondering if it's someone connected to one of the members of the nocturne I expelled when I learned they were in league with Leticia. That seems more likely than a woman I haven't seen in an age. My people knew I adored Elise.

Those guys were real dicks.

Indeed. We'll deal with that later. Tonight, I need you on your toes, on edge and hyper-vigilant. We don't want anyone to read or manipulate you. Put up your mental blocks. While I doubt she had anything to do with such a flagrant flaunting of our existence, we aren't safe with Garyn in town.

"Come, darling," he said, fully aware that every vampire in or out of the nocturne would hear him. "They're expecting us."

Walking hand in hand to the portico and open door, I began, brick by brick, to resurrect my mental block. I hadn't even realized I'd let my guard down. My aunt, who had loved to invade my thoughts and trap me in visions, was gone. Clive and I were happy, so very happy, squeezed into my tiny apartment behind The Slaughtered Lamb, in our dragon-made folly, and now in our new house. Finvarra, the fae king, occasionally sent assassins after me—long story—but they couldn't manipulate my mind.

I hadn't even realized that I was no longer blocking. That needed to change tonight.

The vampy butler inclined his head as Clive and I passed him. "The Master is in his study, sir."

Sir was so close to sire. I wondered how difficult it was for the vamps who'd sworn their allegiance to Clive—for some of them, hundreds of years ago—to switch that allegiance to Russell. The long-lived often didn't do well with change.

It was so strange being back. Some things I missed, like our bedrooms upstairs, the library, the study, sitting around brainstorming with Russell and Godfrey, and Norma, the human liaison who got me whatever I wanted. Good times.

I did not, however, miss the fact that a good ninety percent of the vamps hated my guts and wanted me gone, preferably dead. Less good times.

Clive was right, though. When I'd lived here, I blocked hard, not just because of my aunt, but because the vamps' loathing was unrelenting.

The study was the same and yet not. The furniture was the same, but the decorations, the little treasures on the shelves, now reflected the new Master. Something bluesy played in the background, helping to muffle our voices from any overly interested vamps.

Russell, Godfrey, and Audrey stood when we appeared at the door.

Coming around the desk, Russell opened his arms for a hug. This was new for us. While Clive was Master, Russell was his loyal second, keeping me at arm's length and referring to me as Miss Quinn. Now he was the Master and could do as he wished.

I walked into his arms and squeezed hard.

"How are you, Sam?"

It still caught me off guard when he used my first name. Grinning up into his dark, handsome face, I said, "Good. Clive said he'd teach me to drive a motorcycle."

"Oh, no," Godfrey laughed. "I wouldn't recommend that."

I looked over Russell's arm to glare at Godfrey. "What's that supposed to mean? I have excellent reflexes and balance."

"You do, Missus. The problem is the fae king sending his soldiers to take you out. At least in a car, you can run them down. On a motorcycle, you'll bounce off them into the road." Shaking his head, he turned to Clive. "Bad idea, S—Clive."

Godfrey had been with Clive the longest. For him, the change of address was probably the most difficult.

Russell patted my shoulder and then let me go, reaching for Clive's hand.

"Welcome to you both." Russell gestured to what had been my

bench along the side wall and had, since Clive stepped down, become our bench.

"Not so fast, Missus." Godfrey held out his arms and I hugged him as well.

"I've missed you guys." I waved a hand toward the door. "The rest of them not so much, but you guys yes."

Audrey stood back and watched.

Letting go of Godfrey, I took a step toward her. "What are your thoughts on hugs?"

She laughed. "Oh, I'm very much in favor of them, ma'am. I mean Sam."

I gave her a big hug and then stepped back, taking in her outfit. "You look fabulous. I know these guys are all about the black suit thing, but this? Gorgeous."

She smiled, her hands brushing down the soft draping fabric of the one-button charcoal jacket over wide-legged trousers.

"Those shoes!" I smacked Godfrey's arm. "Hey, since I hear you're my closet fairy, I want those shoes." They were a take on men's wing tip shoes: chunky-soled black and white leather with a thin accent of sky blue, the same sky blue she wore under her jacket. Color! She was wearing color. The silk camisole was the same summer sky blue as Audrey's eyes.

"You look amazing," I said. "Stylish with a side of badass."

She started to duck her head and then remembered herself. Standing straight, she looked me in the eye and said, "I appreciate that." Audrey had been a ladies' maid when she'd been turned. The vampire had then mentally controlled her so that she wore the yoke of servitude for another two hundred and fifty years. She'd only recently been freed of that invisible cage, though, and some habits were hard to break.

"Speaking of nice togs, do you like the dress?" Godfrey asked.

"Yes." I sat on the bench with Clive while they resumed their seats. "How did I never know that you were the one filling my closet?"

Godfrey shrugged one shoulder while brushing lint off his

perfectly tailored trousers. "Beats me. I clearly have the best taste in clothing—present company excluded, Audrey. Clive had originally asked Sire to pick you up some clothes, so you'd know you were welcome here. Thankfully for you, I told him he could pass that task to me." Godfrey laughed.

"Could you imagine," he continued, shaking his head. "Our current Master would have purchased a dozen pairs of black jeans and matching t-shirts. Done. Our former Master suggested more baggy blue jeans, silly long-sleeve tees, and running shoes."

"I wanted you to be comfortable as you are. Or were." Clive patted my knee.

"Yes, yes. Very sweet. The fact remains you look great because of me. And you're welcome."

Godfrey grinned and I couldn't help but laugh. He was right.

"So, tell us how the folly is coming." Russell barely spared a glance at his mocking third. They'd been together for at least a hundred years. He was used to it.

"The Shire is complete," Clive explained. "It looks incredible. You're all welcome to visit and see for yourselves."

"Yes," I jumped in. "You each have your own hobbit holes. If you want to get away from all this, we have a Middle-earth village you can visit."

Godfrey stretched out his legs and turned back to Russell. "Sire, I've been meaning to ask. When do I get some vacation time? I'm owed at least a decade."

"What are they working on now?" Audrey asked.

Clive grinned. "Mind you, we're not allowed to be anywhere near where they're working, but we might have sneaked around one night and saw the next space." He held my hand, rubbing his thumb back and forth. "It's looking remarkably like the farm I grew up on. It's uncanny. I had the strangest case of déjà-vu. Like I should tie my hair back and hook up the plow."

Godfrey shook his head, scoffing. "You're oddly romantic about grueling physical labor. When will we get the tropical island and magical ocean? That's what I'm waiting for."

"I don't even know where they'll fit it?" I said. "With the Shire and Middle Ages Canterbury, how do they fit an island and ocean too? I'm so worried houses are going to start falling into sinkholes, crashing though the sky of our folly."

"I asked that question," Clive said. "Granted, no one wanted to speak to me, so their response was quite brief, but it amounted to, 'It's magic. Fuck off.'"

Godfrey and I laughed.

"Meanwhile," I said, "you all need to come visit the Seal Rock house. We just moved in and it's perfect!"

Russell nodded. "Once our visitors have left, we'd love to."

The mood in the room deflated. We were all together tonight for a reason, and it wasn't to catch up.

"Have you learned anything more?" Clive asked.

Russell sighed. "No. The Historian is tracking down the expelled. As you know, we have people in the police department who can pass us information, but we've learned nothing new on these two deaths."

"Saliva," Godfrey prompted.

"Yes," Russell continued. "They found saliva at the neck wounds. They're currently testing DNA, hoping to identify the killer. No matches or familial connections so far. As for Garyn, she seems to be traveling with her entire inner circle, which is odd. At least to our way of thinking. Perhaps she has no enemies who will attack while she, her first, second, third, fourth, and assorted others are on another continent, but from what we've heard, she's unconcerned."

"Hopefully," Godfrey put in, "it'll be a quick how-do-you-do in the foyer and then we'll send them on their way."

Russell nodded slowly, fingers drumming on the desk.

My phone started buzzing in my jacket pocket.

Godfrey looked around the room. "Who could be calling you? We're all right here."

"Ha ha. Dumbass. I have friends." The call was from Arwyn, a Corey wicche cousin I'd just found out about. She was a clairvoyant and an amazing artist. Tapping the screen, I said, "Hi."

"Something dark is coming for you," she hurriedly said. "It's almost there. Be careful. The nightmare woke me."

Every vamp in the room was staring intently at my phone.

"Is it a vampire?"

She breathed slowly for a moment and then said, "Old power and blood. A bottomless well of longing. Protectiveness with a— what is that I'm feeling?—with a resentment and... maybe fear? I'm not sure. I'm feeling hollowed out, empty. Envy and hidden grief. A perfect veneer hiding a void." She let out a sharp gust of breath, like she'd just been punched in the gut. "She's there."

We were up, Audrey already opening the door, when we found a vamp preparing to knock. His gaze moved to Russell. "Sire, the visitors' cars are pulling through the gate now."

FIVE

I Think I Might Have Underestimated the Situation

C live and I waited in the foyer. We had no standing in the nocturne and therefore no place in the welcoming party. Another ten vamps waited with us, spread out in the expansive entry. It was such a dance, respecting a visitor without letting it tip over into fawning. Russell had to strike the proper balance, enough vamps to welcome magnanimously but not subserviently.

Russell was the Master of San Francisco, of all the supernatural beings in this city. While Garyn was old and very powerful, he was still the one in charge here.

When we'd visited Lafitte in New Orleans last year, he'd only had two vamps acting as guards, and it had been seen as an insult. Ten vamps now said we see you and acknowledge your strength. If he'd had the whole nocturne here, it would have been more like he was readying the troops for her review.

And I'm rambling because this woman frightened me. I couldn't explain why, not even to myself. The image that always popped into my head when I thought of her was a black widow spider, waiting for an unsuspecting insect to get caught in her web. After hours or centuries of stillness, she pounces, wrapping her prey in silk and carrying it off to her nest to consume.

That was my fear. After a millennium, we'd done something to pluck a thread on her web and she was coming to devour us.

First through the door were members of her entourage. They were wearing the ubiquitous black but looked more like Secret Service than vampires. I couldn't put my finger on exactly why. I'd seen a glimpse of her when we'd been in the UK, so I knew Garyn wasn't like Amelie, Liang, or Suzette—drop-dead gorgeous, powerful female vamps—but I'd assumed she'd be taller, more formidable. What the hell? She looked like a children's librarian.

Garyn was someone who faded into the background. She wore dark brown woolen trousers with sensible heels, a cream blouse, and a brown tweed blazer. Her golden-brown hair was tied back in a chignon.

"Isn't this lovely?" She studied the foyer, the high ceilings and stained-glass dome, the huge spray of cut flowers, the marble floors, the artwork, until her pale blue eyes finally fell on Clive.

Tsking, she shook her head, eyebrows raised. "And here's the naughty one." Smiling indulgently, she walked toward him, her arms open. "You didn't call, didn't visit. Never even invited me to see this beautiful city of yours." The hug was overly long, during which Clive seemed to glow.

Stiffening, she pulled away, turned her back on him, and moved to Russell's side. "How good of you to open your doors to me." She patted his forearm and then left it where it was.

Russell preened under the attention while Clive looked as though he'd lost his best friend.

"Look at what you've done here," she said to Russell. "So young to be so powerful." She glanced down the hall. "Show me everything you've built."

He led her toward the library, pointing out rooms and objects he thought might interest her. Meanwhile, Clive followed behind, dejected.

Ostensibly, she was taking in the nocturne, appreciating what-ever Russell pointed out, but I caught the sly glances. She wanted to make sure Clive was by her side, hanging on her every word and gesture, while she was focused elsewhere.

She was petite and fragile-looking, her head sometimes resting against Russell's arm as though clinging to her protector. For his part, her reliance on Russell made him hypervigilant about who was near her and what they wanted. Even Clive, who Russell loved and trusted, was regarded with suspicion. When Garyn noted the growing animosity between the two, she closed her eyes, a small smile on her face.

When she opened them a moment later, she pinned me with a glare. It felt like a punch to the side of the head. Shoring up mental blocks that were starting to buckle under the onslaught, I tried to keep my expression pleasant and unconcerned.

"And who have we here?" she asked, her voice sickly sweet.

Clive followed her gaze, staring at me blankly a moment before blinking rapidly and responding, "Garyn, may I introduce you to my wife Samantha?" He remained at her side, turning his back to me again. "And this is my maker Garyn, to whom I owe my very long life."

I smiled, pretending I couldn't feel what she was doing. "Then you have my sincere gratitude. If not for you, Clive and I would never have met."

She laughed, patting Clive's chest. "Perhaps I'll start a matchmaking service. I know a few who could use mates."

Her men looked on adoringly.

"Please allow us to slake your thirst." Russell nodded to the vamps with trays holding cut crystal goblets of blood. "When you're ready, we can move into the library."

I tried to catch Godfrey's eyes, but he too followed the large party down the hall and into the library. Only Audrey glanced my way before bringing up the rear of vamps.

Left alone in the entry, I wondered what the hell had just happened. I'd liked the hi-now-leave plan. It was a good one. Clive hugging her? Russell doting on her? No.

Following down the hall, I kept my mental blocks in place. I didn't try speaking to Clive mind to mind. Garyn—I assumed it was Garyn who'd tried to invade my mind, but I suppose it could have been one of her people—was too strong. It'd taken everything I'd had not to wince in pain. Right now, though, it felt more like someone leaning their full weight against a door. They weren't pounding on it anymore. It was a low-level constant push.

I took a moment in the hall to relax my face before I walked in. The vamps were ranged around the huge library in assorted small groupings with Garyn, Russell, and Clive garnering all the attention. Audrey was standing by herself, leaning against the wall to the left of the door. Deciding she had the best observation spot, I stood beside her.

Neither Clive nor Russell looked our way. Both were transfixed by Garyn. She was the only one who occasionally glanced my way and it felt like a sucker punch to the back of my skull every time. Forcing myself to breathe through the pain, I kept my expression open and friendly.

Turning to Audrey, I pretended to start a conversation. If any of the vamps were focusing on us, they'd know we were silent, but I hoped the triad in the middle of the room would prove far more interesting than the two of us.

Audrey nodded, as though she understood what I was doing. I hadn't seen Audrey interacting with other vamps since she'd become Russell's second, so maybe this was the persona she'd taken on, the strong, silent, observing type. I wanted to get her away from all the others, though, and talk with her. From the look of things, we were the only ones who weren't mesmerized by Garyn.

It wasn't a gender thing, though. Russell had a few women in his nocturne, and they were as transfixed as the men.

Clive reached out a hand, cupping Garyn's shoulder. It wasn't sexual or really even affectionate, so much as protective. He was keeping her safe from all the others. Which was ridiculous, as they all seemed ready to fall on their swords for her.

Turning to Audrey again, I closed my eyes, tapping into my

necromantic abilities. Cold green blips filled the room, the brightest ones huddled in the middle of the room and—surprisingly—right beside me.

I knew Clive and Russell's blips, so I bypassed theirs and slid around Garyn's, not making any sudden or invasive moves. I did *not* want her to know I could do this. As long as she thought me an unremarkable wolf, she might let up on this probing pressure.

Owen, my good friend and bar manager, had once said that it was hard for wicches to read werewolves' auras because of our dual nature. I wondered if it was the same for mesmerizing. Garyn may not have been able to enthrall me as she did the others, but neither was I resistant or combative. If I blended into the scenery, perhaps she'd forget about me.

Keeping my voice low and unobtrusive, I said, "I'm thinking about changing my hair. What do you think?"

Audrey's gaze sharpened. She fluffed out my long waves and then studied a hank of hair. She wasn't fooling me though. Her gaze was downcast, long eyelashes hiding that her focus was trained on the three in the middle of the room.

Keeping her voice as low as mine, she replied, "Well, you have lovely, healthy hair. If you're looking for a change though..." She went on for quite a while, discussing my options. Our voices were barely audible, easy to miss, but if anyone did decide to listen in, they'd hear nothing but hair care and style tips.

Relief overwhelmed me. I wasn't alone. Audrey knew there was something going on too. While Audrey discussed the merits of various hydrating masks, I tried something different. I'd been taught to think of my magic like a long spool of gold thread. Mentally, I unraveled a length and wrapped it around myself before approaching Garyn's blip again.

The room was full of vamps and she was distracted with Clive and Russell. Hopefully, she wouldn't notice me. I *really* needed her to not notice me. Anyone strong enough to cast a thrall over Clive was not someone I wanted to go head-to-head with. I needed to be sneaky-like.

Nodding and *mhm*-ing to Audrey, I closed my eyes again, found Garyn's green blip in my mind, and reached out with a magically gold-wrapped hand. Yes, I know this sounds stupid, but it's how I picture it in my head, so shut up.

My hands slid around her blip, looking for a crack, a weakness of any kind. Her defenses were impressive, but she was also quite old. Much like St. Germain in New Orleans, there were spongey bits, parts where I almost sank in. I held back, fearful it was a trap. Nothing had to be done now. I'd wait until daybreak when she was asleep and unable to separate my head from my body.

With the way Clive was acting, I wasn't positive he'd stop her from killing me. Pulling out, I patted Audrey's arm and thanked her, telling her I'd come to her once I'd decided on a style.

As the night wore on, my eyelids got heavier and heavier. I considered just leaving, as I needed a few hours of sleep before I opened The Slaughtered Lamb, but I didn't want to leave Clive with her.

Shaking myself awake, I pushed off the wall and headed for the little vampires' room. I'd just flipped on the light of the chandelier —why vampires had posh potties when they didn't use them was beyond me—when three vamps shoved me in.

"Okay fellas," I began, backing up a few steps, as that was all I had in this powder room, "You're going to need to wait your turn."

When they leapt forward, I was pulling my blades and swinging. At the same time, the bathroom door slammed open, knocking a vamp into me. I took his head with my axe while slashing the second one across the chest.

Eyes vamp black, Audrey stood in the doorway, the dust of the third vamp at her feet. She stomped one chunky-soled shoe on the midsection of the slashed vamp, pulled out a gun, and shot him between the eyes. It all happened so fast, it was only in hindsight I pieced it all together.

"What the hell was that?" I yanked the hand towel off the

counter and used it to wipe down my blades before returning them to their sheaths.

Audrey stared down at the dust piles. "Those were Garyn's men. They attacked a friend of the nocturne. The compact on which their visit was predicated has been broken."

The bathroom door was hanging off its hinges. Down the hall crowded a group of vamps, Garyn, Clive, and Russell in front, watching us. Everyone but Garyn wore the same oddly blank expression. Beside me, the tension in Audrey's body drained, her gaze becoming vaguely confused.

Aware I'd have twenty vamps attacking me any minute, I changed tack. With the old ones, it was all about doing the unexpected. I smiled broadly, hopping over the corpse dust, and walking down the hall to Clive. He stared through me as though unsure of who I was. He'd once told me he recognized my heartbeat from miles away. Tonight, though, it seemed a few feet was too great a distance.

Resting my hand on his arm, I felt him flinch. "I'm so sorry to interrupt," I began, "but we need to go. I'm afraid I have to be at work in a few hours." Anger hit me from all directions. They were outraged that I'd spoiled their lady's evening. I wasn't used to feeling anger from Clive or Russell, but I sensed their signatures amongst the others. This close to Garyn, I felt her annoyance.

The smile momentarily dropped off her face before she regained her composure. Forgoing subtlety, she slammed into my mind, ordering me to shut up and go away for good. Eyes watering, trying to fight her off, I pretended to yawn behind my hand and shook my head as though attempting to wake up while blinking away the tears.

"You can go," Clive said.

"Good," Garyn said, touching his arm, finally giving him the attention he'd been craving all night. "We're having such a lovely time, aren't we? You know, I'm staying at my penthouse down the block. We're neighbors. You should see it. It's exquisite." She leaned in and he wrapped an arm around her. "I've missed you," she said. "It's been too long."

"When it came on the market a decade or so ago," Clive said, ignoring me, "I was thinking about buying it, but overnight, it was sold."

She laughed warmly. "To me. If I couldn't be close, I enjoyed thinking about my real estate being near you. And the building is a jewel in this city. You must come, all of you."

Clive was already nodding when I linked my hand in his and again felt the flinch. "I'm so sorry, but Clive and I need to go home now. I'm sure we'll see you again before you leave."

Clive was struggling. I felt the turmoil, which was unusual. He normally kept everything locked down tight.

Taking advantage of his confusion, I smiled brightly, waved, and wished everyone a good evening while I pulled Clive toward the front door. The farther he moved from Garyn, the more easily he came with me. She almost snatched him back. I could see it, feel her intent, but it would have marred the evening she'd choreographed. She let him go. For now.

SIX

It Must Be in the Genes

I walked Clive out of the nocturne to his motorcycle. "Can you drive it?"

He stared at me a moment. "Of course I can. What a ridiculous question." Brow furrowed, he stared at me as though he didn't know me. Or didn't want to. "And I don't appreciate being treated like a child and dragged away from my people. If you want to leave, go. We're not joined at the hip."

"I'm not leaving without you." I knew they could hear us, but I needed to get him safely away from her. I hoped proximity made a difference. If he remained in her thrall miles away, I didn't know how to fix this.

I put my hands on either side of his face, forcing him to look at me. "I want you to drive me home now. Can you do that?"

Long blink. "Yes, but I'd prefer not to."

"I understand, but let's do it anyway." I got on the motorcycle and patted the seat in front of me. "Fergus will be so sad. We've been out far longer than we planned."

Haughty. The look he gave me would definitely be described as haughty.

"I'd really appreciate it if you drove us home now," I said. Please let Clive still be in there. How strong was her pull?

He climbed on, shaking his head, irritation apparent. I knew she was influencing him, that this wasn't his fault, but I really didn't want to hear my husband say hateful things to me.

Gunning the engine, he shot off. I almost flipped right off the back of the bike. Grabbing his waist, I held on for dear life. My knee got scraped going through the gates. The vamps hadn't had enough time to open them, and he didn't seem to give a shit if I got hurt. Tucking my legs in tight behind his, I prayed we made it home safely.

A few blocks away, at the bottom of the steps to Alta Plaza Park, Clive pulled over and I was suddenly slid around, crushed against his chest, his head cradled in the crook of my neck. He was shaking and I began to finally let out the breath I'd been holding for hours.

"I'm sorry. I'm so sorry. Please forgive me." He pulled back, his gaze narrowing on my bloody knee. Cursing under his breath, he leaned over it, licking away the blood and sealing the wound. "Does it hurt?"

I shook my head. "I heal quickly. You know that."

He tipped his forehead to mine and closed his eyes. "Yes, I know. But I should never be the one causing you pain."

I felt his shame, his self-loathing, so I kissed him. "You didn't know she'd have that effect on you."

"No," he breathed.

"If you'd known, you would have warned me. We'd have had a plan."

Nodding, he tucked my windblown hair behind my ears. "I didn't even make sure you were wearing a helmet." He flipped open a storage box, pulled out a helmet, and secured it on my head.

"We're okay now. Let's just go home."

"Of course." He repositioned me so I was sitting on the seat in front of him. He kept one arm tight around my waist, steering with the other.

Some tension drained out of me when the reinforced garage

door slid down behind us. We had distance and wards on all the windows and doors. Soon we would have a bed, but first we had a very large pup to take care of.

We took the elevator up from the garage to the bedroom and found a yawning, tail-wagging buddy waiting for us.

"I need to let him out to potty."

He crouched down to pet the wiggling pooch. "Yes, and I'll go with you both. As long as

Garyn is in town, I don't want you out at night on your own." He looked up at me, the pain still fresh. "Please."

I didn't want to make a promise I couldn't keep, so I said, "I'll do my best."

Sighing, he stood. "I suppose I can't ask for more than that."

After Fergus had a quick sniff and a long piddle, we were back upstairs and getting into bed. Clive pulled me close, and I rested my head on his shoulder. Exhausted, I snuggled in and had started to go under when I heard Clive say something.

"What?" I slurred.

"I don't trust myself around her."

I patted his chest, part of my brain already nodding off.

"You shouldn't trust me either."

———

IT WAS A GOOD THING FOR ME THAT FERGUS HAD ADJUSTED TO OUR late-night schedule. He bounced the side of the bed to wake me a little after ten, which was very patient of him. I strapped on my blades, stepped into flip-flops, and ran him downstairs. On beautiful mornings like this, I brought his food and water bowls out to the back patio and then sat sipping iced tea while he ate his breakfast.

The landscapers were geniuses. Or magical. Probably magical. We had a good-sized yard behind the house, one they'd turned into a chaotic English garden. The back wall was stone and tall enough to block the view from the one-story house next door.

There were a few small well-manicured lawns—one on the side of the house that we'd trained Fergus to use as his potty spot—as well as two more directly off the patio. Around the grassy areas were slate slabs creating paths through wild patches of vibrant plants with lush blooms. Hummingbirds moved from blossom to blossom as I breathed in the heady aroma.

I loved our new home. So much so, I often felt the urge to knock on wood, afraid someone was listening in on my thoughts and just biding their time until they could rip it all away from me. I glanced up at the pergola over my head, dripping with sprays of huge purple and white wisteria blossoms. It was all so unbearably lovely that it made my heart hurt.

Fergus trotted back from the side of the house and laid his huge head in my lap. Scratching behind his ears and under his chin, I closed my eyes and sought out the vamps in town.

Wait. There were a lot more than there should have been. The nocturne had its usual assortment. Some had left when Russell had become the Master—that was normal when power changed hands. What was cool was the number of younger vamps that sought out San Francisco *because* Russell was now Master. He might downplay it, but Russell had a reputation for integrity, intelligence, and strength within the vampy community.

The nocturne wasn't the problem. It was the building a couple of doors down. Garyn's penthouse, I presumed. She'd visited our nocturne with twelve of her own people, which had seemed like a lot to me. Now, though, I counted twenty-seven vamps in the penthouse.

Why the hell had she brought so many with her if this was a friendly visit? Suspicious of all of them, I skimmed over the cold green blips resting at the penthouse. Yes, vamps believed they were dead during the day, but I contended that if they could speak or move—as Clive could in emergencies—then they weren't actually dead, just in a regenerative stasis.

Most of Garyn's people had pretty strong mental blocks, even during the day. I could probably have broken through them, but that wasn't my plan right now. I wanted to get a feel for why they were here and then see if I could dip into Garyn's memories without her noticing.

I texted Owen I might be late and then began to slip and slide around the blips, looking for information. Many of the vamps seemed to believe this was just a visit. A few had been ordered by their Masters, who were connected to Garyn, to protect her from a hostile nocturne. No one questioned why San Francisco was being labeled as hostile. Huh. Now that I thought about it, none questioned her at all. They were all happy to help her in any way she saw fit.

I found Garyn but held off on trying to slip past her defenses. I wanted one of her people first. Eventually, I found one whose defenses were weaker than the rest.

As gently and quietly as possible, I began to push in. I hated this part. It was so creepy, like walking through a thick wall of rotting rubber. I could do it, but it felt toxic. Once in, I wandered the darkness, looking for synapse trails, waiting for the sudden flare of memory.

Thankfully, it wasn't long before one lit beside me. I stepped in and found myself in the sitting room I'd seen when I'd found Garyn in England. It was a fussy room with chintz sofas and floral rugs. A woman who looked like Garyn, but not quite—a sister?—sat at a desk, writing a letter.

"Mistress?" The vamp stood with his hands clasped before him, not wanting to bother her but needing to pass on a message.

The woman turned, sunny blonde hair falling in waves to her waist. "Yes?" Her eyes were a vibrant aquamarine, her beautiful heart-shaped face and cupid's bow mouth more than he could take.

"I-I'm sorry to interrupt. I—that is to say—Robert asked that I give you this missive." He glanced down at the folded parchment in his hand with the name *Garyn* written in dark ink.

She held out her hand and took it, then turned back to her desk, the befuddled vamp continuing to stare. She glanced over her shoulder, eyebrows raised, reminding the vamp it was time to go. She was enough like Garyn to be her, and yet not.

The vamp fumbled an apology and backed out of the room. Garyn nodded benevolently and disappeared as he closed the door.

I pulled out, opened my eyes, and stared out at our garden, considering. What I'd felt in the vamp wasn't lust. It was devotion. She was like a goddess to him, entirely unattainable and far too beautiful and powerful for the likes of him. He was stunned to be in her presence.

It was almost like she'd been using a glamour, a kind of magical disguise demons and the fae can create. Hmm...

Clive, can you hear me?

It took a moment, but then I heard, *Yes?* in my head.

Can you show me what you see when you look at Garyn?

It took a few more minutes, but then I saw an image in my mind's eye. Again, it was enough like Garyn to be recognizable, but she was dowdier than the goddess, older. She had what looked to be soft skin, starting to crease around her eyes and mouth. Her eyes were a warm, dark blue and her hair a burnished russet. Interesting.

Love, can you show me one more thing? Can I see what your mother and sister looked like?

Again, there was a pause and then an image of a young woman standing beside an older one in front of a small cabin. I couldn't believe I hadn't thought to ask for this before. Clive's family!

The image changed and then there were three people, an older man now included. *I can't believe I never thought to do this either. In my defense, you're the first person I've been able to share images with. I can speak to my people mind-to-mind—or rather, I could speak to my people when I was their Master. They couldn't speak back, though, like you and I can.*

Damn, your whole family was beautiful!

Handsome, darling. I'm handsome, not beautiful.

Your dad was a total hottie.

Stop. I beg of you.

Your mom was a real looker too. Your sister, though. Wow.

She was even more beautiful on the inside.

She's like a fairy princess.

She was. Why so interested in seeing my family?

I want to show you a couple of things. This is what one of Garyn's men sees when he looks at Garyn. I showed him the image and felt his humor and then puzzlement.

Are you—

Wait. I have one more to show you. This is what I—who was not mesmerized by her—saw. I shared another image and then felt his confusion.

This is what she looks like? I don't understand. Making herself younger and more beautiful, all right. That's vanity. Why does she appear older to me?

That's just it. I don't think vanity plays in this. I think she chooses how she appears based on what that person will respond to. She wanted you to be a part of her family. You had recently lost your mother and so she made herself look older, more matronly. Her eye color is the same as your mother's. You and you sister have light gray eyes like your dad. Only your mother has deep blue. Her hair color is closer to your mom's auburn as well. You're blond like your dad.

So, since I'd be less likely to walk away from my mother, she made herself look like that to me?

It's a theory. I felt his sluggish turmoil, so I added, *Sleep, love. I'm just thinking.*

When I felt him wink out, I moved on to my next vampy convo. Searching the nocturne, I found Audrey and did my own version of knocking on a door. *Audrey? Can I speak with you?*

After a very long pause, I heard. *Hmm?*

Hi, it's Sam. Would you mind if we had a chat?

What?

It's Sam. Can I talk with you?

What?

Okay. This was going to take a while. After a bit more back and forth, she seemed to be aware enough for a conversation.

Sam? You're in my head?

Yup. I just wanted to ask you about last night. How were you able to fight off Garyn? And were you really mesmerized there at the end?

She was slow to answer. I wasn't sure if she didn't know the answer or if communicating this way was too difficult for her.

No. We were outnumbered and I'd just said out loud—like a ninny—that she'd broken the compact. I hoped if I looked brain dead, no one would attack us.

Good one!

I've been wondering why her commands slide right off me, though. Leticia kept me under her thumb for hundreds of years, but her far older, more powerful maker can't? It doesn't make sense. Except, maybe… I've been—now, don't laugh—I've been reading books on leadership and confidence. She paused like she was waiting for me to laugh.

That makes sense. You're second in command of the nocturne.

The Master's been working with me, helping me to see myself and my place in this world differently. Do you know the Master's personal history?

She was asking if I knew that Russell had been born into slavery and had fought his way to freedom by becoming a vampire. *Yes. Russell told me his story. Probably like with you, he shared his story to illustrate that we can't let others define us, let them decide the trajectory of our lives. I have a problem with assuming everyone else's needs and wants should come first. That my pain is a small price to pay to ensure another's safety and happiness.*

I felt her smile.

You too? Hundreds of years in service is not something you just shake off and forget. The Master's also trained me in hand-to-hand combat and the use of firearms.

I saw that last night. And I gotta say, bringing a gun to a fang fight was epic.

I often worry that in the moment, I'll falter or freeze, but I didn't. That felt good. As I was saying, though, I've been taking books from our library on confidence and leadership. One of them talks about neural pathways. I won't get this exactly right, but the author said that when we do what we've always done, we reinforce the paths we've already created. We make ruts that seem impossible to break out of. But when we train ourselves to think differently about ourselves, our place in the world, our own power, we begin to change those neural pathways that before seemed impossible to alter.

I think I'd like to borrow that book when you're done.

I felt her relax.

Yes, Missus. I can do that. So, I've been wondering. Maybe Garyn thinks of me as a servant, just as Leticia did, but I've created new pathways, ones that don't recognize her authority over me because I no longer see myself in that role.

Interesting.

Or it has nothing to do with that and it's just a fluke. I don't know, but I like believing it's because I know my own power and don't accept her authority.

I like that idea too.

So, can you do this with all of us, talking to us like this?

Can you keep a secret?

Yes, ma'am — Sam.

Then, yes, I can. And you know what? She may scare me, but I don't accept her authority either.

Long pause. I'm awfully tired, Missus. Could we talk about this later?

Of course. Rest well, Audrey.

Thank — and she winked out.

I had a lot to mull over and one more thing to track down. Pulling out my cell phone, I searched for the god visiting Stheno. He'd said his name was Thoth or Djehuty.

Oh, shit. Thoth's an Egyptian god, born from the lips of Ra at the beginning of creation. He's closely associated with divine order and justice. He's the god of many things, including the moon, which is probably why I reacted so strongly to him, my second nature being tied to the moon.

Wisdom, celestial calculations, judgment of the soul, the more I read about him, the more awed I became in retrospect. I'd sat beside this god, chatted with him. Assuming I hadn't made a bad impression on him, maybe…

I tapped the phone screen.

"What the hell? It's too early for calls." Stheno paused a moment. "How is it already eleven? I forget how much I hate working. Times goes by, I get bored, and then I watched you and it seemed like fun, so I suggested our next business venture be a bar. I need to hire people to do this shit so I can just sit in a booth and drink like my sister."

"Sounds like a plan. Listen, will Thoth be in again today? I'd like to talk with him, if I can."

"Sounds serious, kid. Is something up?"

"I'll explain when I get there."

SEVEN

Another Brick in the Wall

I texted Owen again to inform him I would definitely be late. Fyr was at the bar with Owen. Meribella, my recent hire, would be showing up after school let out. Meri was seventeen and only worked in the bookstore. I loved having someone, even part-time, devoted to maintaining the shelves and helping customers find the right books. Meri was an avid reader and seemed to be enjoying the job so far.

She lived with her human mom and went to the local high school. Her dad, however, was water fae, a merman to be exact. I didn't know if she could change her form or just carried fae blood. That was far too personal of a question to ask an employee.

She was an absolute stunner, as in I didn't think I'd ever seen a more beautiful person in my life—well, other than Gloriana, the fae queen. I got the feeling Meri enjoyed working at The Slaughtered Lamb because she was surrounded by other supernaturals who might notice her beauty but weren't terribly interested in it. Each day, I could see her relaxing a bit more.

Anyway, as The Slaughtered Lamb was covered, I got cleaned up, collected Fergus, and went down to the garage. After Garyn left town, I was holding Clive to his promise to teach me how to drive a motorcycle. I wanted one with a sidecar, though. I'd get Fergus a pair of goggles and we'd go on adventures.

Since that wasn't an option yet, I chose the most low-key of Clive's cars, a safe little Volvo. After loading Fergus in, I headed to The Viper's Nest. We were barely a block from the house when my huge—and getting huger everyday—buddy had the front half of his body between the driver's and passenger's seats, huge paws on the console, so he could better keep an eye on the action. And his nose in my ear.

It was a beautiful day, so I opened the sunroof. Fergus was ecstatic, lifting his nose into the rushing air. I found a parking spot around the side of the building. Snapping on Fergus' leash, my stomach rumbled. With all the hubbub, I'd forgotten to eat. Guess who was having pie for lunch?

Swinging open the heavy door, I came face-to-face with a guy I hadn't seen last night. He had thick, light brown hair brushed back in what seemed to be a cross between a pompadour and a mullet. He was about my height, muscular, and stern.

"No dogs."

"Hey!" I followed his gaze. "Oh, him." I pointed in Stheno's direction. "I'm a friend."

Stheno looked up and waved us over. "Stand down, Dalton. These two are always welcome."

He gestured for us to go and then stopped the guy behind me for ID.

Thoth was sitting on a barstool near Stheno again. Hopping up on the one beside him, I had Fergus sit between us.

"And who have we here," Thoth asked, his voice gentle as he held out his hand for my pup to sniff.

Fergus rested his big head on Thoth's thigh, looking up adoringly.

Thoth chuckled, scratching behind his ears. "How old is he?"

"Seven months." I patted my Irish Wolfhound's back.

Thoth rubbed a thumb over Fergus' head and down between his eyes. "Smart, this one. Courageous too."

"Yes."

"Good dog," he pronounced before taking a sip of his tea.

Fergus leaned into me, his eyes still on Thoth.

"So," the Egyptian god said, "I've been told you'd like to speak with me."

"Yes, sir." I still felt the heat radiating off him, but it was nothing like last night. He had his godly power buttoned up.

"Take a booth," Stheno said, waving us to the one closest to the bar. "I'll join you guys in a few." She slid a soda and a piece of the lemon meringue in front of me.

"How did you know?" I took a bite of the pie and it was heaven, the tartness setting the back of my tongue to tingling.

"Like I didn't notice you staring last night." She rolled her eyes and shooed us away.

We moved to the booth, Fergus flopping down at our feet. I offered Thoth a bite. The corner of his lips quirked up, but he shook his head.

"Now, child, finish your dessert and tell me what you wanted to talk with me about?"

I explained Garyn and her strength of mind, her hold on the vamps, and her constant battering of my defenses.

"Vampires," he said with distaste. Magnetic golden-brown eyes pinned me to the spot. "You married one of these denizens of the night. Why?"

"I love him. He's"—my chest ached, thinking about him—"my mate." As he was still looking pretty judgy, I went on. "And I've got a lot of baggage too. When we started spending time together, I had a sorcerer aunt who was doing everything in her power to kill me. Not to mention the fae king who keeps throwing his assassins at me. And then there were those demons, but honestly, that wasn't really my fault. All I'm saying is that I'm no walk in the park either."

"And this vampire feels the same about you?"

"He's stupid in love with her," Stheno said, bringing over a teapot and refilling Thoth's cup.

I grinned. "He is."

Taking a sip, he stared into my soul. "All right. Let's see how strong your defenses are. Block me."

I erected the mental wall, focusing on keeping him out. With almost laughable ease, I felt a stab of pain and then heard his voice.

Were you trying to block me?

Yes. Yes, I was.

Good. You have strong mental skills, but not the strongest defenses. Most do not have the ability to speak to me this way.

My husband and I communicate like this all the time.

Ah. You've built the muscle memory for it. When I spoke to you this way, your brain recognized it and applied prior knowledge to this new situation. If you can, explain to me what you're doing when you block your thoughts.

I'm picturing a big wall—

Describe the wall.

I took a sip of soda and then closed my eyes. *It's a tall brick wall—*

What color?

Black.

And the mortar between the bricks?

Black.

So, a tall black wall?

Yes. I wrap my magic around it to make it stronger. And then I stand behind it, my hands on it, holding it up.

Can you see the top of the wall?

I thought about that a moment. *I don't know. It's dark in my thoughts. I guess I can because when I'm imagining wrapping the wall with the gold thread, I see it coming over the top.*

Exactly. A wall is not an effective defense. The enemy can go over, around, even under. They can, with enough strength, just push it over and crush you under the rubble.

A chill ran through me.

A brick wall is built upon weaknesses. The mortar blends with the brick, appearing to be a solid defense, but it's not. Alter the image in your head. Make the mortar white. Do you see all the places that can be worn away, destabilizing your wall?

Shit.

This isn't just about keeping her from manipulating you like she did the others, correct? You want to keep her out of your thoughts and memories, as well as from your friends' secrets. Yes?

I thought about all the top-secret stuff rattling around up there and said, Yes.

Good. Now, let's try this. Forget the wall. It's an incomplete barrier. It's your mind you want to protect. Your magic needs to encapsulate it.

I thought a moment. Like a Skittle.

He paused. Is that English?

Grinning, I took another sip of soda. Fergus slunk up onto the bench beside me, draping the upper half of his body over my lap. Skittles are candy-coated treats.

Still looking confused, he nodded. If you like. Please envision candy-coating your brain.

Can do! I pictured my squishy, wrinkly, two-lobed brain with a big metaphorical spigot hovering in the air over it. A switch was flicked and a swirl of rainbow colors infused with my magic poured over my super gross-looking brain. The candy coating ran down the sides and pooled below. I concentrated hard on making sure every tiny crevice was covered. There were no breaks or weak spots. My mind was all my own.

I heard a strange, muffled sound. Glancing around, I tried to locate the source but didn't find anything.

"Sam?" Thoth said.

"Yes?"

"Can you no longer hear me in your mind?" Brow furrowed, he studied me.

"Was that you? Sorry. I couldn't make out what that was." I scratched Fergus' head.

"We'll come back to that. Have you changed how you picture your protection?"

"Yes. I'm just waiting for the candy-coating to harden."

Shaking his head, he muttered, "So odd," and then looked out the window, waiting for me.

I closed my eyes and again pictured my mind coated in my magic. Then I remembered. "Can I use my other nature to help protect my mind too?"

"You aren't?"

Opening my eyes, I said, "Nope. I've been using the magic from my necromancer side to block out the vamps."

"Let's fix that. You are one of the Quinn line."

It wasn't a question, but I answered anyway. "Yes."

"You possess Apex Transformation?"

I let my eyes lighten to wolf gold.

His smile was sharp and approving.

"Good. Just as you shifted your eyes, shift your mind." He sipped his tea and waited.

I considered a moment and realized I had no idea how to do that. "When I shift, I'm always me. I mean, I like chasing rabbits and don't mind eating them raw—in fact, I rather enjoy that as a wolf—but my mind is always the same."

"Hmm." He stood and gestured for me to follow. "Stheno, we need your back room."

She nodded, patted the other bartender on the back, and followed us. Hey, she *did* have a pool table and dart boards. This place was so cool.

"Is that a mechanical bull?" I pointed to the far side of the room, where padded mats lined the floor.

"Hell yeah it is. So far, no one but Medusa and I have stayed on longer than six seconds. And we have it set for beginners." She shook her head. "Disappointing."

"Come," Thoth interrupted. "I'd like to try something. This could cause you to shift—which is why I brought you in here—or it might help us reveal your instinctual wolf brain."

I was kinda wishing I hadn't agreed to this. "This won't make me a permanent wolf, will it?"

Stheno laughed. "You'd have one pissed-off bloodsucker on your hands."

When I didn't move, she shoved me toward the god. *Shitshitshit.*

I didn't even see him move. He was that fast. Stheno shoved, my forehead exploded, and then darkness descended.

EIGHT

Deathmatch: Wolf vs. Bear

N ose twitching, my eyes flew open. I was on the ground, head resting on my paws, reveling in the scents of the forest. Trees towered in every direction, as far I could see, which was remarkably far. Rich, fertile soil, crushed pine needles, a decaying tree trunk a quarter of a mile away that now housed shrews, birds chirping and hopping from branch to branch overhead in the canopy, moss clinging to rough bark, the musk of rodents who had been nearby recently but no longer were, dew beading on my fur...

Surging to my feet, I trotted and then ran, muscles bunching and lengthening, the mouthwatering scent of rabbit perfuming the air. He'd left crisscrossing trails as he searched for his own food. I arrowed straight to the sound of little paws kicking up needles and earth. He scurried at the soft thuds of my paws, diving under vegetation, trembling, waiting.

Lunging, jaws snapping, I broke its neck. Claws ripping through fur, I devoured the steaming meal. It filled an aching hollow in the pit of my stomach, but it wasn't enough. There were more out here. The forest was alive. I followed the fading scent trails of rabbits to their warren. My nose twitched. There were two in the nearest burrow.

I sprang, long, sharp claws digging at the entrance, tearing through the walls so I could get at them, waiting for one to panic and bolt. A moment later, it did. I snapped, enjoying the satisfying squeal, the blood spattering my muzzle.

I stilled when I heard the soft tread of paws. Wolf. He'd heard, smelled. He was coming for my meal. I waited, the rabbit at my feet. A gray wolf appeared through the saplings, gold eyes fixed on my kill. I growled and its gaze met mine. This was my kill, my meal. No way was I walking away from this fight. When I took a step forward, my growl reverberating through the forest, he retreated back into the trees.

How did that feel?

The voice caught me off guard. I'd forgotten all about Thoth and the bar. I'd been deep in my wolf brain, more lost in the animal than I'd ever been when I shifted each month.

Good. Strong. I was having a hard time altering my thoughts for speech. *Angry. He tried to steal food.*

Yes. How did you get him to run?

I considered that, trying to find the words. *I'm stronger. He'd die, so he ran.* The rabbit smelled too good and I was still hungry, so I ate.

When you finish, I'll bring you back.

Like it here.

I understand, but Stheno tells me your husband would be heartbroken.

Clive. It all came rushing back: my life, The Slaughtered Lamb, Fergus, my friends, the new house, all of it. My stomach roiled and I vomited rabbit.

Ah. I see the problem. Come back now.

Eyes fluttering open, I stared into Fergus' face. When I reached up to pet him, he flopped down on me, his head on my chest. I was lying on the floor, the back of my head throbbing.

"You guys just let me hit the ground? No one thought, hey, maybe letting her bounce her skull off the floor might be a bad idea?" Jeez.

"Oh, fuck off. You're tough and you went down fast." Stheno offered me a hand and I took it, pulling myself up. "If it makes you feel any better, Fergus tried to help."

Actually, it did.

There were tables and booths in here as well. Stheno directed us to a table in the corner that already had drinks on it. I gave Stheno a confused look.

"You were out for a while. Thoth said you'd need something to eat when you came around."

The memory of raw rabbit coming back up should have been enough to make me lose my appetite, but he was right. I was ravenous. After downing the full glass of water, I bit into a sandwich piled high with meat.

"Where's this come from?" I asked once I'd swallowed.

"Your demon. I think his woman—"

"Maggie," I said before another bite.

"Yeah, her. I think she's helping him. She was the one who dropped off the food today." She paused a moment. "Does that make me an asshole, not even thinking to ask about her?"

I nodded.

Thoth said, "You haven't needed to know. Now, though, she's involved in the food you serve, so you're asking the question."

I swallowed. "She owns a flower shop in the Marina District. She may be a banshee, but her fae blood helps make her plants and flowers grow healthy and strong. It's a successful shop."

"Huh," was Stheno's only response.

"Tell me about your time in the forest," Thoth said.

I filled up my glass from the water pitcher Stheno had put on the table—look at her being thoughtful—and then drank it down, considering.

"It was different. I'm never that deep in my wolf brain. I'm always Sam. I'm just furry Sam going for a run. This time, though, I wasn't Sam. I was wolf. My vision was clearer than it's ever been. My hearing was ridiculous, and my sense of smell was unreal."

"And how are those things now?" he asked.

I did an internal check on the sights and sounds of The Viper's Nest. "Back to normal."

Nodding, he said, "And that's the problem. The wolf and the woman are not one. To be dual-natured, one must fully embrace both sides. You don't. You're a woman who sometimes shifts into the shape of a wolf. Do you see?"

"Yes." I thought back over the last almost-exactly eight years of my life. "I think the wolf scared me too much. I had a hard time accepting it. I hid when I shifted. I stayed in familiar places. Close to home. It brought it all back every time I shifted—not that it didn't hang like an albatross around my neck all the time—but turning into a monster, the same kind of monster that had tortured me, was hard to reconcile."

"I would imagine you were experiencing a great deal of pain, fear, shame." At my nod, he continued, "Because of that, because of the memories stirred up every month when you needed to shift, you distanced the monster—as you thought of your other half—never fully becoming one with her."

I'd thought I was doing so well, but he was right. I was just trying to bury what made me uncomfortable.

Stheno punched me in the arm. Hard.

"What the hell?" That freaking hurt. Fergus was up and sitting between us, growling at Stheno.

She glared, one-eyed, at him, her long coils of hair moving menacingly. I'd expected him to hide behind me, but instead he stood, his butt pushing my chair away from Stheno.

"What was that about?" I demanded.

Thoth tapped Stheno's arm. "It would be best if you moved to this seat," he said, indicating the empty chair beside him. "He's very upset. He thought you were a friend so he could relax, but you hurt Sam. He's failed at protecting her. Give them some space so he feels she's safe."

I rested my hand on my protector's back.

Stheno grumbled but moved. "I could see it on her face. She was kicking herself for not being stronger. This chick has been through it. She's a warrior. I didn't want her hearing what you said as her being weak, so I punched her."

"And that was a very you way of dealing with it," he said with a smile. Turning back to me, he added, "I hope that isn't what you took from what I said."

I shook my head, but it wasn't true. Stheno's raised eyebrows said she knew exactly which direction my thoughts had traveled.

"We need to find a way for you to accept your dual nature. Not tolerate, but to accept and embrace."

I stared at him blankly. "I don't know how to do that."

Stheno scoffed. "No shit."

He laid his hand down on the table, palm up. "I can help."

I didn't like having anyone in my head, but I had to do something if I wanted to keep Garyn out. Resigned, I placed my hand in his and, again, I felt like I'd taken a punch to the forehead.

I was back in the forest, walking along a mossy path in dappled sunlight, Fergus trotting along beside me. I sensed a presence on my other side. A tall Black man—a god—with the head of a long-beaked bird walked with us, the soft swish of yellow robes the only noise in the unnatural hush.

"May I walk with you?" he asked.

I chuffed my agreement.

We'd traveled a good distance, deep into the forest, when a bear cub crossed our path. I stopped, beginning to back away, pushing a very interested Fergus away from the cub, but Thoth continued on. I knew where there was a cub, there was a mama bear, and I had no desire for any of us to be swatted with ten-inch claws.

After a quiet moment, during which no thousand-pound protective animal came barreling toward us, I caught up with Thoth. I was alert to every sight and sound, wondering about the bear, but we continued our walk, the trees growing closer, the forest getting darker.

A strange snuffling and rustling in the bushes had my fur

standing on end and proved too enticing to Fergus. He shot forward on a bark.

Knocking him sideways, I changed the trajectory just as mama bear, a cub between her massive paws, trampled the bushes to get at Fergus. He barked again, this time deep and threatening.

She charged and I leapt, my hind legs shoving her back, the claws on my front paws slashing down her muzzle. Fergus tried to move forward to help, but I snapped at him, pushing him back with my body again. My pup wasn't getting mauled today.

The bear went down on all fours and roared at me. I knew I should have been terrified, but all I could think about was getting us out of here. She lumbered forward, all muscle, mass, and intent.

I moved to the left, blocking Fergus. Hackles raised, my growl vibrating through the ground, I lowered my head, gold eyes staring into hers. I didn't want to hurt her, but I would.

Her bulk swayed back and forth, as though sizing me up, and then she was on her hind legs again, making herself huge and terrifying. I was not, however, terrified. I was trying to figure out how to get us all out of here—bears included—without any major injuries.

She lunged and I dodged, racing behind her and scrambling up her bowed back. With razor-sharp claws, I dug into her heavy coat, my jaw crushing her thick neck. I shook my head. Contorting herself, she tried to buck me off, but I'd already leapt clear, skirting her and glaring at Fergus, who was slinking forward.

Keeping my eyes glued to her, I pushed him back with my body again, giving her the space she needed to settle. We were about ten yards away when she gave one last warning, a sound between a huff and a growl, and then took her cub deeper into the forest.

I searched up and down the path, trying to decide which way to take Fergus when I noticed Thoth sitting in a tall, ornate chair tucked into the woods behind us. He beckoned us forward. Pushing Fergus toward the god I checked over my shoulder to make sure the bear hadn't decided to pursue us.

"Come. Rest and talk with me a moment."

Fergus dropped his head on Thoth's knee. I, however, kept my body aimed where the bear had disappeared. I could listen to whatever he had to say while guarding us.

"How do you feel?"

Fine.

"Oh, good. You can speak with me again. Did she hurt you?"

I blew air out of my nose. As if.

I heard a low chuckle and glanced over my shoulder at the bird-headed god who had his hand resting on Fergus.

"Why didn't you kill her?"

Why would I? She was just protecting her young.

"Yes, but she threatened your young."

Only because we trespassed. I wasn't going to let her hurt Fergus, but she didn't need to die.

"Could you have taken her down? She was six or seven times larger than you, with incredible strength and long, sharp claws. A lone wolf is no match for an enraged bear."

I huffed, annoyed but trying not to offend a god.

"Why does that bother you?"

I'm more lethal than a natural wolf. I have a human's intelligence and knowledge of battle along with enhanced physical gifts. Added to that, a wicche's magic. It wasn't a fair fight.

"I'm glad you realize that. When you need to protect others, the self-doubt falls away and what is left is a canny warrior. You need to put those skills to work in protecting yourself the way you do others." His hand remained on Fergus' head as he waved me forward with his other.

I glanced down the path one more time and then went to his side. He cupped my muzzle, stared into my eyes, and then—BOOM—my thoughts exploded in light and noise.

NINE

Wolfie FOMO

M y head was killing me, and I was getting really sick of waking up on a barroom floor. "You guys mop these floors every day, right?"

"What's a mop?" Stheno gave me her hand again and helped me up.

Fergus bumped me over and over with his nose, trying to figure out what was wrong with me. I sat, pulled him close, and wrapped an arm around him.

"Did it work?" Stheno asked.

"You don't need to shout. And did what work?" I wished I could take aspirin. My body processed the medication too quickly for it to help, though.

"Look around. Take a sniff. What do you notice?" Stheno asked.

Thoth sat silently, waiting.

Okay. I turned in my seat. "Hey, that's a cool paint technique. They made it look run down—splintered wood, peeling paint." I went to the wall and ran my hand over the smooth, fresh coat. Perfect. "That's so cool. Oh, and someone peed in that corner by the restroom."

"What?" Stheno stood, glowering into the corner. "It's

lunchtime. Who's already too drunk to find the toilets?"

"Last night," I clarified. "It was mopped but it still stinks."

"Good," Thoth said. "Have a seat and we'll try this again."

Stheno stomped off toward the backroom.

"You are something they can never be," he began.

"Alive," Stheno said, rolling out the mop bucket.

Thoth tipped his head. "Yes, that too, but I was referring to your anima, life force, soul. Vampires are cold, self-centered things. They understand power, hierarchy, revenge. There's cold logic there but not warmth and protection."

I leaned forward. "I hate to argue with you, but that's not true. My husband is kind and loving. Russell, Godfrey, Audrey, they're all very caring."

He stared, clearly not buying it.

"It's true. There are good ones that are still very close to their humanity."

"So why have you asked for my help?" He raised one eyebrow, waiting.

Sighing, I said, "Okay. Yes. There are a lot of really shitty ones but not all—" I stopped talking. I needed to know how to defend my mind against vamps. Trying to argue they weren't all bad was stupid.

"Sorry. Please continue." I folded my hands before me, an attentive pupil.

He gave a slow nod. "That's exactly what I mean. A vampire would try to get as much information out of me as possible before plotting to kill me in order to keep that information from others. It's cold calculation. I can't fault the logic. You, on the other hand, are more concerned with my liking your husband and friends, seeing their goodness, their humanity, as you say.

"You must use what sets you apart to protect your mind from them. Let that protective wolf of yours prowl around your candy-coated mind, guarding you from attack."

I could do that. I closed my eyes and visualized the multicolored, hard candy shell, and then I let my wolf loose, let her pad through my mind, familiarizing herself with the territory. When she was done, she sat, ready to repel all comers.

"Okay," I said.

"Block me," he demanded.

My wolf was ready. When I felt him push, she howled. Thoth winced. It was subtle, but I saw it. He pushed harder and she pawed at the air, her claws slicing through it. He blinked.

"Much better," he murmured.

He had clearly been toying with me before. This time, it felt like a vice around my head. My wolf shook out her fur, growled, and snapped at the intruder.

Thoth let out a quick breath and lifted his hand, studying the fading bite mark. His gaze shifted to me. "Interesting." Leaning back in his chair, he said, "That's all for today."

Understanding I was being dismissed, I stood. "Thank you, sir. I'm incredibly grateful for your time and wisdom."

He nodded, his expression thoughtful.

"Bye, Stheno," I called.

"See ya, kid," floated out of the restroom.

I tapped my thigh and Fergus popped up, taking his place at my side. We were almost to the short hall leading to the bar, when he spoke again.

"If Stheno was correct and you were doubting yourself earlier, I'll be quite disappointed." He stared into my soul, his keen avian gaze stealing my breath. "Don't disappoint me."

I bowed, as that seemed appropriate, and then backed out of the room. Fergus stayed close beside me as we made our way across the barroom and out the front door. The stench of the harbor was overwhelming.

"How do you do this, dude?" I asked Fergus, opening the back door for him. I caught a scent then. It was a man who had been at the Viper's Nest last night. Tipping my head up, I scented the wind and unraveled multiple scent markers. If I'd had to, I could have tracked down everyone working on the dock now who had been in the bar last night. Damn, that was handy.

I slid in and started the engine, catching Fergus' eye in the rearview mirror. "I mean, it's great and all, but does everything have to stink?" I'd thought I'd had a strong sense of smell before. Now? It was ridiculous. Seawater, fish, dock workers sweating in the sun, produce baking in crates, trucks belching exhaust—oh, nice—flowering trees, a bakery, coffee, leather seats—eww—unwashed people, human waste, steaming tar...

As we got closer to home, the strong wind off the ocean blew downtown's lingering scents away. I parked the car back in the underground garage—had it always smelled so strongly of gas and oil? I took the elevator up to the first floor of the house and went out to the garden. Fergus ran around the corner of the house, and I breathed deeply. It was no wonder this was his favorite place to hang out. It smelled wonderful out here, rich, dark earth, jasmine, honeysuckle—oh, the heliotrope was amazing—wisteria, tuberose...

I lay down on a shady patch of lawn, stared up into the blue, cloud-filled sky, and breathed in the garden. I could hear and smell what waited beyond our walled paradise, but it was perfect here. Fergus trotted back and lay down beside me. I almost nodded off before I remembered The Slaughtered Lamb.

Dragging myself up, I said, "Come on, bud. We need to go to work."

Fergus was slow to stand, and I totally understood.

"You can stay if you want." I gave him a quick side scratch and went in search of food. I'd found a butcher in town who made delicious turkey meat sticks. I grabbed two out of the fridge and headed for the front door.

"I love you! Sleep well!" I called up to Clive. When I opened the front door, Fergus was back by my side, leash in his mouth. Smiling, I locked the door, snapped on his lead, broke off half a stick for my trusty sidekick, took a bite myself, and headed across the green to The Slaughtered Lamb's steps.

Some days, the area above my bookstore and bar was more crowded with tourists. On those days, we had to mill around a bit until the others had moved past the warded steps that humans could neither see nor walk through. We watched them follow a path along the ocean or go down to the lookout for pictures. Once everyone was distracted, Fergus and I moved forward, stepping through the ward, following the magical steps down to The Slaughtered Lamb.

Emerging from the darkened staircase, I was once again taken by its beauty. The bookstore stood to the left of the steps, through the archway. The shelves were finally filling. We weren't there yet, but we were close.

Ahead was a glass wall, holding the ocean back. Waves splashed on the window, the water swirling about four feet above the mahogany floors. At high tide, the water was above my head. Right now, though, white clouds dotted the bright blue sky, the green hills of the North Bay rising up over the waves. Seaweed bobbed under the surface, a gang of little silver fishes streaking through the water.

Huh. I'd thought my eyesight was perfect before, but now I could see the people on the sailboats, the couple climbing the hill across the Bay. And…

"Is Meri here yet?"

Owen came around the bar to pet Fergus. "Soon. I think school let out about ten minutes ago."

I tipped my head toward the window wall. "I think I see her dad, coming to check on her."

"Really?" Owen squinted, trying to see through the water.

Fyr nodded. "He comes every day she's on shift and sticks around for most of it."

Kick ass! My eyesight was almost as good as a dragon's now.

Light steps danced down the stairs. Turning, I found Meri drowning in a huge hoodie, her white-blonde hair in a messy bun. I totally got it. I wore stuff like that for almost eight years to hide my scars. Meri dressed in baggy clothes to hide as well. In her case, though, it was beauty she was hiding, not scars.

She had large purple-blue eyes, luminous golden skin, bee-stung lips, and straight white teeth. The poor thing got double takes on the street, people pulling out phones to snap pictures, and creepy adults hitting on her. That was part of why her dad kept an eye on us while his daughter was working. I didn't blame him at all. She was heartbreakingly lovely and clearly uncomfortable with the attention.

I took a sniff. And then another. "Are you wearing snickerdoodle perfume?"

Turning red, she shook her head.

I leaned in closer. "You just naturally smell like vanilla, sugar, and cinnamon?" What the hell?

Fyr nodded.

Meri shrugged.

Dang, I was making her uncomfortable. "Sorry! Don't mind me. I'm just hungry."

"Hey, Meri," Owen said, thankfully taking the focus off my creepy sniffing. "We got a shipment of books yesterday."

Her eyes lit up.

"Sam's already inventoried them. They need to be shelved," he added.

She was already nodding. "Is the cart in the back?"

"Yep." He went back behind the bar and began brewing another pot of tea for the wicches in the corner.

She smiled at me, nodded to Fyr, and then went into the kitchen to drop off her backpack on Dave's desk and grab the cart from the storeroom. She came out a few minutes later, eating a cookie and pushing a full cart of books, Fergus trotting along behind.

"There are cookies?" I headed for the kitchen.

On a grin, she nodded before ducking into the bookstore.

I glared at Fyr and Owen. "I've been standing here all this time, and no one thought to mention cookies?" Traitors, that's what they were.

On the island in the middle of the kitchen was a plate half-filled with chocolate-dipped peanut butter cookies. I'd seen these in

Stheno's pastry case and had wanted one. Hot damn! Maybe we were getting the extras or funny-shaped ones. I took a bite. Mmm, heaven. Arwyn's tutorial videos were doing wonders for Dave's baking skills.

When I strolled back into the bar, I was in a much better mood. With a great big cookie in my hand, what could be wrong?

I needed to remember not to ask myself questions like that.

I walked past an elf I hadn't noticed before. He sat at a table by the wall, which was odd. We had empty tables by the window. No one chose the wall when a window seat was available. I felt the air move, almost like a prickle in my fur and then an oh-so-faint scent of Finvarra.

I didn't think. My wolf and I reacted, grabbing my blades as I spun. His head was spinning across the floor, severed arms dropping near my feet before he'd had a chance to lunge.

Fyr came around the bar, picked up the elf's head by his hair, and then tossed it to the body. We were all watching when the body disappeared, returning to Faerie. Fyr handed me the bar towel he tucked into his waist so I could wipe off my blades.

"How did you do that?" Owen asked. "You moved so fast." He shook his head. "You were a blur and then his head was rolling."

Once my blades were clean, I returned them to their magical sheaths, and they vanished again. "Um." I pointed to the blood. "Could you take care of that?"

Owen did a scouring charm, cleaning up the mess.

Meri's father swam up to the window, expression outraged.

"Meri? Can you please come explain to your dad that I killed a bad guy, not a good one?"

Meri walked in a moment later. "Can I wh—" She saw her dad and rushed to the window, a huge grin on her face. She pointed to the magical entrance for water fae and mouthed, *Please*.

He swam out of sight, into the swaying seaweed, and then his head and chest popped up through the entrance. Meri plopped down, leaned forward, and hugged him. He hugged her back, his narrowed gaze still locked on me.

TEN

It's Like They Have a Different Word for Everything

He thundered, shouting what sounded like dire threats, but I didn't speak Mermish. Meri patted his shoulder, speaking the same language in soft tones.

"Can you translate for me?" I asked her.

She nodded.

Where to start... I had lots of fae secrets in my head. I needed to tell him something, though. I didn't want him to make Meri quit because he thought I was a homicidal maniac. "The king wants me dead." We both knew who I was talking about, and names have power.

Meri translated and her dad's expression became even darker. *Shit.* Maybe he was buds with Finvarra.

"I've done nothing to deserve it. Promise. I just know some stuff, so he wants me silenced. The queen had her Captain of the Guard spell my axe so I could kill any fae who went against her orders and attacked me."

I waited for Meri to translate and realized that everyone in the bar was hanging on my every word. Damn, I lost my cookie. Owen must have cleaned it up with the blood. I wondered if I had enough time to go grab another one. I didn't know how complicated Mermish was.

When Meri paused and looked over her shoulder, I continued.

"The queen caught him and imprisoned him after I told her what he'd been up to—which was no good. Unfortunately, he's broken out and is looking for revenge." I paused again.

When Meri finished translating, I continued. "I'm not his top priority, so I think when he's feeling particularly put out, he sends one of his people to kill me. That's why I always have the blades on me." I was pretty sure I was telling him too much, but the angry dad face had me talking. I'd never experienced it before, so I had no defense against it.

Meri translated. "If you think it'll help," I whispered to Meri, "tell him we have cookies."

"I don't want cookies!" he roared.

What the hell was with all the translating if he spoke English?

"I want to know if my daughter will be safe here. How many times has the king sent his warriors after you?"

Jeez, too many to count. "Here, in The Slaughtered Lamb? Twice. *But*, remember, your daughter is well protected here. None of us would let her get hurt."

He grunted at that and scowled.

"Of course, if you wanted to help us out, you could let us know if you see any fae who don't belong here, especially kelpies—they really seem to hate me."

After what seemed like a ridiculously long pause, he finally said, "If you let anyone—and I do mean *any*one—hurt my little girl, I'll pluck your head off myself, and I won't need an axe."

"If I were you," Fyr began, his Welsh accent stronger than usual, "I wouldn't threaten Sam. My dragon's breath works just fine underwater. And what I could do to you is nothing compared to what her Master vampire husband would do." Smoke billowed from Fyr's nostrils. "We like Meri. As Sam said, we'll look out for her. Your threats have no place here. And if you'd been paying attention to what just happened, you'd realize that Sam was faster and deadlier than a fae assassin. Remember that."

Meri spoke to him softly in Mermish. Grudgingly, he nodded, kissed her on the forehead, and sunk back into the ocean.

She popped up, looking sheepish. "He's just very protective of me," she began.

I held up my hand. She didn't need to apologize. "He loves you. We understand. Many of us, myself included, wish we still had a father to watch over us and occasionally lose his temper." I glanced around the room. "Okay, people, show's over." I pointed at Meri. "You, get back to work. Those books aren't going to shelve themselves, you know."

Once she'd returned to the bookstore, I let out a gust of air. I didn't need merpeople after me too. I was just a bookish werewolf. Why did I seem to attract so much trouble? I patted Fyr's arm as I passed him on the way back to the kitchen. "Want a cookie?"

"No, thanks. I already had four."

I didn't get what one had to do with the other, but whatever. More cookies for me.

The rest of the afternoon was quiet. Dave arrived, Meri went home—she had homework—Owen went home, and then it was Fyr and me behind the bar. He'd be leaving soon for his night shift at The Viper's Nest, but for now, he was helping with the early evening rush.

Good evening, darling.

I was pouring a cup of coffee when I heard Clive's voice in my head. It was quieter and more muffled than usual, but I heard him. I'd been worried my candy-coating would block him out. *Hello, love!*

I can't hear you very well. Is everything all right?

Yep. I've been working with Thoth today so I can keep Garyn and her peeps out of my head. I delivered the coffee to Liam's selkie friend. *Also, I've gotten more in touch with my wolf—she's helping to protect my thoughts—and now, consequently, my senses are stronger and I'm faster. On the one hand, everything stinks—except our garden. On the other, I killed one of Finvarra's men before I even consciously thought,* Hey, I bet that guy's here to kill me.

What?

It's cool. I'm fine. I can explain all this when I see you. It's too hard to explain and listen to orders at the same time. Oh, by the way, there are more vamps in town. I checked Garyn's penthouse after you all went to bed and found another dozen or so with her.

Interesting.

Isn't it? Okay, love you. See you when you get here.

Clive was an early riser, due to his age and strength. I wondered if Garyn was too. I was used to Clive being the bell-wether that other vamps would soon be up, but maybe they already were.

I patted Fyr's beefy shoulder. "I'll be back in a minute."

He nodded and I ducked into the bookstore, going straight to the back where there was a bookshelf with a hidden release button. I hit it. When the bookcase swung open, I went into the apartment bedroom and shut the door. Could I have gone through the kitchen without all the cloak-and-dagger? Of course, but what fun would that be?

Actually, I was just avoiding Dave. Every time I ran back to the kitchen to grab clean glasses or load the washer, he was there with samples of something new he was baking that he wanted me to try. Mostly, this was awesome, except when I was in a hurry and didn't have time to give him a detailed critique in triplicate, high-lighting the flavor profile, visual, and mouth feel.

Leaving the lights off, I rolled onto the bed, closed my eyes, and sought out the green blips in town. With the candy-coating, it was harder than usual.

The scent in the room changed. Fergus must have lost me in the bar and so came looking. I flipped my hand over, palm up, and he dropped his head into it. "Hey, buddy. Good job finding me." I scratched under his chin. Trying to maintain my defenses, I searched for vamps. Russell was up. Godfrey and Audrey were waking—not together. There was movement at the nocturne.

Widening my gaze, I located the penthouse. Garyn was up, as were many of her people. Too many. Wait. How were there even more? I counted the blips in my head. Thirty-seven. *Holy crap!* Was this a war?

The air in the room changed again. The mattress dipped as Clive pulled me in for a kiss. When his hands started roaming, I pulled back.

"Thirty-seven."

"Hmm?" He continued kissing down the column of my throat.

"She has thirty-seven vamps in her penthouse."

He drew back and stared down at me. "War?"

"That was my thought. Should we call Russell, or do you think he's still under her influence?"

Clive rolled off the bed and pulled out his phone. "You keep searching. I'll check on the nocturne."

Blocking the low voices as best I could, I focused on the penthouse again. They were all awake. Garyn was in a room with three vamps. I tested each one, looking for a weak link. None were, so I switched to the strongest, hoping he was her second.

My wolf paced, growling at the vampires. *Shh, we're hunting.* She quieted immediately and I began to worm my way in. Voices. Clive's name. I pushed harder. If they were aimed at Clive, I needed to know. I felt a pop and then—

"Do we know where he and the dog are living if they're no longer in the nocturne?" Garyn asked.

They were in a sitting room with buff Italian plaster on the walls. To the right of the vampire whose mind I was visiting was a marble fireplace with a huge gilt mirror hanging above. Brocade curtains hung on either side of the open French doors which led to a terrace high above all the surrounding buildings. The sky behind Garyn was purple going to indigo. She sat in a high-backed antique chair, looking every bit the goddess, her golden hair perfectly coiffed, her aquamarine eyes growing impatient.

"Yes, my lady. We've located the house. Richard is there now. He says no one is inside and the entrances are warded," a light-haired vamp responded.

"Have him bust through a wall," she said, as though talking to a toddler.

"I misspoke, my lady. He tried getting in, doors, windows, chimney, walls. He said the warding is the strongest he's even seen. He tried jumping over the wall into their back garden, but even the air over the yard is warded. He bounced back into the front yard."

Hot damn! The magical builders took my concerns seriously.

"What about that pub of hers?" she demanded.

"No, my lady. We know the general area, but no one can find it. Max is our best tracker. He's with Richard. He said he tracked her scent to a tourist spot close by, but then her scent disappears. He thinks he smells magic, so it could be right where he's standing but the warding is keeping it invisible to us."

"I've never heard of warding that strong," my vamp said. "Who are the wicches who created it and where do we find them?"

"Reginald," Garyn said to my guy, "find out. If they built the wards, they can break them."

The blond vamp said, "Max thinks he might smell sulfur. If she has demons creating her wards, they'll be harder for us to tear down."

Garyn stood, and Reginald swallowed. His mistress was impossibly beautiful and powerful. He'd do anything to make her happy. Her stiff movements, though, betrayed her annoyance. She walked onto the terrace, gripped the wrought iron rail, and stared over the city. "Fine. I'll visit the nocturne again and have Russell explain how to enter her pub. Be ready to take her there."

Pulling out of Reginald, I said to Clive, *Tell Russell if he can't fight her influence, to get the hell out. She's coming back to pry info on us out of him.* I was pretty sure Clive heard me, as the whispered voices became more urgent. Meanwhile, I pushed back into Reginald's mind and crouched, spying once again.

"What about Clive?" Her fingers drummed on the balustrade.

"No sign yet, my lady," Blondie said. "Max caught his scent. It was faint, but again, disappeared where hers did."

"So," she said, "they're both most likely in the pub." Glancing over her shoulder, her radiant expression turning fierce, she muttered, "Must I do everything?" before leaping over the railing and plummeting ten floors.

If I hadn't seen Clive do something similar countless times, I might have panicked, alerting my vampy host to my presence. As it was, I just hoped Russell and his crew made it out in time.

The blond vamp who had yet to be named got back on his phone. My guy, Reginald, went out to the terrace. While he was occupied, I wandered around, following faint synapse trails, waiting for a memory to light up. And then one did.

ELEVEN

We Don't Need No Stinking Rules

We were in Garyn's English sitting room again, the one I'd seen when searching for cold green blips when we'd been visiting the UK. Her clothing and hair were different, as was the décor; it looked like historical dramas set in the seventeen-ish hundreds.

Her golden hair was pulled up into intricate coils. Her dress was a deep blue satin, with a low-cut bodice, a lace fichu making the daring cut more modest. The sleeves were tight to the elbow, where they loosened in a profusion of ruffles and bows. Her waist appeared impossibly small in her corset. Gold bows continued down the front of her grown, glistening against the dark blue.

The men, Reginald—through whom I was reliving this memory —and the blond vamp from the penthouse, were wearing white linen shirts, long strips of fabric tied at their collars and tucked into embroidered silk waistcoats, with jackets over breeches buttoned below the knee. White stockings and shiny black pumps completed the look. They made quite the picture, the men in black and Garyn in midnight blue.

Candles flickered in the dim room, casting shadows over the delicate gilt furniture. Large portraits hung against burnished walls. Garyn walked to the brown marble fireplace and pulled a white peony from the spray on the mantle.

"What have we learned? Where is he?" The seeming disinterest with which she asked the question was belied by the focus with which she studied the flower. This was not an idle inquiry.

"Clive continues to move about Europe, my lady. He was most recently in Paris, but the outbreak drove him back to England. He's returned to London and from all reports has made no noise about moving on yet," the blond one responded.

Her fingers brushed over the velvety petals. "And is he seeing anyone?"

My guy inclined his head in an almost bow and said, "Quite a few women, my lady. He was with the redhead in Paris, but they parted ways again. Since he's been back in London, there have been various women, but they have been human or our kind. From the reports, none have been serious partners."

Garyn nodded, throwing the bloom into the smoldering embers in the fireplace, watching the soft white flower blacken. "Good. I want to know the minute he does get serious."

"It may not be a romantic relationship, my lady," the blond vamp said—I really needed someone to use this guy's name.

Oh! Reginald, my vamp, just thought the name Stephen. Thank goodness. I was getting really sick of referring to him as the blond guy.

"He may find one and keep her as a pet," Stephen continued.

Garyn was already shaking her head. "No. She said nothing about a pet. She said love and partner." She brushed her hands down the front of her gown. "Have them bring the carriage around. We have a ball to attend."

Turning to Reginald, she added, "Make sure our people are on their best behavior. I like this house. It suits me. I don't wish to abandon it because our people were too lazy or stupid to hunt in the proper places."

"Of course, my lady. I'll see to it." Reginald bowed as she swept from the room.

The memory went dark, and though I considered jumping into another one, I really needed to get back to work. Fyr had probably left by now, meaning Dave was holding it down on his own. Fearing for my customers, I pulled out of Reginald's mind and found Clive sitting on the side of the bed, waiting for me.

"Is Fyr still here?" I sat up.

Clive shook his head, stood, and pulled me with him. "He left about thirty minutes ago. Dave knows you're occupied. He's got the bar."

"I need to tell you what I saw; see if you understand what it means."

He nodded. "Russell evacuated the nocturne. He's also declared her in breach of compact. She and all her people must leave the city immediately or it's war. Also, Dave said he strengthened our wards here against vampires, just in case."

"Good." I squeezed his hand. "Will she go?"

"No. She wouldn't have gone to all this trouble just to slip back out of the city. She wants war, though I have no idea to what end." He shook his head in disgust. "Russell may be new, and the nocturne may have the fewest members it's had in a century, but she has no idea the hell she'll rain down on herself and her people if she stays. This city is unique. We have every manner of supernatural living here and they will fight anyone who threatens them."

The smell hit when we stepped into the kitchen. A new plate of cookies sat in the middle of the island. Ooh, they were large meringues. I bit in. Chocolate-filled giant meringues. "Am I drooling?" I wiped at my mouth.

Clive patted my shoulder, following me through the swinging door into the bar.

"Dave, these are—" I took a last bite and moaned. "You need to hide them. I'm going to make myself sick, gorging on them until my stomach explodes. And honestly, all I'll regret is not being able to eat more."

"Good," he said as he walked past me, toward the kitchen.

"Wait," I shouted before the door swung shut.

He gave me his shark gaze. "What?"

"Can I have—" I tried to determine the maximum deliciousness I could consume without stomach pain. "Three. Three more, please, before you hide the rest for tomorrow's crew."

I kept the plate of cookies behind the bar. No way was I letting any sneaks steal one.

Clive stood to the side while I filled orders and cleared tables. Dave had dealt with the rush on his own. It was moving into the quiet time of the evening, with only a few tables needing service. Low conversation and reading; this was my favorite time of day, watching the sky change colors, sitting on my stool, and reading a mystery between requests.

Clive sat at what used to be his usual table, back when he would visit the business once a month to check on me, long before there was an us. He didn't like standing behind the bar. He thought it encouraged patrons to ask him to make them drinks, which he flatly refused to do.

He might not be the Master of the City anymore, but he was still a Master vampire. For our safety, as well as the safety of San Francisco, Clive couldn't be one of the guys. His threat needed to be such that only an idiot— or a very old narcissist— would consider invading our territory.

While we sat, he at his table, me on my stool behind the bar, we spoke mind-to-mind, our voices a little muffled because of the candy-coating, but not too bad. I explained to Clive what I'd seen and heard at the penthouse as well as in Reginald's memory. I shared an image from the memory, and he agreed it looked to be the eighteenth century.

What I don't understand is her interest in your love life.

He nodded slowly, drumming his fingers on the table.

It didn't feel like jealousy, I continued, *more like concern you might have met a lover she feared.*

Exactly. But also someone I might consider a pet.

Yeah. It makes no sense for her to be referring to me, though. I wouldn't be born for another two hundred and fifty years. I took a sip of tea. *Have you dated other werewolves or shifters? Maybe fae? Vamps can be so snotty. What other species do you consider pets?*

Not me, darling. As for others of my kind, well, it's hard to say. I agree with you, though. The use of the word pet *does make me wonder if it's a slur for a shifter.*

I couldn't count the number of times vamps at the nocturne referred to me in their heads as Clive's scarred pet. Assholes. *Did you know she had people following you, collecting information on you?*

He gave a small shake of his head. *And that really bothers me. How did I not notice spies following me?*

She could have planted her people in whatever nocturne you were in, like she did with Leticia. They weren't hiding in the shadows, following you around town, so much as living in the same scary house and regularly reporting back news of you.

He considered. *Possible. Quite possible.*

While Clive contemplated, I checked the tables. No one needed me, so I took another bite of heaven, closed my eyes, and went vampire hunting. Eight—no, ten—were milling around above us, no doubt trying to trip the ward. *Shit.*

How do we get these guys out of here safely? There are ten vamps up there, trying to get in.

Clive looked around the bar. *Liam and his friend will use the water entrance. The others are powerful magical beings. Ask them.*

Good call. "Hey, everyone? Sorry to bother you, but we're dealing with some hostile visiting vampires."

I was met with looks of concern but not panic, which was good. "I'm told there are about ten vamps at the top of the stairs, trying to figure out how to trip the ward to get in." I held up a hand. "No worries. Dave reinforced the ward against vampires."

Dave came out of the kitchen and leaned against the wall.

"My issue is I don't want you guys to go up the stairs and get attacked. So, any ideas on how you can safely get home?"

They looked at one another as though assessing their weapons. Who was still here and what were their strengths?

A tiny wicche in the corner said, "I can do an invisibility charm on people before they go up the stairs." She looked apologetic, adding, "It'll only last a few minutes, but it should get everyone to the parking lot."

"What if we go through the ward and then run right into them?" another asked. "That happened to me last summer. Luckily, the stairs were crowded. The humans were surprised, but no one screamed or fell or anything."

"I can leap out of Meg's entrance," Clive said to the group, "and take two at a time, depositing you on the ocean path, away from the stairs."

Thank you, love. I knew no one was going to choose the big, scary vamp exit, but I really appreciated his offer.

"I could go first," Dave said, "shoot a little fire, turn some vamps to dust. The rest will scatter and then these guys can get away."

Clive smiled at that, and he wasn't the only one. Quite a few of the wicches liked the idea of taking the vamps out permanently.

"We can do both," the little wicche piped up. "I'll do the spell, and you use your fire. The bloodsuckers—sorry, Clive; no offense intended—will scatter and our people will leave without being seen."

I looked at Clive. "Will we be lighting a powder keg by setting her vamps on fire?"

The smile he gave me was terrifying. "Most definitely, but not to worry, darling. She's in breach, remember."

"Those rules are for vampires," Dave grumbled, "not me. They want to start shit, trying to break into a private business, well," he said, fire shooting up from his open palm, "there are consequences. Garyn will have far fewer bloodsuckers by the end of the night."

Clive stood abruptly and the patrons flinched. "I've been working within the system for so long, I'd forgotten. Proper protocols don't matter. Enemy combatants are attacking. All bets are off." He turned to the tiny wicche. "Letty's right. She should cast her spell. Dave and I will go first to deal with vampires while your customers get to their vehicles and head home."

How did he know the tiny wicche's name? Oh, right, Master of the City. It was his job to know all of them.

"What say you?" Clive asked all assembled.

The wicches nodded. Some looked scared, the others quite excited. Liam and his friend went to the water entrance while the wicches moved to Letty's corner. Okay, we were doing this.

TWELVE

The Saddest Little Vampires in the Land

Letty worked her magic on herself and the seven other wicches, while I ordered Fergus to sit and stay. I knew he was going to try to follow us, but I needed him to stay down here.

"I mean it. Stay." I let my eyes lighten to wolf gold and he plopped his butt down. Clive and I were running into danger. Fergus wanted to protect us. I got that, but I also knew that the vamps wouldn't hesitate to kill him just because we loved him.

Dave and Clive disappeared up the stairs, moving faster than I could track. The invisible wicches ran far more slowly up the stairs, while I brought up the rear. I gave Fergus one last look, jabbing my finger at the floor where he sat, and then jogged up behind the already winded wicches. In their defense, it was a lot of stairs.

By the time I emerged, dust was blowing in the wind and Clive was helping one of the older wicches up the last of the stairs to her car. Ah, well. It looked as though I'd missed the battle. At least none of our not-so-invisible-anymore wicches had been hurt, thank goodness.

Clive was by my side a moment later.

"That was quick." I was itching for a vampire melee. Heck, I would have settled for a skirmish. Alas, I'd missed the brief fisticuffs. This was probably how Fergus was feeling.

"Dave is quite accurate with his fireballs. I'm afraid there wasn't much for me to do either."

"We good?" Dave asked, hands at his hips as he scanned the area.

I closed my eyes and looked for nearby green blips.

I nodded. "We're good. You can go. Thanks for your help."

He jogged up the steps, still glancing around, on his way to his beloved Shelby Mustang.

I nudged Clive, tipping my head toward the road. "We have visitors." A shiny black truck pulled into the parking lot. A moment later, Russell and Godfrey were coming down the stairs toward The Slaughtered Lamb entrance.

"Gentlemen," I said, "you missed all the fun. Of course, come to that, so did I."

By the time I got to the bottom of the stairs and found Fergus waiting for me, I realized that the three vamps weren't following me. Huh. Giving Fergus a full-body scratch, I thought, *Let Clive, Russell, and Godfrey pass through the ward.*

A moment later… "What gives?" Godfrey's outrage made me laugh.

As we all had excellent night vision, I turned off the lights so we could watch the moonlight dance on the waves. "Sorry, guys. Apparently, Dave upgraded my wards. Garyn's people were swarming up there, trying to get in."

Godfrey dragged out a chair and dropped into it. "Sodding cow," he groused.

Clive leaned against the bar while Russell paced, their expressions saying they agreed.

I freshened up my tea and took the chair across from Godfrey.

"It's bleeding embarrassing, is what it is," Godfrey elaborated.

Clive and Russell nodded.

"Maybe you guys should take lessons from Audrey. Where is she, anyway?" I took a sip of spicy orange tea.

"Making sure our people find secure resting places," Russell said. "I hate evacuating our own home, but—"

"You had to," Clive finished. "She's too powerful and too close. She had the whole nocturne eating out of her hand last night." His jaw clenched. "We can't let her steal your people. The only way to keep them safe is to hide them from her. In the short term, anyway." He crossed his arms over his chest and stared at the waves crashing against the window.

Russell rubbed his hands over his face. "I'm Master and I can't protect my people because if I come within fifty feet of her, I fall over myself wanting to serve her." He roared in frustration, causing me to jump, though neither of the other two flinched. "How do I kill her if I can't get near her?"

"Sniper rifle?" Godfrey suggested.

Russell grunted in agreement.

"She didn't mesmerize the whole nocturne," I finally said.

"We weren't talking about you, Missus," Godfrey said.

"Not me. Audrey."

All three men looked at me with varying expressions of confusion.

"She didn't tell you? Why didn't she tell you?" I gave Russell and Godfrey my squinty-eyed suspicious look. "Are you two not including her in your planning sessions?"

Russell looked indignant. "Of course we are."

I snagged a nearby chair with my foot and dragged it over before resting my feet on top of it. "If that were true, you'd know that we were the only two people in that room who weren't in her thrall."

Godfrey leaned forward. "Are you telling me that Audrey was the only vampire in that room that Garyn couldn't mesmerize?" Gesturing at Russell and Clive, he added, "Two Masters in the room and she was the only one able to fight her off?"

Nodding, I took another sip. "Yup." I patted Russell on the arm. "By the way, she's going to be a Master herself someday. Audrey's strong. She felt what Garyn was doing, saw how she'd ensnared all of you, but didn't know how to stop it. If either of us had moved against Garyn, we would have had the whole room to contend with."

A large wave swamped the window. "We couldn't talk freely then, of course," I continued, "but we've spoken since. Ask her about it. She has a good theory. Now Garyn, she's an odd one. For most of you vampy guys, power seems to be the goal. Power, prestige, blood, fear, sex. For her, though, I think it's adoration. And especially from men. I was watching her last night. There are no women in her entourage. Even now, with a couple dozen more vamps in the penthouse, no women. Last night, she completely ignored the women in our nocturne.

"I'm not sure she even noticed Audrey, and she only occasionally glanced at me when she was trying to screw with my head," I explained. "Some of her minions gaze at her as though she were a goddess walking amongst them, and others like a beloved and doted-on maternal figure."

Clive scratched his jaw. "Yes. Sam and I were discussing this. I see Garyn as a maternal figure." He ran his hand through his hair, a sure sign of agitation. "It was why I was so horrible to you last night," he said, catching my eye. "You were separating me from my mother." He shook his head, disgust written all over his features.

Godfrey nodded, watching the waves. "Mother."

"Goddess," Russell said. "I felt special, singled out to be in her presence."

Godfrey nodded again. "When Sam took Clive away, though, it changed."

"Yes." Russell had stopped pacing and was, like Godfrey, watching the seaweed bob. "I felt it too. She was angry Clive was leaving her orbit, enraged at Sam for pulling him away from her. Some of the goddess shine dimmed then."

Godfrey took over. "Her face changed. She was angry mommy and I wanted to back up. Thank Christ I still had the presence of mind to know I couldn't retreat from a rival vampire."

Crossing his arms over his chest, Russell added, "Exactly that. She had me mesmerized until that moment. Her whole demeanor changed from benevolence to wrath."

"Isn't that interesting," I said. "She could mesmerize an entire room of—what?—twenty-two vampires for hours without a chink in the armor but let one vamp—the one who walked away and never looked back a millennium ago—follow his wife out the door and she loses control. That's some fascinating psychology there."

Godfrey grumbled under his breath, gaze fixed on the hypnotic movement of the ocean.

"She's right," Clive said. "Garyn was strong enough to pull us all in without our noticing."

"And her change of emotion wasn't enough to break the spell for any of you," I added. "It just allowed some of her polish to dim."

We sat in silence for a few minutes, each, I think, wondering how we could win when proximity caused enemies to become allies. It was untenable. My stomach growled, so I got up to look for food. Dave usually made me something to eat—besides cookies, that was.

Pushing through the kitchen door, I realized Fergus was following. I wasn't sure if Fergus had been fed yet. He sniffed at his bowl and then looked longingly at me. "I've fallen for that before, dude." I texted Dave to see if he'd fed Fergus. Given how late it was, I assumed he had, but I wanted to be sure.

I searched the fridge. Score! He'd made shepherd's pie for dinner and left me a huge serving. By the time I was pulling it out of the microwave, I got a text back. "You big fibber. Dave said he fed you." Fergus flopped down beside his bowl, appearing to be the saddest dog in the land.

I couldn't do it. I couldn't eat in front of him. Ducking into the storeroom, I got him a bully stick, which made him the happiest dog in the land, and then took my dinner back into the bar. After pouring myself a soda, I sat behind the bar to eat.

The guys were talking quietly, looking like the most dejected little vampires in the land, an observation I intended to keep to myself.

Clive looked over his shoulder, eyebrows raised.

"I'm very hungry, so I figured it would be more polite not to make you guys watch me right now. I do have stuff to tell you, though." Using Clive as my interpreter while I ate, I explained what I'd seen through Reginald's eyes and memory. *Proximity is important. She tried to regain control of the nocturne but couldn't do it from a hundred yards away.*

Clive passed on the information and then added, "It's more like two hundred, but I see your point."

"How do we get rid of her?" Godfrey asked.

I shrugged. "Short of throwing her on an airplane and sending her back to England, I think we need to keep her rattled. If we let her hit her stride, all three of you and the rest of the vamps will be handing over the key to the city."

"Thanks so much for your high opinion of us," Godfrey replied, but I knew his annoyance was aimed at Garyn, not me.

"It's not that," I began, sitting back down with them, dinner a warm, delicious weight in my stomach.

Clive rubbed my thigh. "She's right and we all know it. Garyn had us in her palm all night."

"We need to separate her from her people," Russell said. "We can fight them. How, though, do we keep her from influencing the battle?"

Clive turned to me. "You walked across a library filled with hostile-to-you vampires, interrupted their mommy goddess, and pulled me—against my will—away from her." Leaning in, he kissed my cheek. "And as thanks, I was cruel to you. I'm so sorry, darling."

Clutching his hand on my thigh, I squeezed. "Not your fault. You snapped out of it."

Shaking his head, he clarified for his friends, "Once I was blocks from the nocturne, like an elastic band, her control snapped back and I was left cold and horrified. My wife had had to plead with me to take her to safety."

"And you did," I assured him.

He stared at me.

"Eventually."

Godfrey shook his head. "We're so screwed."

Nudging Clive, I pointed at the back of Godfrey's head. "Smack him. He's being defeatist." Plus, they all needed to lighten up so they could think. Whacking Godfrey upside the head often cheered up Clive and Russell.

"Unfortunately, darling, he's right."

THIRTEEN

Beware of Lurking Thieves

I felt a push on the ward. Closing my eyes, I checked to see what manner of supernatural had come calling. I couldn't see wicches in my head at all. Most of the others had a kind of signature color: vampires were a poisonous green, the fae were a healthy spring green, dragons were red, the ancient immortals, the gods and goddesses, were purple.

"Hey, guys, would it cheer you up if I told you we had seventeen of Garyn's vamps at the top of the stairs?" And they were gone. I raced up the stairs after them and found myself in the middle of a good old-fashioned vampire brawl.

A head rolled past me before turning to dust. Oh, good. That ought to brighten Clive's mood. All these vampires carried Garyn's scent. They were hers, all right. One flew at me and I spun, razor-sharp claws taking his head. When two more came at me from opposite sides, I flipped backward, letting them careen into each other, and then leapt, dragging my claws through both of their necks.

The fog sitting at the coast and the roar of the surf hid the fracas from nearby humans. Unless someone with excellent sight was walking by and saw the dark blurs, the vamps were safe from discovery. Vampires were incredibly quiet fighters. Godfrey skidded backward on his ass right in front of me before flying back into combat. Clive and Russell were fighting multiple vamps at once. They were both crazy fast, but so too were the other guys. They weren't like Lafitte's poorly trained popinjays. Like my guys, these vamps were old, powerful, and motivated. Still, somehow, their dust was blowing in the wind.

Stupid. I knew better than to watch when I was standing on the battlefield. I sensed someone a moment before he attacked. Ducking his grab, I spun and came up with my sword, cleaving him in two.

I had a moment of satisfaction and then I heard something that chilled my blood. Fergus whined. *Damn it!* A vamp held him by the neck, dangling him above the ground. "Come with us now," he said, voice low, "or I crush its head." He knew he had me.

Sam.

I've got it.

"You're going to put my dog back on the ground and you're going to step away from him." A vamp was racing up behind me, but I kept still, my focus on the asshole threatening Fergus.

Sam!

I know.

Never taking my eyes off asshole, I swung the sword, jabbing it over my shoulder, right through the head of the vamp sneaking up on me. His body weighed down the blade for a second before it slid through, his body turning to dust.

Shock registered on the asshole's face. I let my teeth lengthen and then gave him my most feral grin. Fear. You love to see it.

"Put. My. Dog. Down."

Instead, he leapt up, arrowing toward a nearby tree. I found his blip in my mind and crushed it. Head pounding, I raced over the rocky terrain to be directly beneath him when he turned to dust. Fergus yelped, free-falling right into my arms. Another vamp raced toward us. I found his blip in my mind too and crushed it. Who did these bastards think they were, going after my dog? I put

Fergus down and he leaned into my side, trembling. I howled my rage.

Clive was suddenly there, holding me with one arm, a hand on Fergus' head. "It's all right now, love. You're okay."

"I was always okay. He tried to kill my dog! I want to pop his head again. Bastard."

Crouching down, I hugged Fergus. His head rested on my shoulder as he sniffed my hair. "My poor little buddy," I crooned softly. "We need to have George check him. That piece of crap was dangling him by his neck."

"Is anyone else coming, my lady?" Russell asked.

"Let 'em come!" I shouted. "Try to hurt my dog? I WILL DESTROY YOU!"

"Clive?" Russell said.

"Right you are," he responded.

Suddenly I was up and being carried down the stairs. In the blink of an eye, we were back in the bar, Russell and Godfrey, who was carrying Fergus, right behind us. I slid to the floor, my back to the bar, and Fergus did his best to sit his oversized pup's body in my lap. I held him close, trying to reassure him that Mommy wouldn't let those pointy-toothed shitheads hurt him.

"I know you've been training, Missus, but I've never seen you move so fast," Godfrey said.

"Nor have I," Russell agreed.

Clive crouched beside me, brushing hair out of my face. "They're right, love. Even I had trouble tracking you. Your scent is different as well."

I'm sure my cheeks flamed as I sniffed at my top. "Do I stink?"

"Stink is such a harsh word, Missus. Not an inaccurate one, but —" Godfrey got a head smack from Russell.

"No," Clive said. "You have a hint of forest that you didn't before."

"Oh, that." I gave Fergus a snoot kiss and then stood. "Thoth helped me today to get more in touch with my wolf. I was able to keep Garyn out last night, but just barely. I need to get stronger if

I'm going to be able to hold my own against her." I looked at my guys, the bar, Fergus. "She can't have you," I said to Clive. "Not any of you. She can't have this town."

"You know," Godfrey said, "that howling thing was pretty hot." *Smack.* I didn't even see Russell's hand move.

Godfrey recovered quickly. "You said you killed ten before we got here. We just took out seventeen more. How many will she sacrifice?" He still had the flush of victory on him.

"All of them," Russell said. "She wasn't here. I assumed she'd use her control over us to help her people win, but she's not even here." He turned to Clive. "Is this all a distraction?"

"I have no idea what she's playing at." Clive stared out over the moonlit ocean, our voices barely audible over the surf.

"Is it connected?" I asked. "The dead guy at the Viper's Nest and Garyn instigating a war? One she's not attending?"

"She was always one to let others get their hands dirty, but what's the bloody point?" Clive ground out. "She's been keeping tabs on me for hundreds of years. Why? She's got spies watching who I date. For what purpose? I can't anticipate next steps because nothing she does makes any bleeding sense."

"Unrequited love?" Godfrey asked.

Clive and I both shook our heads. "We don't believe so," he said.

We were silent, each trying to fit the puzzle pieces together correctly and failing.

"Have more arrived tonight?" Clive asked.

I closed my eyes and began counting the unfamiliar vamps in town. "She has forty-two—no. Wait. She has fifty-seven. A private plane just landed."

Clive checked his watch. "The time is wrong. We just did this flight. It's a very tight window to get from London to San Francisco before the sun rises."

"And you said it couldn't be done in the summer," I added.

He shook his head. "Not safely. Yes, the plane can be sealed up against sunlight, but the pilot needs to know what we are and protect us. The problem is that the plane will need to land for refueling. Once the plane is on the ground, you run the risk of inspections. They rarely happen. Officials don't like inconveniencing the wealthy, but it only takes one door being opened to sunlight and half the plane has turned to dust. It's not worth the risk."

"Unless you consider them cannon fodder. Then the benefit outweighs the risk," I volunteered.

"These could be North American vampires," Russell said. "Her reach is long. She has people in her pocket all over the world, ones who owe her a great deal. She's probably calling in favors."

Clive sighed. "Good point."

"Make that seventy. Another plane just landed. Wait..." I touched all the cold green blips in the latest plane. "Canada." This was going to hurt, but we had to do something.

Uncoiling my magic from my chest—it was just how I pictured it—I looped it around all the vamps in the plane, including the pilot. Reginald, Garyn's second, was waiting on the tarmac to welcome them. Gathering the thirteen on the plane in my mind, I began to squeeze.

One down. Two. My head felt like it was splitting with the pain, but I channeled it into the white streak of hair at my temple and the wicche glass around my neck. I couldn't stop or I'd lose the rest. Three. Four. They were panicking now, trying to get off the plane.

Pulling the magical loop tighter, I strained to keep them contained. Five. Six. My heart was racing, sweat running down my back. And then I remembered I had my wolf to call on.

No sooner had I thought of her than she was stalking through the cabin. Claws long, she swiped at one who was trying to break a window. Seven. Another tried to pry off the door. Eight. It was too much. Light exploded behind my eyes.

Reginald was getting agitated, wondering why the door hadn't yet opened. The ground crew had already placed the stairs against the side of the plane. Why wasn't the door opening? He didn't want human officials investigating, so he jogged up the steps, muttering.

I was shaking, needing food and sleep, but I wasn't done yet. Drawing in a breath, I howled—hopefully just in my head or I'd never hear the end of it. My wolf hopped up onto the seat beside the Master vampire. His eyes were black, his fangs locked and loaded. My wolf lunged, jaws clamping around his neck. We worked together and when she finally ripped his head from his body, I dropped to the floor.

Or would have if Clive hadn't caught me. "Sixty-one." And then I was out.

———

I WOKE LATER IN BED.

"You need to eat something, darling. Nine. You gave nine their final deaths. That was astounding, but it took so much out of you." A lamp went on and Clive was passing me a plate holding a huge meat sandwich and another meringue cookie. Yum.

I sat up in bed and then thought about the crumbs. Moving to a reading chair, I curled my legs under me and took a big bite. Famished, I barely swallowed the first before taking the next. Had more vamps arrived while I was sleeping?

I opened my mind, calling on my necromancy, and found nothing. "I seemed to have fried my circuits." I took another bite. *Can you get me a glass of water?*

Clive continued to watch me eat, concern lining his face.

Damn. I'd apparently fried those too. Once I'd swallowed again, I said, "Can you get me a glass of water?"

He glanced at the nightstand and then was gone. A moment later, he walked back in with a tall glass of ice water and a full pitcher. "Sorry. I thought I had." He placed them on the small table beside the chair. "How are you feeling?"

Tipping my head back and forth, I considered and chewed.

"Mostly better," I finally responded. "My head is still pounding, but it's getting better as I eat."

He waited until I was done and then asked, "Fried your circuits how?"

I bit into the meringue. *Mmmmmm.* "I tried to see if more vamps had arrived, but I can't see them right now. I can't talk to you mind-to-mind either, which sucks. I like having you up here," I said, tapping my head gently with my cookie.

"I had a bad moment, wondering if you were well and truly pissed off, as you'd say, when you were ignoring me a few minutes ago."

"Ha," I said after swallowing the last of my cookie. "I wondered that about you too. Anyway, I wanted to see if another plane had come in, but that part of my brain is currently on the fritz."

Clive came to me, moved the plate from my hand to the table, and then picked me up, carrying me back to our bed. "Russell has sent a team of his best fighters to the airport. The goal being to keep out more enemy combatants. We're severely outnumbered, though.

"Oh," he added, settling between my legs, "you'll enjoy this. Russell called Garyn, telling her we'd given thirty-six of her vampires their final death, and that if she didn't want to choke on the dust of the rest, she'd leave now."

I slapped his shoulder. "He didn't."

"Oh, but he did. It was brilliantly done." He gave me a smacking kiss. "And it answered a question we had as to whether she could influence others with her voice."

"That was risky."

"Hmm, not really. If his eyes had glazed over, we would have disconnected the call."

I laughed and he rolled us over into the center of the bed. He kissed my chin, sliding his nose along my cheek. "How is your head feeling now? Did the food help?"

"It did." I looked around the small bedroom. We'd spent

months squished in here with all our belongings, waiting for either the Seal Rock house or the folly to be ready. "I didn't think we'd be sleeping here again so soon."

"Nor did I. Still, home is wherever you are, darling." He kissed me, and all concern for the outside world drifted away. He could do this to me. Every time.

"Tricksy vampire," I said breathlessly. "Where did my pajamas go?"

"Did you lose them?" He looked down at our naked bodies. "Goodness, mine seem to have disappeared as well." He glanced over his shoulder. "There may be thieves lurking."

I wrapped myself around him, the soles of my feet resting on the backs of his thighs. "Whatever shall we do?"

He grinned, taking my breath. "I'm sure we'll think of something."

FOURTEEN

The Dreaded Wet-Nose Wake Up

I woke when a wet nose was strategically pressed on my wrist. "Dude," I whispered—no idea why. Clive was out for the day —"I just saved your life. You're supposed to do me a solid and let me sleep."

I checked my phone. I'd slept about six hours. That was probably the best I could hope for. Sliding out from under the covers, I picked up my pjs from where Clive had tossed them, ran to the bathroom, used the facilities, dressed, and then toed into a pair of running shoes.

I pulled a hoodie over my head as I snatched his leash off the hook by the kitchen door. "Okay, buddy. Potty time."

In my head, I heard the phantom of Clive, Stheno, and Dave all yelling *Blades!*, so I stopped, went back to the bureau in our bedroom, and strapped them on.

I usually remembered, except when I was tired and taking Fergus out first thing in the morning. We were safe from vampires during daylight hours. The fae, though, could attack at any time, so I needed to stay armed.

Fergus went through the ward at the top of the stairs first. I caught a glimpse of his tail starting to wag and worried we were appearing right in front of a friendly tourist when I stepped through and saw Thoth. Part of the magic of the ward meant we didn't just pop into sight. It was like Owen's look-away spell. The human's eyes just passed over us until it seemed as though we'd been there all along. It was very sophisticated magic, but I often had a quick tug of panic that this time it wouldn't work.

Thankfully this morning, it was the case of a god seeing through spells. He crouched down and looked into Fergus' eyes before placing his hands on my pup's neck.

"I see," he said, voice low and deep. "It seems you had some excitement here last night." He looked up, studying me, as though making sure we were both okay. "This one had some strained muscles and trepidation about coming out here." He patted Fergus' side. "He's fine now."

"Thank you so much. I've been worried about his neck. I was going to take him today to see a friend who's a veterinarian."

Thoth stood and reached for my head. "I've saved you a trip." He brushed his fingertips over my forehead. "Much pain," he murmured.

Leaning into his hand, I said, "It's mostly gone now."

Then it was all gone. My shoulders slumped in relief. "Thank you again."

Fergus made a quiet noise.

"I need to take him for a potty walk. Would you like to walk with us?"

He nodded and gestured for me to lead the way. "So," he began once we were away from the stairs, on a path along the cliff edge, "tell me about last night."

I did, explaining everything that had happened, including my circuits being fried. I tried to locate the vamps in my head. This time, they were all back. "You fixed it. I can find them again."

"Good. And how many do you see?"

Fergus was having a grand time sniffing everything while Thoth and I spoke.

I paused, closing my eyes to count. "Still sixty-one. Looks like we didn't get another plane after we dealt with the last attack."

The rush of wind through the trees covered our low voices from all but the most sensitive of supernatural hearing. I didn't sense anyone nearby. More importantly, Thoth didn't seem to either.

"And the local nocturne? Have any of them been lost?" He had a strong, calming presence, one that allowed me to relax. It felt as though everything would be okay when he was around.

Fergus leaned into my side, waiting to continue his walk. I scanned the city for Russell's people. A few were far-flung, but I eventually got them all.

"Why are you smiling?" he asked me.

"Most of them are sleeping in the stadium where the Giants baseball team plays. I'm guessing they're in tunnels beneath the field." I checked my phone for the team's schedule. "Smart. The team is on the road. There aren't any home games scheduled for a few days."

"They haven't lived this long by choosing their daytime resting spots unwisely."

There was something about his tone. "You don't care for vampires, do you?"

The corner of his mouth quirked up. "My dear, I think you'll find that the vast majority of the world does not care for vampires, your excellent husband and friends excepted, of course."

I thought about it a moment. "Fair."

"A friend of mine created the first one. I told her it was a bad idea." He pushed a branch out of our way. "We have enough trouble in the world with wars, ignorance, and famine. Why add reanimated corpses?" He sounded tired, as though it was a very old argument he was sick of having. "I believe even she now realizes they were a mistake, but she is far too stubborn to admit it."

"I'm mostly on your side, with a huge exception. If vampires didn't exist, Clive would have died a thousand years before I was born."

"Perhaps that was how it should have been, how it was intended?"

We walked around a curve and there was the Golden Gate Bridge, gleaming over the sparkling water, white sailboats dotting the bay.

"No. If there's one thing I know, one utter truth in my life, it's that Clive and I were meant to find one another. Across oceans. Across time."

He pointed to a bench. "I like this spot. Can we sit a moment?"

"Of course." I enjoyed this spot too. The pooch plopped down on my shoe, his gaze following the progress of a dragonfly bobbing in the wind.

"How are you and your wolf getting along?" He lifted his dark, handsome face into the wind.

"Good. I think we've come to an understanding. The guys said they'd never seen me move as fast as I did last night."

He breathed deeply. "And what concessions have you made to your wolf?"

"Concessions?"

He half turned, one of his hard avian eyes pinning me to the spot. "She is helping you guard your mind, your family." He gestured to Fergus. "What are you doing for her?"

Oh, well shit. I kinda sucked, didn't I? "I'm eating more meat."

He shook his head. "That you should have always been doing. What does she enjoy?"

"Running. Hunting." She'd been so happy in his forest vision.

"And how often do you let her run and hunt?" He interlaced his fingers, resting them over his trim stomach.

"I shift every month at the full moon."

He gave me a disapproving frown. "Once a month is not enough. She is integrating herself into your human life. You must do the same, becoming more at home in your fur. She is not your subordinate. You are two halves, the woman and the wolf."

I started to protest. I had a business, a husband…

"I'm not saying that there must be parity with the time spent in fur and skin, but when you are able, let her out to run and hunt.

Not just once a month." He raised his eyebrows, waiting for me to agree.

He was right, but it wasn't exactly easy to hide a wolf in San Francisco. I could take the tunnel in The Slaughtered Lamb apartment to—wait a minute. I had a completely hidden, underground folly I could run in. Granted, I couldn't really hunt there, but what she really loved was running. And I did still have the tunnels to the Presidio and Mount Tamalpais for hunting...

"Yes. You're right. I can do that." Fergus would be my running buddy.

He stood. "Are you heading back or continuing on?"

"Back," I said, looking at the time on my phone. "I've got time for a run before I open for business."

"Good," he said.

We walked in companionable silence, Fergus renewing his quest for interesting scents.

"How long will you be visiting Stheno?" I hated to see him go.

He gave the barest of shrugs. "We'll see. I find myself invested in this vampire drama." He turned his head, grinning. "I want to know how it all plays out. Garyn is far older and a very powerful predator, but Stheno says I should be betting on you. Not much intrigues me anymore, so I think I'll be staying for a little while."

"Good," I echoed.

At the parking lot, Thoth went to a shiny black sedan, tipped his head toward me, then got in and drove away.

"What do you say, bud? Shall we go for a run?"

Fergus knew that word. He danced around my feet, waiting for me to start sprinting toward the beach.

"Come on. We're going to try something new." I unleashed him as we started down the stairs to the bar. There was still an hour before opening. I needed time to get cleaned up afterward, but I didn't need to be the one who opened. Owen was my manager. He could do it.

We went back to the apartment, and I gave Clive a kiss on the cheek.

Coco, George's jewelry-making sister, had made me a replacement necklace for the one Dave had melted. She used beautiful stones with protective qualities and then added her own dragon magic. It didn't hide my own magical gifts, like the necklace my mother had made me when I was a child. Coco's necklace helped me protect my mind from intrusion.

Now that I thought about it, the necklace may have been helping to keep Garyn out. I unclipped the choker, threaded my wedding ring and Gloriana's ring, and then clipped it back on. It was a little longer than a standard choker, which made it the perfect length for when I shifted. Stripping down, I called on my wolf, letting her take the lead. Shaking out my fur, I nosed Fergus and then took off at a run, my pup fast on my trail.

Bursting through the sheets of plastic at the door of our unfinished folly, I skirted the small pond on the right, lovely purple water lilies floating on its surface, and went to explore. The dragon folly was a marvel. Like the bookstore and bar, the folly was deep underground, but it felt as though we had been transported to Middle-earth. Or New Zealand, at the very least.

Dragons are deeply magical creatures, and this construction crew had used *all* the magic to create Hobbiton. High above our heads, I knew there was rock, but what we saw was a clear blue sky. If our folly was anything like George's family folly in Wales, there would also be a hidden control panel somewhere that allowed us to change the time of day in our false sky.

The dragons didn't want us in here while it was under construction, didn't want to be reminded that they were working for a vampire and a werewolf, though I think it was the vampire bit that bothered them the most. As Thoth had said, no one liked vampires, often not even other vampires. Don't get me wrong, though. It wasn't as if the dragons loved werewolves. We weren't a threat to them, so I doubted they gave us much thought. Dragons cared about other dragons. And treasure. That was about it.

All of that is to say that we weren't officially supposed to be here yet. Yes, they'd finished Hobbiton, but they were still working on the other spaces down here: Clive's family farm and—we guessed—a magical ocean filled with prehistoric and mythological creatures with a lovely island, perfect for lounging with a fruity cocktail.

We had given the dragon architect and his foreman our list of wants. They decided amongst themselves which ones they'd build. I couldn't overstate just how much they didn't want to think about who they were working for. They were charging a ridiculously exorbitant fee for their trouble, but I think it was more the principle of the matter. These magical places were intended for little dragons.

There were fewer and fewer dragons being born, though, as there were fewer and fewer dragons in existence, so they'd made an exception. It was also in our favor that Benvair was the one who'd hired them. George's grandmother was the matriarch of the Drake clan. She was well-respected and wielded a great deal of power within the dragon community. Had Clive or I tried to hire them, they wouldn't have answered the phone. As it was Benvair's request, they met with us, took all the money, and began to create magic.

FIFTEEN

Wait. How Do You Know My Dog?

Our folly ran underground between The Slaughtered Lamb and our new home on Seal Rock Drive. Above ground, the house was across a parking lot and green area, maybe a hundred and fifty yards from our door to the steps of the bookstore and bar. Below ground, Hobbiton had to be a mile long, maybe the same wide. How, you might ask, could that be? No idea. Dragon magic was the only response I'd ever been given.

A trodden dirt path ran the length of Hobbiton. On it, a cart was pulled by a disturbingly realistic horse. The road meandered past a tall hill, under which were the hobbit holes, round-doored homes dug into the earth. Before the hill was a serene pond, its water reflecting not only the colorful doors but the huge, sheltering tree growing at the top of the hill.

Directly under the tree was the largest door. It was green with circular windows on either side. That was our home. I mean, technically, they were all ours, but the middle door was modeled after Bilbo's, so that was the one Clive and I called home. Russell had claimed the light blue door, Godfrey the dark blue, and Audrey the yellow. They'd claimed them based on a photo.

I'd sneaked in for brief peeks, but this was my first time exploring the whole area. Rolling hills, bushes, trees, cows grazing, horses cantering, vegetable patches, a tavern; it all felt so real. With every step, my claws dug into rich, dark, fertile soil. I knew this wasn't really Middle-earth, but my senses swore it was.

When Fergus tired, I led him to the green door and flopped down, giving the pup a breather. Resting my head on my paws, I looked out over the Shire and felt peace. It occurred to me that the small pond by our apartment entrance was the only one I'd seen with water lilies. I bet they'd done that so we'd know where the exit was. Clearly, the dragons didn't think much of our navigational skills.

The run did both my wolf and me good, but I was no doubt late for work. When Fergus seemed ready to move again, I trotted down the hill and over the path. We were close to the apartment entrance when I heard a strange sound and hit the dirt in the tall grass. I was, after all, still trying to avoid angry dragons. With any luck, Fergus had followed my lead.

I turned my head and found that Fergus had *not* followed my lead at all. I chuffed to get his attention, but he was standing tall. Looking toward the far end of the Shire.

At the sound of a whistle, he went running. Oh, I see. Too tired to run with me but not too tired to answer a whistle. Real nice. Slinking through the grass, I searched for the whistler. I needed to make sure Fergus was okay while trying not to draw attention to myself.

"Come on, boy," a deep voice said. "Come help me eat my sandwich." One of the workmen appeared to step out of a wall, offering my dog half of his huge sandwich. Fergus chomped it down in a few bites. Another man came out of the wall and petted my dog too.

So, when I thought Fergus was disappearing into the apartment to take a midday nap, he was actually coming out here to mooch food from the construction crew. As the dragons were very sweet to him and I had to get to work, I slunk back to the apartment to get cleaned up. Fergus knew his way home, the scammer.

After I shifted and got cleaned up, I put my blades back on and went in search of my own food. Owen was in the kitchen, loading dirty glasses into the dishwasher.

"Hey, boss, what gives? I have to hear from the knitting circle that we had a vampire bloodbath here last night?" Owen, wicche extraordinaire, friend, and Slaughtered Lamb manager, had been my right-hand man for almost eight years. The bookstore and bar had only been open a week or so when he came in for a book and ended up staying.

I shrugged. "It was more of a dust bath. We took out thirty-six of her vamps last night, but she just keeps shipping more in. I don't—" I hopped up on the counter, shaking my head. "I don't get it. What's her endgame?"

"Kill Clive? Take over the city?" Owen picked up a meringue cookie and bit in. He blinked rapidly and then dropped his head. "Oh my God, how does he do this?"

"My cousin Arwyn sent him tutorial videos as payment for a demon job. I told Dave he had to hide those before I gorged myself into a coma. Even now, what I want to do is jump over the island and rip that cookie out of your hand." I let my eyes lighten and Owen stepped back.

"Kidding." I slid off the counter and went to the fridge. I needed meat. "Clive isn't the Master of the City anymore. She'd have to attack Russell, and she hasn't. Although I suppose mesmerizing the Master of the City would be seen as an attack. I don't know. None of it makes sense. She had them all in her thrall the night before last. She could have done anything and they all would have supported her. If she wanted Clive dead, she could have influenced any of them, hell, all of them, to give him his final death, but she didn't. Why is she okay with thirty-six of her people being destroyed?" I needed to do more snooping today.

Owen tentatively took another bite. "We're talking vampires here. Their logic isn't ours. For us, we'd need some big, complicated, high-stakes scheme to justify losing that many people. For them, the loss may not even register as a big deal."

"Like that old *Twilight Zone* episode?" I said. "You know, the kid who could psychically control his parents, the whole town. They spent their lives one tantrum away from being banished to cornfield death. They weren't real people with their own lives to him. They were more like Army men to be set up and knocked down on a whim. It might be the same for Garyn, and we're over here trying to find meaning where there is none."

"That's a disturbing thought," he said.

"Yeah. By the way, I like the look." Owen had toned down his usual style a couple of months ago. When he'd started working here, he had spikey black hair with blue streaks, pierced ears, and an eyebrow ring. He was gorgeous and sparkly.

All that changed when he was set to meet his boyfriend George Drake's family, as in Benvair Drake, George's grandmother and the matriarch of the dragon clan. Owen had been nervous and wanted to make a good impression, so his streaks and rings disappeared. George had told him from the start that it wasn't necessary, that he was already perfect, but Owen worried George's family wouldn't accept a wicche, even one from an ancient and gifted line of wicches, like the Wongs.

"Do the red streaks mean you're feeling more comfortable around Benvair?"

Owen laughed. "Not hardly. The woman is terrifying. It's more that as far as she's concerned, I can do no wrong."

"Nice. How'd you manage that?"

"According to George, she believes that if he hadn't starting dating me, George wouldn't have met you and Clive, which means they wouldn't have found Alec." He shook his head in wonder. "You can't believe how happy they are to have him back. All of them; they're so much lighter and they can't stop themselves from touching him, patting him on the back, wrapping an arm around him."

"Reassuring themselves he's really there," I guessed.

"Exactly. George has always been a horrible sleeper. Now, especially when Alec is staying with us, he's out like a light and down for eight."

"And how is Alec doing?"

He tipped his head back and forth, weighing his answer. "Better. Better every day, but it's going to take a while."

"And he may never get there. But *better* is something to celebrate." George's twin brother Alec had been taken as a child and kept imprisoned by a psychotic vampire to feed on. Twenty years. He'd grown up in a dark, stinking cell, starved, set upon by guards, fed on by Aldith, one of Garyn's vamps. When we'd found him, he'd been little more than skin and bones in filthy rags. A couple months of sun, food, and freedom, and Alec was actually beginning to look like his handsome brother George.

Owen nodded, smiling. "We celebrate often. Every milestone involves cake. Alec loves cake." Owen patted his flat stomach. "George and I are gaining weight right along with Alec."

"Take him one of Dave's meringues," I suggested.

"Already packed two away for both of them." He moved toward the door again.

"Listen, are you okay out there?" I pointed to the bar.

"Yeah. Fyr just got in." He checked his watch. "Meri will be here in another two hours or so. Do you need to go somewhere?"

I found a large bowl of beef chili in the back of the fridge from two nights ago. Perfect. I vented the lid and put it in the microwave. "I need to go in there"—I gestured to my apartment—"and do some sleuthing."

"You should come out and eat that. Let them all know you're okay." He pushed open the door, holding a tray of clean glasses in his other hand.

Yeah. He was right. It wasn't that long ago I worked seven days a week, opening to closing. It felt strange to not be in the bookstore or behind the bar, like I was visiting my own business. I would never want to give up all the new complications that limited my work hours, though. I hadn't had a good work-life balance before. I had no balance. I worked, slept, and ran, hiding away in my Slaughtered Lamb.

Now I had a home away from work, a husband I loved more

than should be allowed, and a dog who was sidling up to the dragons for meaty handouts. I had friends and enemies, though thankfully more of the former. I'd met gods, the fae queen and king, Abaddon, gorgons, a Fury… My life was often out of control, but so much fuller and happier than I'd believed possible. It was good to remember that.

I went out to the bar, sat at the little-used side table by the wall, and then went behind the bar to pour myself a soda.

Letty, our invisibility caster from last night, waved me over.

"Did everything work out last night?" She and the other wicches at her table, one of whom Clive had helped up the stairs, leaned forward to listen.

"Yes, and thank you so much for your help. Dave took out most of the vamps before we got to the top of the stairs."

"But—" They looked at one another. "We understood even more came afterward."

"How did you…" Oh, what difference did it make? "Yes, and we got rid of them too."

"Is Fergus all right?" Letty's friend Carol asked.

I glanced around. "Do you guys have surveillance cameras set up in here?"

Laughing, they shook their heads. Letty said, "Carol was scrying last night."

"Well," I said, "then you probably saw that we took them out too. Fergus had some strained muscles, but he's better now. Thank you for asking."

"We don't want to keep you from your lunch," Letty said. "We just worried."

"And I thank you for that. Owen?" I called.

He walked around the end of the bar to Letty's table. "Yeah, boss?"

"I believe these ladies could use a fresh pot of tea. My special reserve. On the house," I added as he leaned in to pick up the pot.

His eyes widened. "Of course. Coming right up."

I went back to my table and dug into the chili that was thankfully still hot. It was a gorgeous day, the sky a bright blue, the ocean dotted with white sailboats. Fergus trotted out of the kitchen and sat beside me, his head on my thigh.

"Nice try, buddy. This is *my* lunch. Your breath smells suspiciously of lunch meat, anyway."

He huffed out a sigh and slid down to the floor while I finished eating.

When I was done, I bussed my table. "Hey, Owen, do we have any cookies left?"

Owen shook his head, pointing at Fyr.

"Sorry. Didn't know we were saving one for you." Fyr, like Alec, was a dragon who had been imprisoned by the vampire Aldith. Unlike Alec, he'd escaped maybe ten years ago. He'd been on the run for a while and then opened a pub with a hobgoblin he thought was his friend but who was actually spying on him for the fae king. His family had been killed while he was imprisoned, so while he was a member of the Fyr clan, he'd come to America with the Drakes to be near others of his kind and to start over. He was working for me and Stheno while he decided what to do next.

"No problem. I ate a ton last night. I was just hoping." I patted the bar in farewell. "I'll be back later."

The apartment was dark and quiet. Fergus went to his bed, and I went to mine. The nice thing about a vampire husband was that he didn't thrash around in his sleep and didn't snore. He was exactly where he'd been when I slipped out of bed this morning.

I fluffed the pillow, got comfortable, and closed my eyes, locating the cold green blips in my head. It was time to do a little research.

SIXTEEN

Want to Tag Along?

I considered trying to worm my way into Garyn's mind but I was hesitant, as I didn't know the extent of her abilities. I was able to do what I did because they didn't know I was a necromancer. I wanted to get more info on her and the situation before I tried to breach her mind.

I did, however, want to try something new. I had no idea if it could be done, but I didn't want to experiment while dealing with her.

Clive? Can you hear me?

It took a moment, but I eventually heard, *Yes, darling?*

I've had a thought.

Dangerous.

I know. I'm wondering if I can keep you in here with me while I visit one of Garyn's lieutenants' minds.

We can try, but why?

You know these people. You know vampire customs and rivalries and norms. I try to explain everything I see, but I worry that my leaving out the type of clock that sat on the mantel will make all the difference in how a conversation should be interpreted.

Important clock.

Haha. You might recognize it as a clock stolen from Lord Bitey, the impetus for a war between him and Lord Fang, but you seeing it in the sitting room of Lady Bloodie means that Bitey and Fang were duped into battling one another instead the of the puppet master Bloodie.

You make an excellent point.

All my points are excellent.

Let's not go too far.

The problem is I have no idea if it can be done. And if it can, how.

I'm afraid I won't be much help. My thoughts are quite sluggish.

I know. I probably shouldn't have woken you, as I don't know how to do this.

Nonsense. I wasn't busy.

I elbowed him.

Ow. Darling, you're overthinking. Your magic is innate. Picture it, believe it. Do it.

Easy for you to say. Even to me, I sounded petulant. Okay, I had a candy-coated brain with a wolf guard. I could do this. How... *Can you keep talking to me?*

Of course. What would you like to discuss?

Nothing. I just need you to talk, so I can find you in here. Recite something.

I see. Shall I compare thee to a summer's day? Thou are more lovely and more temperate...

I couldn't see him, but I could hear him and knew the direction his voice came from. She was always there, but I called my wolf to me. She came around the far side of my hard-sided mind. She was guarding me and didn't like being pulled away from her job.

Do you hear him? Can you bring him to me? We need to get him in there. I pointed to my multicolored mind.

She chuffed her agreement and stalked off.

...but thy eternal summer shall not fade—Darling? Why does my ankle hurt?

My wolf returned, dragging Clive by his ankle.

Not sure.

It took all my self-control not to laugh. Perfectly-in-control Clive was lying on the floor of my mind, his suit jacket rucked up, one leg caught in my wolf's mouth. Well, I had asked her to bring him to me.

She used her claws to make a slit in the candy-coating, and then she dragged his body closer to my brain. Hmm, I really hoped I wasn't about to mind-meld us. I didn't want Clive in here all the time.

As I lifted him up, he became smaller and smaller, so sliding him past my hard shell was easy. I ran my finger up and down the slit until it reformed. And again, I don't want to get into any arguments about Science and how all of this was impossible. Of course it was impossible but that didn't mean it couldn't be done.

Can you hear me?

Quite clearly. Shall I continue reciting sonnets?

I thought about that. *Maybe later.*

I felt him grinning. *As you wish.*

We want to experiment, to make sure this works before we try it on Garyn's men.

Take us to Russell.

Ooh, good idea. I need to know whether or not they can hear you or if only I can. Hold on. I located cold, green blips in my head. *Can you see what I see?*

I don't see anything, no.

Hmm, that's kind of the point of all this. Wait. I found most of the nocturne under Giants Stadium. Let me locate Russell.

I knew Russell and Godfrey so well, it was easy to home in on their blips. I decided at the last minute to jump into Godfrey's mind instead. It felt rude to invade the privacy of the Master of the City, whereas Godfrey was far less formal or guarded. I wasn't sure if he'd care. So, Godfrey it was.

I wasn't concerned about discovery, so I burrowed in and arrived with a pop. *Godfrey? Can you hear me?*

Is that you, Missus? Is everything all right?

It is. I'm experimenting. I'm trying to bring Clive with me when I do this. Clive, say something.

Sorry to disturb your rest.

How long do I need to wait?

Yay! Clive, shout at him.

GODFREY!

Did you hear that? I asked him.

I'm only hearing you, Missus.

Kick ass! Is it okay if we jump into a memory? I want to see if Clive can see what I see.

That makes me far less comfortable, but I suppose so.

Thank you. I felt Clive take my hand and then we walked through the dark. Occasional lightning strikes of firing synapses lit the dark. *We're looking for a memory to light and then we jump in. It'll look like a dim soap bubble. There!*

I tugged and we both jumped into a very fancy bathroom. How odd. Then I heard the splashing and giggling. Godfrey was in a tub with two very naked women. I turned away, finding Clive standing beside me.

Can you see them?

I can and I know the two women. He studied the bathroom, looked up at a chandelier. *I believe this is his bathroom in the nocturne.*

I glanced around too, everywhere that didn't have naked people consenting to all manner of activities. *You're right. I recognize the countertops and the tile. Time to go.*

I pulled us out and we were back in the dark of Godfrey's mind. *What the hell? Of all the memories you have stored from hundreds of years of living, you show us a bubbly ménage à trois?*

Apologies, Missus. You said soap bubble and that popped into my head. I never intended for you to see that.

Tell him he can expect a smack to the back of his head when I next see him.

I passed along Clive's threat. *So, you could hear me talking to Clive about finding a memory, but you couldn't see or hear him?*

I can't see you either. I just hear your voice in my head. If I didn't already know what you can do, I'd be worried I was being possessed.

Ooh, that presents some interesting possibilities. Okay, go back to sleep. We're leaving.

I pulled Clive out and we were back together in my mind. *Cool. Now we know you can ride along, but if I talk to you they'll hear. Was the memory clear?*

Yes, I could see and hear quite well.

Good. Now, who knows the most? Garyn's second Reginald or someone else?

Lawrence. Try to find a man named Lawrence. When she turned me, he was her second. They seemed quite intimate but when she visited the nocturne, he wasn't even in the entourage. He might be at the penthouse, or he may be dead. If he's not around, let's go for Reginald. He'll know more than the others.

I was in Reginald's head last time. Let me look for a Lawrence. You can rest while I search.

I'm not feeling sluggish anymore. I believe being joined like this with you is energizing for me. If you don't mind, I'd like to watch. Maybe I can see what you do, maybe I can't. Either way, I'll be with you. And if I tire, I'll drift off.

Okie-dokie.

I let out a long breath, relaxed my muscles, and cleared my mind. Focusing on the penthouse, I brushed each one, finding Garyn, Reginald, and Stephen. Among the sixty-one, there was no Lawrence. Perhaps he'd been left in England.

Moving farther afield, I searched for cold green blips across the Atlantic Ocean. When I hit the UK, I slowed, focusing in the southwest of England, where'd I found her before.

It took a while, as there were only two vampires there instead of the dozen or so the last time I'd searched. They were awake and feeding. The first was Martin. He was young and didn't have the mental walls that the rest of her people did. Without even trying, I was in. While I doubted he had any information that could help me, I didn't see the point in wasting this opportunity.

I breathed Garyn's name in his mind, wanting it to feel like his own thought, and then waited for his memories to light up. And one did, right next to me. I hopped to the left and then...

"Come in, Martin." Garyn looked as she had a couple of nights ago. This must have been a modern memory. Her shoulder-length golden brown hair looked far more blonde than brown in this memory. Oh, right. This was Martin's recollection, so I was seeing her as he saw her. She sat regally, a halo of light around her. Ah. For Martin, she was a goddess.

"My lady, I've heard from the New Orleans nocturne." He stood just inside the doorway, his hands clasped in front of him.

She nodded and he continued.

"She's with him and she's just like they said. A scarred werewolf. Darrin said he was there when Clive visited the nocturne with his second and third. Clive brought her."

Garyn leaned forward, a slight furrow between her brows. "He brought his pet to Lafitte's nocturne?" She tapped her fingers on the arm of her chair, her gaze on her woolen trousers. "Now why would he do that?" she wondered aloud.

"Darrin told me Clive said, 'Is it any wonder I love you?' about the werewolf."

Her head reeled back as if she'd been slapped. Martin stepped forward, wanting to help his mistress but unsure of how.

"He said he loved her in a room full of our kind?" She lifted her chin, considering. "What have we learned about her?"

"Not a lot, my lady. Her birth certificate says her mother was named Bridget and her father Michael, last name Quinn. Both parents are dead. We can't find anything else. No high school diploma, no college degree, no government ID. She fell off the radar after birth."

"I see. And what does Leticia tell us?" Her fingers drummed on the armrest again.

He cleared his throat. "She wants to talk to you directly. She said she wouldn't waste her time with me."

"And what did you do to persuade her?" Garyn raised one eyebrow, waiting.

His shoulders drooped. "She made it very clear that she wouldn't talk to me, so I called her assistant, Audrey."

Garyn released a breath in what was almost a laugh. "Yes, I remember. She gave her lady's maid the dark kiss so she wouldn't have to train another one. Fine. What did Audrey tell us?"

"She told me Miss Leticia had left the nocturne a few weeks ago and hadn't reached out to her. As for the dog, she said she'd never met her and hadn't heard anything about her." His eyes became keen. "I don't believe her, though."

"And why is that?" Garyn tilted her radiant head, as though waiting to be dazzled by Martin.

Dang, this dude had it bad.

"I phoned Richard as well. He said the Master's infatuation is the talk of the nocturne. They're shamed and angry that their Master is showing such poor judgement."

Man, I hated that dick and was super happy he was dead now. Well, more dead.

"So, was Audrey lying or is she being kept separate from the others?" she murmured. "What does Richard tell us about the wolf?" Garyn asked Martin.

"Nothing complimentary," he said, brushing a hand down his gray sweater, "but also not terribly helpful. The one thing he did tell me was that she owned a bar named The Slaughtered Lamb and that it was oceanside. She may or may not have a demon working for her. He wasn't clear on that point."

"Demons?" She gave a mock shiver. "I'd never stoop so low, but it does tell us something about her."

"My lady?"

She gave him a patronizing smile. "It tells us her morals are gray, at best. It tells us she can be bought and manipulated. It tells us that Clive is not the golden boy he once was. Yes, this is good work. Leave me and keep digging." She turned back to her desk and he bowed out of the room.

The memory went dark and I slipped out of Martin's mind.

And that tells us, Clive said, *that she doesn't know either of us.*

Hey, I wasn't sure if you were still with me. I couldn't speak or Martin would hear.

There's no place I'd rather be than with you. I'm so glad my brilliant wife had this idea. It's fascinating to watch another's memory. And you were right. I did notice a few things.

SEVENTEEN

Now I Can't Stop Thinking About Vampires Sneaking Around in Squeaky Shoes

W *hat did you see?*
She's relying on a fledgling. Why? She has far more experienced and powerful people she could have given that job to, ones Leticia would never have dared to say no to.

Which tells us?

Either she actually doesn't care about you and therefore isn't concerned with his pitiful report or she enjoys the adoration more than she should. The flinching, the stepping back, the straightening of his sweater, all of those ticks give us information. For him, she is a terrifying goddess and he has no idea how to behave in front of her.

He's new.

He's absolutely new, which again begs the question: Why is she giving him tasks when he should still be learning to control his reactions? He belongs in the basement with his mentor, learning to be a useful member of the nocturne, not doing research. And where's her Historian? This is exactly what a Historian does. So, where's hers? Why is this star-struck fledgling being given a task that's far too complicated for him? Leticia didn't answer him because she knew he had no power. Audrey lied to him because, though she believed herself to have little power, she knew she had more than him, and Richard told all because he wanted to smear my name and spread rumors about you.

That guy was a dick.

As you've always said. Did you see the way she toyed with him? The raised eyebrow, the smile, pretending to talk to herself. She's creating an intimacy between them.

Maybe that's part of how she keeps them in her thrall.

Perhaps. She has a great many to keep under control, but it feels off. He sees the goddess when he looks at her. She should be aloof, not familiar.

Maybe she doesn't know how they see her. Or, perhaps how she sees herself is what she thinks she's projecting to all, not realizing they see her differently.

I like that.

I'm just spitballing over here.

Lovely image, but that makes the most sense. Keeping track of what everyone needs to see in her is far too complicated. She projects a manipulated version of herself, and they see what they see.

It's like a filter.

What is?

What she's doing is like those social media filters. Owen was showing me one. You set the filter and it displays you how it's been programmed: older, thinner, younger, different eye or hair color, whatever. She projects an image and those she ensnares see her as either a goddess or a mom.

Interesting.

I wonder if it bothers her?

What?

Well, neither is the sexy filter. She's either worshipped or doted on. No one has the hots for her.

Excellent, darling. And what does that tell us?

You guys should have a vampy psychologist on retainer. You all desperately need therapy.

I'd be offended if it weren't true.

That she doesn't want that. I'd been thinking she was in love with you or something, that that was the reason for the obsession, but I don't think that anymore. She's not looking for lust. Hmm... Does Russell have a Historian we can borrow to research Garyn?

Yes. We have an excel— they *have an excellent Historian.*

Stepping down as Master of the City has been a hard transition. *If they haven't already, maybe they could look into her life when she was alive.*

I'll call when the sun goes down.

Okay, ready to dive into Lawrence's thoughts?

You found him?

Yep. He's holding down the nocturne back home with Martin.

You can read us that far away?

I can.

Is this new?

No. I did it once before, when we were in New Orleans.

You've known for months and never told me?

Yeah. It sounds bad the way you say it. I tried to think how to explain it. *I didn't tell you at first because we were fighting bad guys nonstop and I worried about putting yet another target on my back. I thought I showed you when we were in England. I mean, I was sitting in Canterbury and searching the UK for Aldith.*

The UK isn't very big.

Okay, yes, but what if I was wrong, Clive?

About what?

You. What does a stupid, traumatized twenty-four-year-old who's been hiding most of her life know about the world, about love? You were hundreds of years old, been everywhere, knew a million people, dated a million women. What if you got bored and moved on with information that would cause every vampire in the world to want to kill me? What if you didn't even do it maliciously? You're just sitting around with friends and you accidentally let something slip, something you don't even remember being problematic for me, and someone puts it together, maybe someone who wasn't even there? People talk. You were on the phone with all those vamps on the flight to New Orleans, pumping them for info they didn't realize they were giving you. So, I spend the rest of my possibly long life flinching at shadows because I'll never know when the one who puts it together comes to get rid of me. Look what just happened. We were choosing between Russell and Godfrey for running our experiment. Both know what I can do. There are currently three vampires who know most of what I can do. Four, if Russell told Audrey.

My heart ached. I never meant to hurt Clive. *So, any of those four people could share that info with someone they have complete faith in—because vampires are well-known for never betraying one another and starting wars—but shouldn't have. Or they should, but the conversation was overheard and passed on. There are already a ridiculous number of ways I could end up with thousands of fangs aimed at my jugular. I'm sorry to have hurt you, but I did just show you what I could do. You didn't catch me in a lie. I'm sharing with you the thing that could get me killed. I—*

You're right, he interrupted. *I told you before that we had our long lives to learn about each other and then I jumped on you when you didn't share something incredibly sensitive the minute it happened, when you were still processing what it meant. I'm sorry, love. Sometimes I am... stunned by what you can do. There's a plan. There has to be a plan for someone so special, someone with skills so unique, who's gone through what you have. There has to be a reason for you poised right here, right now. I lose myself wondering what it is. And, yes, I fear what will happen if anyone else learns. What if I'm not there? What if I can't protect you? One of Garyn's men was threatening Fergus while another was racing up behind you and I had to stand down because you said you had it. Our lives flashed before my eyes in that half second I waited for you to move. And then you dealt with them both and got our dog back.*

He paused. *I'm sorry, darling. I've derailed our offensive. Let's go find out what Lawrence knows.*

You're sure?

I'm sure.

Relaxing back into the task, I found Lawrence quite easily. He was walking the streets, looking for a meal. Bagged blood existed, but he much preferred live donors. He was walking silently behind a young man who had just left a pub. He'd noticed the slight bobble when the man had crossed the street, the gentle sway, leaning a few degrees right of center.

He's hunting.

Lawrence moved so quickly, I almost missed it. The drunk walked past the mouth of a narrow alleyway and then Lawrence and the drunk were at the far end, behind a dumpster. The guy's face was to the wall as Lawrence slipped his fangs into drunk guy's neck.

Do it now. He's too preoccupied to think of anything but blood.

Instead of just plastering myself to his blip and listening, I burrowed inside. Clive was right. That was easier than it should have been.

As Lawrence had had so much longer of an association with Garyn, I didn't think whispering her name would get me anywhere. I considered while he walked back to the nocturne, his shoes silent on the cobbled stones.

I needed to ask Clive about that. Did they own a vampy silent shoe company?

I breathed, *Left behind,* and waited. I was afraid he hadn't heard, or it didn't register, but then memories flared to life around me. I jumped into the largest light directly beside me...

"I don't understand. How have I displeased you, my lady?" They *stood in a stone chamber. A lantern hung from the rafters overhead. Rivulets of water snaked down the walls and gathered on the far side in a shallow, fetid pool.*

Lawrence wore a long dark tunic over light hose. His garments appeared ill-fitting and threadbare. Garyn's dress was a simple green wool over a white linen tunic. Her long sleeves flared at the wrist and hung far below her fingertips.

Given their clothing, Clive said, *I'd guess this was the twelfth centur—*

When Garyn began speaking, Clive shut up.

"Not displeased, dear one. Disappointed." She shook her head, expression sorrowful. *"You're loyal and you know what that means to me. I've given you one task, though, and you've failed me. How can I rely on you as my second when you couldn't complete this simple request?"*

"I've tried, my lady. I've tracked down every sighting. After he slaughtered the Atwoods, he left Canterbury. If he's made it as far as

London, I'm not sure how we'll find him." He looked miserable to be disappointing Garyn.

"And that is why you disappoint me, Lawrence. If you truly cared, you'd already be halfway to London to find him for me. I need to know if he has fallen in love." She paced along the damp stones, away from the pool of stagnant water. "My survival depends on it. You know that."

He moved forward, his arms twitching at his sides as though wanting to reach out and comfort Garyn. "We don't even know if it's true. You said she was a child. Her prophesy could have been the ramblings of an imaginative child."

Garyn shook her head, still pacing. "Her mother was a wicche. You didn't see her. She was in some kind of a trance."

He closed his eyes a moment and then opened them with a new resolve. "I'll go now, my lady," he said, his hand over his heart.

She stopped and her face transformed, the approving mother. "I knew you couldn't be so cruel. I knew I could count on you."

"Always, my lady." Lawrence bowed his head.

"Good. Well, you better get started. You should be able to get a few hours of walking in tonight before seeking a daytime resting spot. Get word to me when you learn something useful." She turned her back on him, took the lamp, and ascended the stone steps.

"Of course, my lady. Right away," he murmured, alone in the dark basement.

EIGHTEEN

Everyone Smile Like Angry Psychos Wouldn't

I pulled all the way out so Clive and I could talk. *That was interesting.*

Wasn't it? I'm beginning to think this doesn't have anything to do with me.

It must. She identified you as the vamp who would fall in love with a woman who would endanger her in some way.

Kill her. She wouldn't be this worked up about an injury.

But I wouldn't have had anything to do with her if she'd just stayed in England. If she was worried about me, why announce herself and set up shop in my backyard? Maybe a thousand years of waiting for the shoe to drop has made her nuts.

There's that.

You guys are so weird. If she'd snuck into the city on her own and waited until I was walking home after closing, she could have killed me without anyone being the wiser. But, no, she has to make it a big deal and arrive with an entourage. Pompous dumbass.

Which tells us what? I heard the humor in his voice.

That we're dealing with a narcissist who can't imagine it not being all about her. And her strategy stinks. She's got all these minions and none of them can pull her aside to say, Yo, sister, bad idea?

And that is precisely her problem. They see her as goddess or mother, both authority figures you don't question. They don't tell her the hard truths because she can't handle being gainsaid.

So how do we fight a vamp who can mesmerize all of you?

I have no bloody idea, other than what we've been doing. We avoid her while taking out as many of her people as we possibly can. Clive's frustration was palpable. *That first image we saw in the alley? It reminds me that Garyn's nocturne prefers live donors. We have sixty-one vampires in this city who will be feeding on our citizens tonight.*

We need to warn Russell.

Darling, this is war and every member of the nocturne is braced for it. He was silent for a while. *The sun will be setting soon. Are there more planes waiting in hangars for nightfall?*

Oh, shit. I forgot we had the threat hanging over us of still more flooding into our city. I closed my eyes and scanned the airport. *Three private planes holding twenty-nine more vamps in total. We're going to have ninety vamps feeding tonight.*

I checked my phone. Shit. I'd been in here for hours. *Sorry, babe. Gotta go.* Strapping on my blades, I ran out, through the kitchen, and into the bar. Owen had his backpack on and was leaving.

"Sorry, guys!"

A group of three wicches were just leaving as well. They waved on their way out while I bussed their table and Fyr mixed a cocktail. I took the teacups in back. The dishwasher was already going, so I left them on the counter to put in the next load and went back out.

"Sam, I need to go now. I'm meeting George and Alec. Meri's almost done shelving the last cart. You should go look." He gestured to the bookstore. "It's finally looking like a bookstore in there."

I clapped and moved quickly to his side, looking through the archway into the bookstore. Oh, he was right. The shelves were filling and customers were back to browsing.

Owen threw an arm over my shoulder. "You've created a fantastic collection. I bought a few myself and a couple for Alec today."

"That must be so hard. He wasn't able to read after—what?—eight years old. What type of books are you getting him?"

"Young adult." He pulled his backpack off and unzipped it, handing me a few books in a great sci-fi dystopian series.

Nodding, I passed them back. "Those are perfect. If the language is a little too difficult, let me know. I can look for high-interest books for struggling readers."

"George says Alec was always a really strong reader, testing at least a few grades ahead, so we're hopeful." He zipped his bag and shouldered it. "Gotta go."

Waving, I added, "Tell them I said hi," before wandering into the bookstore. I found Meri at the shelves in back, putting away books on local history. I picked up one on Alcatraz, the former high security prison on a small island in the Bay.

Sliding the book into its spot on the shelf, I asked, "How was today?"

"Better now. School was…school." She grinned and added, "I helped Owen find books for his boyfriend's brother. And then I also helped a couple of older wicches find the books they were looking for." Her beautiful lavender eyes lit up. "All they remembered was that the cover was green, and they thought there was a tentacle."

"And you figured it out?"

"Yes!" she whisper-shouted. "I'd just shelved copies of that one two weeks ago. I read the inner leaf and the blurb on the back, so I recognized it when they said it had a woman living in a seaside town."

"Great job. It makes me so happy to have someone working here who loves the books as much as I do."

"I really do," she said, grinning broadly.

Helping her shelve the last few books, I said, "Given what happened yesterday, I was sure your dad was going to forbid you from coming back."

"Oh, that." She waved her hand. "He's fine. He was really upset but then I explained how much I loved it here and he agreed to let me stay." She began to wheel the empty book cart away and then stopped, her silvery blonde hair covering most of her face. "I'm really sorry he yelled at you."

"Don't be. He was worried about you. That's all. He's your dad. He just needs to make sure you're safe. That's what dads do." I assumed, anyway. How the heck would I know?

Shyly peeking over at me, she said, "Thanks, Sam," and returned the cart to the back room.

When she returned to the bookstore, I moved to the bar. "Everything okay?" I asked Fyr.

"Sure. No problems." He delivered a fresh pot of tea to a table by the window.

Heavy boots pounded down the stairs and my salivary glands went into overdrive. When Dave hit the bottom step, I rounded the bar.

"Please tell me you have more meringue cookies. I'm begging you."

He smacked the bag in his hand against my stomach and kept moving toward the kitchen.

Hoping, I opened the bag. Two meringues and one brownie. "I love you!" I pulled a meringue out and took a big bite. *Mmmmm...*

"I love you too, darling. You needn't shout it, though. I can hear you just fine." Clive swung through the kitchen door. "You should ask Dave if he'd be willing to make more pastries for you to sell here."

My brain exploded in happy thoughts. "You know I'm just going to eat most of them, right?"

Clive shrugged, unconcerned. "You need the calories and you'd be the one paying for them. I don't see the issue."

Dropping the rest of the cookie I was eating back in the bag, I handed it off to Clive. "Guard that with your life." I needed to go negotiate with a certain grumpy demon.

The kitchen door flew open, almost taking my face off. Standing in the open doorway was a huge, very angry dragon. Clive was suddenly there, between us, pushing me back. I appreciated the help, but his hands were empty. What the hell did he do with my cookies?

Meri, looking terrified, picked up the dropped bag and placed it on the bar.

Shit! Not again. Her dad was going to make her quit for sure. "Thank you! This is no problem. Don't worry," I said as brightly as I could manage with a raging dragon looming over me, smoke billowing from his nostrils.

"You're damn right it's a problem." He glanced over at Meri. "Not for you, though." He jabbed his finger at Clive and me. "These two, however, we are done with. When we agreed to take this job," he ground out, "we said no bloodsuckers. We don't want to see any *fucking* bloodsuckers!"

"I live here," Clive said. "And you've busted into our home to threaten us."

Red sparks flashed in the dragon's eyes. I knew this one. He was the foreman. No one had introduced him to me, so I didn't know his name, but I remembered his face. He was one of the men petting Fergus this afternoon. Speaking of which…

"Where's Fergus?" If they did anything to my dog, I was going to kick some dragon ass!

Fyr was there a moment later, his beefy arm holding back the other dragon. "Stand down. You can't demand they leave their own home."

"I've got him," Dave answered me.

"Not them!" the dragon roared. "It's his friends, coming in through our entrance, trying to sneak by us."

Clive pushed me farther back, which made sense as we both saw fire licking around his lips as he thundered.

Speaking over Clive's shoulder, I said, "I get that you're mad, but we don't even know where your entrance is."

He glared at me. "Your scent is all over the folly."

"Not *all* over, just in Hobbiton, and you guys are done with that part. My wolf needed to run and that was a safe place to do it. We weren't bothering you. Why're you being such a dick all of a sudden?"

The smoke billowed darker.

"Sam," Fyr said quietly, "that's not helping."

"Your problem, I believe," Clive began, "is that vampires used your entrance into the folly. Are they in there now?"

We need to go hunt them down.

On it.

"No. Dragon's Fire puts down bloodsuckers for good."

"Oh." Clive's shoulders relaxed. "Let us offer you thanks, then. We appreciate your help."

The red disappeared from the dragon's baffled gaze.

"You see," Clive continued, "San Francisco is currently being overrun with warring vampires. We've taken care of"—he looked over his shoulder, including me in the vampire hunting—"thirty-six of them last night. How many did you get today?"

"Six."

Clive looked at me again. "Six to take us both out? I find that offensive."

"They weren't friends of yours?" he growled.

"No indeed. We'd love it if you burned up any you find trying to sneak in. We still have quite a few to track down and kill."

"We're not doing your dirty work for you." Knowing they'd inadvertently helped vampires seemed to have him confused as to where to place his anger.

"Rupert, mate." Fyr patted the other dragon's chest and let go. "You know you need to secure the worksite. This is their home and you're out here raging about assassins breaking in as though it's their fault."

Hands on hips, Fyr stared the other man down. "You know what these two did for our kind. You also know they're paying ten times your normal fee."

I knew it!

"And she's right," Fyr continued. "You're done with The Shire. What the hell do you care if she and her dog go for a run in their own. Damn. Home?" Fyr had some smoke billowing from his own nostrils now too.

I glanced behind me and saw Meri's very angry dad in the window. Seaweed fronds bent with the force of his pissed-off tail. *Shitshitshit.* "Meri, I think your dad would be happier if you were in the bookstore right now."

She'd been like a deer in headlights watching this all play out, much like the rest of my customers. Flinching, she turned to the window and then gave a huge, totally fake smile. "Hi, Daddy!" She waved frantically.

The dragon—Rupert, apparently—stared out the window. "Huh."

"Be nice!" I hissed. "Her dad is going to make her quit if he keeps seeing raging supernaturals threatening me. He thinks we're unsafe."

Rupert stopped smoking and raised a hand in greeting. I turned to the window, smiling and waving. Thankfully, most of my patrons joined me. They were the best.

Meri's dad shook his head in disgust but swam away.

"Phew! Good job everyone! Hopefully we get to keep Meri a little longer now."

"Sorry, Sam," Meri said.

I waved her apology away. "Nothing to be sorry about. It got a little tense with Rupert storming in here"—I gave him my best suspicious squinty eye—"but that's not your fault."

"Was that really a merman?" Rupert asked, still staring out the window.

"Yes." I pushed him back into the kitchen. "I'm not even going to get into you stomping through our private apartment to come out here, scare my customers, and roar false allegations. Time for you to go until you can be polite." I shooed him away with my hands.

"We can't get through that doorway," he said, pointing at the darkened doorway to our apartment.

"And how would you know that?" What had they been up to?

Fyr stepped in. "Remember when Colin came out to have a beer with me? He tried to go back the way he came and realized the wards bounced him back. He had to go out through the bar."

Rupert had stopped paying attention to us because he was staring at the stovetop. "That smells good."

Dave chuckled, dropping his glamour. With shark-black eyes and red skin, he said, "Like I'm going to feed you after you threatened my boss."

Rupert took a step back. "Demons?" he whispered.

Dave shrugged. "Just the one."

"What the hell kind of place is this?" Poor little dragon.

"It's a bookstore and bar."

Duh.

NINETEEN

A Love Story Told Through Burritos

"I'm getting out of this nuthouse," Rupert said.

"Well, who's trying to stop you?" Jeez. This guy.

Darling? There were six at the folly. Are there any up there now?

Oh no! Did I just let those wicches walk right into a pack of vampires? I closed my eyes, found the supernaturals with me and then found fourteen vamps at the top of the steps. I shared the image with Clive and we took off, Dave on our heels.

"No one leave!" I shouted on my way out.

Dave moved ahead on the stairs, fireballs forming in his hands. I came out on Clive's heels, but he was already engaged with three vamps by the time I could see what was going on. Dave was mowing them down with fireballs. Three ran at me. I unsheathed my blades and started swinging. As much as I enjoyed taking them out with my claws, the blades extended my reach, which was better for hand-to-hand combat with vamps.

I took the first two out quickly. They didn't see the blades until they were in my hands and cutting through their necks. The third ducked and then dove at me. I spun, coming up at his back and running him through the heart from behind.

A jet of fire shot past me, taking out two vamps.

"What the frick, Dave? You almost burned me!"

135

I turned to watch Fyr breathing into the face of a struggling vamp. Oh.

When the dust fell to the ground, Fyr said, "Sorry about that. I'm still working on my aim."

Clive was suddenly beside me, studying my arm and the side of my face.

"I'm okay. It was just really hot there for a minute." I turned back to Fyr. "Can you get all our customers out? If tonight is like last night, there will be more soon." Something in the water caught my gaze. "Damn it!" I whispered. "Meri's dad caught all of that. She's awesome and I'm going to lose her."

Clive patted my back in comfort.

I waved at Mr. Meri's Dad. "Hello, sir. How are you this evening?"

"Is the second wave on its way?" Dave asked, surveying the scattered clothes and mounds of dust shifting in the constant winds off the ocean.

I sought out all the supernaturals in the city. *Clive, there's one in the tree in our front yard.* Clive was gone in a blink of an eye and back a few seconds later, a phone in his hand.

"He was texting when I took his head," he said, dropping more clothes on the ground. "Can you call Godfrey and ask him for another cleanup?"

"The secondhand shops are going to be getting a lot of dusty clothes this week." I dialed Godfrey.

"Hello, Missus. Again, sorry about earlier."

"Not your fault. That's what I get for snooping. Anyway, we need another cleanup on aisle six." While I spoke with Godfrey, Clive and Dave swiped through the enemy vamp's phone.

"How many?" The teasing in his voice was gone. It was all business.

"There were fourteen, but a few of them went up in flames, so no clothes to worry about."

"I see," he said, murmuring to someone nearby.

"Godfrey," Clive said, "another six tried to break into our folly, but the dragons got them."

"Twenty down tonight, so the enemy is at thirty-seven?"

"Nope," I answered. "With the private plane last night and three more today, we're at—"

"Seventy," Clive answered.

"I'll let the Master know." The line went dead.

"That felt very strange. Since when is Godfrey so formal? Do you think she's there with them?" We had enough problems with seventy vampires strolling our streets and using our people as juice boxes. We didn't need our friends under her influence too.

Clive shook his head. "He's third for a reason. He might play around with you, but he knows when to drop the jokes and do the job." *Are they still at the stadium?*

My customers began to hurry by.

"Sorry, guys. I'm going to start closing a little before sunset until the invading vamps go away. Sorry. Goodnight." I smiled and apologized until the last patron was out. Last up the stairs were Meri, Fyr, and the cranky dragon builder. He gave me a dirty look as he walked by, but I ignored him and turned to Fyr. "Can you make sure Meri gets home safely?"

She began to protest, not wanting to inconvenience Fyr, but he shook his head. "It's no problem. We can't have you out walking in the dark by yourself. If it's not the vampires, it could be the humans." He tipped his head toward the stairs. "Come on. Let's get you home."

He continued up and after a hesitation, she followed. Dragons are naturally protective. After what Fyr had been through, he was even more so. He knew how quickly a person could be taken and their lives torn apart. She was as safe as I could make her, so I let it go.

Once Clive, Dave, and I were alone, I closed my eyes and searched out the vamps. "Russell and most of the nocturne are at the stadium. Six of his people are at the airport." Garyn's vamps were roaming the streets, specifically high tourist areas. "Her people have split up. They're at Pier 39, Union Square, Chinatown, and a few seem to be on cable cars, given the way their blips are moving."

"What about her?" Dave asked. "Where's she?"

"I almost said she was at the nocturne, but then I remembered that the penthouse is essentially next door. It looks like the guards cleared out. The nocturne is empty." I paused, testing the blips. "Garyn has two with her. Reginald and Stephen again." I opened my eyes to check with Clive. "Her second and third?"

"I would assume," he said.

"Listen," Dave began, "do you still need me?"

I shook my head. "It doesn't look like we have a second wave coming."

Being a man of few words, he nodded and took off.

"Let's go home," Clive said. "I need to call Russell, but not out in the open."

I went to the steps, took one down to the bar, and found Fergus waiting. "Good boy!" He came out with me, sniffing cautiously at the piles of dust and clothes, high stepping around all of it.

Mentally, I shut down my wards and then raced Fergus to our front door, where we found Clive lounging on the porch. Fergus barked happily and then bounced around Clive.

"Dang! I forgot my cookies." When I started back, Clive grabbed my arm and swung me around, pulling the bag from his jacket pocket. "What? How'd you do that?"

"Darling, I thought you knew. I'm extraordinary." He ushered us in and then locked the door before I reset the wards.

"At least we know we're safe here." I went to the kitchen to feed Fergus.

Clive had his phone out but paused. "We do?"

"I thought I told you." At his blank stare, I explained about the vamp who had tried to break in and couldn't even get over the garden wall.

"Excellent." He walked into the living room. "That was money well spent." He sat in his favorite chair by the fireplace and tapped the screen, leaving it on the arm of his chair so we could both hear Russell. It rang once.

"Clive. Godfrey told me about the cleanup. I have two en route now. Has the trouble continued?"

I poured dog food into Fergus' bowl. If he had already eaten, we'd consider this second dinner. Fergus fell on it as though he hadn't eaten in months.

"Garyn's people prefer live blood donors," Clive said. "And they are currently at Pier 39, Union Square, and Chinatown."

I heard cursing in the background, mostly likely from Godfrey.

"Is she with them?" Russell asked.

"Sam says she, Reginald, and Stephen are in the penthouse."

"Let's go get them, Sire," Godfrey said.

Clive was shaking his head as I sat down on the couch opposite him. I'd left the back door open for Fergus, so he could go out and potty after dinner. Now that we knew the garden was safe, it made our day-to-day routine easier.

"She has you outnumbered, and these aren't poorly trained fledglings like Lafitte had. We've killed"—Clive looked at me—"Fifty-six?"

I nodded.

"Fifty-six of her men, and all have turned to dust. These are experienced fighters."

"Not to mention you guys can't brawl in the streets where the humans can see you," I said. "They tend to notice heads rolling around." I fluffed the pillow on the end of the couch and then tipped over. It'd been a long day already.

"You need to eat," Clive said, "and not just cookies."

Damn. He was right. I needed to feed my wolf. I sat back up and went to the fridge. I ate a meat stick, shelled a hard-boiled egg and ate that. I wanted a quick protein kick while I looked for dinner.

"Bottom shelf," Clive said. "I picked up two of the burritos you like."

I ran back into the living room to give him a kiss. Was there anything better than the gift of Mexican food? There was a little hole-in-the-wall Mexican restaurant not too far away. I used to sometimes run over there for lunch for Owen and me—when we didn't have leftovers from Dave's cooking the night before.

The couple that owned the place were super sweet, subtly trying to set me up with their son, who did the cooking. That was back when I tried not to interact with humans too much and definitely not with men. When the mom, Magdalena, had noticed the scars snaking up out of the collar of my t-shirt, she stopped hinting about dates and instead started adding more chips and salsa to my orders.

When I stopped in after I got married, she saw the ring and came around the counter to hug me. She called her husband out and pointed to my wedding ring. He smiled so wide, it brought tears to my eyes. He didn't touch me; somehow knew not to. He just laughed and said my husband was a lucky man.

I told Clive about them, and he remembered, sometimes going there on his own while I was working, to pick up my favorites and to thank them for looking out for me. I'd found a receipt in the bag once. My guess was Magdalena wanted me to know who I married, as if I hadn't already known. Clive had tipped twice the price of the meal. Yeah, he was a keeper.

The microwave would have been faster, but I preferred the taste when I put them on a baking sheet and heated them up in the oven. Fergus trotted back in, so I closed and locked the French doors to the garden.

"Sam? Russell is asking if Garyn's people have moved."

I returned to the living room and surprised Clive by plopping onto his lap. Snuggling in, I closed my eyes and rested my head on his shoulder.

"Blips are on the mov— wait. Russell, can anyone but you and Godfrey overhear this call?" I was thinking about my conversation with Clive earlier.

There was a charged silence. "Audrey is with us, but no one

else. I didn't ask your permission to share this with her. Please forgive me."

I sighed and Clive kissed the top of my head. With every person who knew, the chances of my secret being out multiplied exponentially.

"Audrey," I began, "I trust you, but please don't share this information, not even in an oblique reference. I'd rather not die by angry vampy mob."

"Of course. I would never do anything to endanger you," she said.

"That's just it, though. Neither would Russell. I know he'd never hurt me and yet, because he was preoccupied, the number of ways I could be found out and targeted has increased."

"My lady, I do—" Russell began.

"No, please. I know it was an accident." Were more vamps listening at keyholes?

"But accidents have consequences," Clive said, his voice harsher than usual as he pulled me in close. "Have you checked that no one is eavesdropping?"

We heard a door open and then, "'Ello, gents. Have you fed? I was about to—" and then the door clicked shut.

I sighed again. Those left in the San Francisco nocturne didn't actively want me dead, but they wouldn't shed a tear over my mangled corpse.

Clive disconnected and threw the phone across the room, bouncing it off the couch.

TWENTY

I'm Feeling Woozy

"**A**t least you didn't crush it this time."

He crushed me instead, to the point of pain, and then he quickly relaxed his grip. "I'd say we should move somewhere far away, but you wouldn't want to leave The Slaughtered Lamb."

Shaking my head, I agreed. I wasn't ready to leave my bookstore and bar. "One problem at a time. Right now, we have Garyn. If at some point in the future we find ourselves facing down an angry vampire mob intent on my demise, we'll deal with it. Okay?" I kissed his cheek.

"Yes. Why don't you lie down on the couch and throw my phone back? I'll call Dave and see if he'd like to do a spot of vampire hunting with me."

"And you want me to nap while you're out?" What the hell?

"No. I want you up here." He tapped his head. "Tell me where they are, where they go. Dave and I can skirt around the large groups and take out the smaller ones. Maybe by the end of the night, we can halve her ranks."

He stood and patted Fergus, who had stood with him. Crossing to a bookcase in the corner of the room, Clive tapped a hidden panel. The bookcase swung out, revealing an elevator. "Let me know whatever you see."

"Clive?"

He held the door open, eyebrows raised.

"Be careful, please. I love you far too much to lose you."

He grinned and my heart skipped a beat. "Right back atcha, darling." The door slid shut and I missed him already.

Making myself comfortable, I closed my eyes and then a moment later, I felt the couch move. Slowly, taking care to be unnoticed, Fergus sneaked onto the couch, trying to fit into the narrow gap between myself and the back cushion. I didn't have the heart to kick him off. Besides, we all knew he napped here when we weren't home. Plus, the weight of his head on my stomach was comforting.

I kept one hand on his shoulder while I waited to hear Clive's voice in my head. Instead, my phone buzzed. I pulled it out of my pocket, swiped, and heard the idling of his motorcycle engine and then the thunk of the garage door closing.

"Thanks for making sure nothing snuck in while you drove away."

He chuckled. "For you, darling, anything." He gunned it, and then there was the sound of muffled tires on pavement overlaying the roar of the engine. "Is our furry child on the couch with you?"

"How'd you know?" I looked down at Fergus, whose attention was focused on Clive's voice coming from my phone.

"I didn't, but I know him. Whenever I'm on the couch, he creeps up, apparently believing that if he moves slowly enough, I won't notice a giant bloody dog snuggling next to me."

"He's not giant yet. That'll come in a few months."

"Something to look forward to." The sound changed. He must have moved to a busier street. "Your voice is often muffled since the great candy-coating experiment, so I decided to call."

"Did you get a hold of Dave?" I really didn't want Clive doing this on his own.

"Yes. He's meeting me downtown. Can you check to see where they are now?" He was idling again. Maybe a red light.

I closed my eyes and searched for green blips in my head.

"Russell and his people are at the stadium. Garyn, Reginald, and Stephen are in the penthouse." I needed to listen in. They were plotting and I was missing it. "The Pier 39 group moved over to Fisherman's Wharf. Lots of touristy spots there. A smaller group moved to the City Hall-Theater District area. Lots of homeless people there. And the last group is moving toward the stadium. I wonder how they figured that out?"

"How many are in that group?"

"Uh, thirty are on their way to Giants Stadium. Twenty-one are at Fisherman's Wharf.... and sixteen are downtown."

"Call Godfrey and warn them, please. I'll call Dave and have him meet me near City Hall. Tell Russell to call me if he needs help. Dave and I can reroute. I'll call you right back."

Godfrey picked up on the first ring.

"Missus, the Master is very sorr—"

"I know, but it's done. That's not why I'm calling." I relayed what was happening and got off the phone as Clive was calling back.

A bell dinged as I picked up the call. What the hell was that?

"Your dinner is ready," he said.

"Oh! Great." I popped up, Fergus following along, and took my burritos out of the oven. I slid them on a plate, got a fork, napkin, and soda. "Did you find Dave?"

An engine revved.

"That was Dave telling you he's here. Are we still headed in the right direction?"

I took my dinner out to the patio and sat at the table. I wanted less interference as I scanned the city between bites. "Uh, yes. They've split up and are moving slowly in different directions." I checked the time on my phone. "The plays and musicals are letting out. They're probably following theatergoers to their cars."

"It'll be easier for them to attack in car parks and parking garages," Dave grumbled.

"Exactly," Clive responded. "Thank you, love. We're going to be busy for a while."

"Be safe!" I said right before the line went dead. I took big bite and checked my immediate surroundings. I knew there were no vamps near me, but what about the fae? Nope. I didn't see or sense anything. Given Fergus' relaxed snooze on my foot, he didn't either.

I checked the vamps. Dave and Clive were already on it. I only saw fourte—thirteen down at the city center. I turned my focus to the stadium. Russell's crew was still there and Garyn's looked to be approaching. Scanning the thirty, I found Darrin, the one who had tried to break into our place and had our ward knock him back.

They were all focused on finding the local vamps and so were a little distracted. I wormed into Darrin but didn't go all the way into his memories. I wanted to see what was going on through his eyes. They were moving silently down the street toward the stadium, across a short bridge, over the main gates, and then swarming the stadium, most moving around the back so as not to be seen by any humans who might be walking on the street.

Some leapt over interior gates and then ran up the stairs; others scaled the outside of the stadium. Darrin climbed up a side wall and flipped over the top, ending up in Levi's Landing, the section between right field and the Bay. He watched the other vamps appear over the stadium walls, a couple ending up in the giant mitt and Coke bottle past left field. Still more made their way down the bleacher stairs, converging on the darkened field.

Darrin reached into his pocket and sent a quick text to Reginald reading:

We're here. It begins.

There was a moment of stilled silence and then a dark wave of Russell's vamps came flooding out of the dugouts, Godfrey and Audrey in the lead. They all carried baseballs bats, the light wood glowing in the moonlight. Some vamps twirled them in their fingers, some flicked them back and forth, readying for the big swing. Unable to stop the momentum—or, more likely, overtaken by our nocturne as they tried to retreat—Garyn's vamps ran right into bats swinging with supernatural force. Heads were caved in, bones crushed, making it easier for our guys to overwhelm their opponents and rip off their heads. When the bats broke, they made excellent stakes. More than a few of Garyn's men got an old-fashioned wooden stake to the heart.

Our local vamps were outnumbered by ones who were older and probably more powerful, but our guys fought dirty. Clive had taught them well. Use what you have and do whatever it takes to win.

Vamps were flying in every direction, only to scramble up and race back into the fray. One was thrown with such strength and ferocity, he hit a railing and was folded backward over the metal bar like a taco shell. It should have snapped him in two; broken his spine at the very least. Instead, he popped up a moment later, shook it off, and attacked again. It was insane to watch, a horrific battle scene with the volume turned off.

Vamps were incredibly fast and strong. When the bats had been reduced to splinters, they punched like sledgehammers and the ones getting hit rolled back, jumped up, and continued the brawl. The punishment they could endure was unreal. Heads did occasionally roll, and dust piles slowly grew.

I'd been so preoccupied by the fight, I hadn't been paying attention to what Darrin was doing. I looked down and saw his phone was still out. He was recording. This felt like it should be against vamp rules. Phones could be hacked. The world would have evidence that vampires existed. Then again, they could probably pawn it off as CGI or AI. He stopped, shared it, and then pocketed his phone, leaping over the wall and landing in right field.

Two of Russell's vamps flew at the same enemy vamp, each taking an arm and ripping it off. I knew vamps could painfully regrow severed limbs, but it took time. This guy was out of time.

They yanked his head off almost as quickly as his arms and then raced back to grab another one.

Darrin ran toward the pitcher's mound, zeroing in on Audrey's blonde hair, a beacon on the dark field. Hands fisted, he intended to punch her in the back of the head and then relieve her of the whole thing.

Russell had just ripped off a head and was turning with the momentum of it, when he saw me-Darrin. Eyes opening wide, he stared at Audrey. She spun in a crouch, punching Darrin's junk with enough force to make him a eunuch while slicing her bladed left hand through the air at his neck. She sent his head flying and my stomach dropped.

I'd never been in a vamp's head when he'd been given his final death. It felt as though my heart imploded while my brain exploded. I was pretty sure I was going to hurl. A horrible scent filled my senses, one of coagulated blood and decomposing flesh. Yep. Definitely hurling.

When I eventually found myself back in my own mind and body, I held the cold soda can to my forehead, pulling out the pain and directing it to the white streak in my hair. Feeling weak, I ate the second burrito and then jogged around the patio, trying to feel more in my own skin and feed the gnawing hole in my stomach. Fergus stayed on my heels. He had no idea what I was doing, but he wanted to be a part of it.

When my head stopped spinning, I went in the house, grabbed four meat sticks, one for Fergus and three for me, and poured a tall glass of water. I went back outside, ate two sticks, drank the water, and closed my eyes.

There were five left at the city center. Clive and Dave seemed to be working well together. There were hardly any left at the stadium. I found Godfrey and slipped in to look out from his eyes.

Sorry! Me again. Just checking on the fight. Pay me no mind.

Shut up!

He was fighting two at once and needed to focus. When he spun one vamp around, slamming him into another one, I saw

Russell was busy with two as well. Garyn's vamps knew who the Master, second, and third were. They were doing everything they could to dismantle the power structure.

They were so fast, it felt like I was watching an old martial arts film sped up. Broken wrist, broken leg, severed arm; it didn't matter what they did to each other, there was no quit in any of them.

I tried leaping into Audrey's mind, but it wasn't as easy. Maybe I was more tired, maybe she was mentally stronger. I didn't want to distract Russell, so I decided to go for one of Garyn's again. If I was going to throw anyone off their game, it should be one of hers.

I leapt into the one speeding up behind Audrey and squeezed him until he popped and his dust rained down on the field. I quickly redirected the horrible pain into my wicche glass. It was faster and more effective than the hair streak thing.

Thanks, Audrey said, *but I had him.*

You can initiate a conversation with me?

Apparently. I felt you a minute ago and assumed you were hovering somewhere nearby.

Can I watch through your eyes?

Yeah. Just don't bother me. She punched a vamp so hard, his neck snapped, head lolling to the side. She grabbed his shoulders and pulled his chest down to her pistoning knee, caving in his chest. She then picked up a shard of bat from the ground and stabbed it through his heart.

Once her opponent was down, she ran to Godfrey, yanking away one of his. They each dispatched their vamp with haste. Both turned, braced for the next, and watched Russell rip off the arm that had been wrapped around his neck. He spun and a head went flying, turning to dust in the weak moonlight.

"Is that all of them?" Godfrey asked.

I checked. *Tell them there are two waiting in the dugouts. They're hoping to take a few out when you move back underground.*

Audrey made a couple of subtle hand movements, her back to the dugouts, and Russell and Godfrey streaked across the infield.

When they each stepped up from the dugouts, they were brushing dust from their hands.

Russell surveyed his nocturne. "We have lost some of our own. We will mourn their loss and we will celebrate our victory. You have made yourselves and this nocturne proud."

Guttural shouts filled the stadium. Russell had lost eight, but they'd taken out thirty.

You're a hell of a fighter, I told Audrey.

I've been training. I've got a lot of pent-up rage in here.

I hear ya, sister. I'm going to go check on Clive now. He and Dave are working downtown.

TWENTY-ONE

Undead Math Problems

Three left downtown.

Hello, my pointy-toothed love.

Just a second, darling.

I sank down and watched Clive sneak up behind a vamp who was silently stalking an old couple to the handicapped parking place in a multistory garage. The woman used a walker and was quite frail. The man kept a hand on her arm, making sure she was steady, as they discussed the musical they'd seen.

The man got his wife in the car and was bent over, snapping in her seat belt, when Garyn's vamp made his move. Before he took more than a step, Clive was at his back, an arm around his neck, ripping off his head and then ducking behind a pillar. The husband turned to put the walker in their trunk but was distracted by the dust and clothes in his way. His wife had just rolled through that spot a moment ago unimpeded.

Brow furrowed, he looked left and right, wary now. Putting the walker away, he looked over his shoulder for trouble, and then hurried to get in the car and lock the doors. The poor couple would probably tell their friends that San Francisco was a scary place. Stupid vamp.

I'm glad you're here. Where's my next one?

I tried to interpret what I was seeing. *It looks like you're standing right next to each other. He must be in that same structure, but up a story or two.* Clive went silent, on the hunt, so I left him to it, checking on the last group. They'd left Fisherman's Wharf and had spread out around the city. *Shit.* They'd be harder to track now.

I checked on the penthouse, wanting to listen in, and was more than a little uncomfortable to see it was empty. *Damn.* Where did they go? Not the nocturne. Stadium? No. The city center was clear. Dave and Clive had finished off that group. The airport? I looked and found two more private jets. How many damn favors could she call in? And why did they keep coming if their predecessors were getting mowed down? And where was Russell's welcoming committee at the airport? Why weren't they taking more of the new guys out?

I counted the vamps in the two planes. Thirty-three. This was turning into an undead story problem. If San Francisco has seventy bloodsuckers and forty-six are taken away and then thirty-three are added, how many bloodsuckers does San Francisco have?

The answer was too damned many! Or fifty-seven, if we were showing our work.

Where was Garyn? If she was moving toward the stadium, I'd need to call Russell and have them move.

Fergus was up, focused on the back wall of the garden, a deep growl reverberating through his chest. I looked up and found vamp black eyes staring at me from the roof of the house next door. Pain clamped around my skull.

Sonofabitch! I'd found Garyn.

Breathing though the pain, I ate the last meat stick, not wanting to be weak while under attack. Head throbbing, I tried to remember if Stephen had said anything about Darrin being able to see over the wall. I knew he couldn't jump into our garden, but could he see? More importantly, was Garyn watching me right now?

Trying my hardest to breathe through the pain, I found her blip and wrapped myself around it, worming in just enough to see through her eyes. I saw wavy colors, like an oil slick in lamplight. Could she hear us? I tapped my soda can on the table. Nothing. Not wanting Fergus too close to the fence, I snapped my fingers. Nothing. He sidled up beside me and I rattled his collar. I heard it all, sitting here, but I didn't hear it in Garyn's mind. Good. I wanted to kiss every one of the magical contractors who'd built this place and erected the wards.

Hello, darling. Dave and I are done downtown. We found a few more prowling around. Russell tells me—

I sent him an image of what I had going on here.

I'm on my way.

If I spoke to him, she'd hear me. I sent him an image of a stop sign. Clive was the last person I needed right now. If he came home, she could mentally influence him to open the door and invite her in.

Thinking through the pain was proving to be quite difficult. I siphoned off as much as I could into the wicche glass, dreading having to take it all back soon. Magic required balance. What I did, invading people's thoughts and memories, required a lot to balance the scales.

My head was splitting, even with the wicche glass. She wasn't casually checking me out this time. She'd lost over eighty of her men in the last couple of days. She was pissed. Anger rolled off her. I sent Clive an image of a marionette and hoped he got it. He'd be the puppet on her strings if he came home.

This was going to hurt, but it felt like the only way to slip in undetected. I showed her my memory inside Darrin, looking down at his phone, texting it was beginning, and then looking up and watching her people being annihilated by a smaller, less experienced crew wielding bats.

She let loose an internal scream of rage, and I used it to slip past her defenses, deep into her psyche. She was leaving, returning to the penthouse to find out what had happened to her men.

Stephen had told her our wards couldn't be breached, but she'd needed to know for herself if it was true. Clive had been nothing but trouble, right from the beginning.

A memory lit up beside me and I leapt in.

Clive, sitting in his family cabin. Alone. Rocking in a chair by the fire, a full bowl of stew going cold on the stool beside him. Garyn was staring through a partially closed shutter into the main room. Flames flickering under a kettle provided the only light.

He looked so sad and lost, I wanted to rush into the cabin and comfort him, but Garyn saw something else. She saw a likeness that drew her. There was something about his light hair, his strong jaw, and gray eyes. I didn't catch the thought, but it made her melancholy.

Lifting his head, he stared, seeing nothing and yet seeming to sense her presence. Taking a deep breath, he let it out as he stood, grabbing an axe from beside the fire. He moved to the door to deal with whatever was skulking around the cabin. Garyn disappeared into the night, and I was back in her mind, jumping into the next memory.

Again, she was looking through an open window, this time into a tavern. Clive sat by himself, a tankard of ale before him. His eyes looked glazed. Perfect, she'd thought. They were so much easier to deal with when they were inebriated.

He drank down what was left and swayed to his feet, unsteadily making his way to the door. The barman and a few of the men drinking watched uneasily as Clive left. They knew who he was and what he'd lost: his whole family.

The fresh air seemed to revive him some. Steadier, he walked mostly straight down the center of the dark dirt road, unaware that a woman followed him. He even seemed the right size to her. It was uncanny.

Eventually, she couldn't wait anymore. She mesmerized him and led him off the path to his farm and into the cabin. He'd do anything she wanted now, and she liked that.

"Why did you leave me?" she asked.

Clive stood before the banked fire, his eyes vacant, saying the words she put in his mouth. "I was forced. I didn't want to."

Smiling, she said, "You'll stay with me now, though, won't you?"

"Yes."

"Good." She stepped forward, tipped his head to the side, and fed.

The memory went dark. I saw another light up straight ahead and hopped into it.

Clive was sitting in the chair by the fire, rocking, eyes blank, again in her thrall.

"But you missed me, didn't you?" Garyn asked, sitting on a cushion in the glow of the fire.

Clive nodded robotically. "Very much. I thought of you all the time."

"I knew it. I knew you wouldn't have left me like that if it were up to you."

"Never. You've always been my favorite. You know that."

She nodded, a smirk on her lips. "I do. And you won't make that mistake again, will you?"

"No."

She stood, replacing the cushion on the chair opposite him, her expression flinty as she appeared to drop the influence. "Why should I offer you the dark kiss?"

Clive blinked a few times, fear jumping into his eyes. His gaze darted around the room, to the spot where his axe no longer leaned, and then to the intruder. "You—"

"Yes, it's me again. I heard about your family. Don't you want to avenge your sister's murder?"

Brows furrowed, still looking as though he wasn't sure if he was dreaming, he said, "Yes?"

"You don't sound sure." Her face pulled down in a sneer. "Are you going to let the men walk free?"

"No." Clive stood, towering over her, and almost immediately his face went blank again, his eyes empty, before dropping back into his seat.

She'd recaptured his mind and put him back where she needed him.

"I want everything you're offering," he said, his voice toneless.

"That's better." She went to him, patting his shoulder. "Tomorrow. I still have a few things I need to get ready. After tomorrow, you'll come live with me, and it'll be as it should have always been."

Clive was still staring straight ahead as she walked out of the cabin and the memory went dark.

I was getting tired and my head was ready to explode, but I felt like I could handle one more, so when I found myself back in the dark, synapse trails firing up, I jumped into the next memory.

Clive was sitting in a room, his chair beside the fire again. Garyn sat in a matching chair on the opposite side of the large fireplace. This room was different, not Clive's cabin and not the house I'd seen Garyn in a few times. It was dark and mostly empty, just a few pieces of furniture. Thick, heavy drapes hung at the windows.

Garyn watched Clive closely. "You never told me where you went when you left."

Staring blankly over her shoulder, he said, "No place interesting. I was always trying to get back to you. I longed to know where you were and what you were doing."

I hated this, hated seeing Clive turned into a mindless doll for her to play with.

Her expression flickered between appreciation and resentment. "If that were the case, you could have returned sooner."

"I tried but I was set upon by marauders. Robbed and beaten, I was left for dead in the woods. All I thought about was getting back to you, though." The words may have been passing Clive's lips, but they were clearly coming from Garyn.

"And now you're here." Her sharp smile should have put Clive on edge, but his gaze was still hovering, unconcerned, over her shoulder. "You learned your lesson and came back. You shall be honored first among all my people."

"I will rule with you," he said tonelessly.

"Yes." She stood, brushing dust from the folds of her skirt. "Too bad she's not still alive. I want her to see that you came back for me." Patting Clive on the shoulder as she walked by, she dragged open the curtains and looked out on the brambles.

Sighing, she turned to the dark corner by the door where Lawrence stood. "Yes?"

"My lady, we understand you think this new one is special, but we don't—" His expression went slack. *"Of course. You know best. May I accompany you on your hunt this evening?"*

"No." She snapped her fingers and Clive rose, following her out the door.

TWENTY-TWO

Unwanted Invitations

reathing in the cold night air, I directed the pain into the wicche glass around my neck before dropping my head to my crossed arms on the patio table. *Please don't hurl. Please don't hurl.* Fergus whined and shoved his big head under my arm, sniffing at me.

"I'm okay, buddy." I whispered. Why was everything so loud?

He rested his head on my thigh and waited, holding himself still. I hugged him. "Good boy. I *will be* okay."

I checked the time on my phone. *Clive?*

Yes.

She's back in the penthouse and I'm out. You can come home now.

On my way.

Grabbing the warm soda can and the napkin, I ushered Fergus back inside. Door locked, I dragged myself upstairs and changed into pajamas. I needed dark, quiet, and sleep. Unfortunately, sleep didn't come right away. My head hurt too much and I was too preoccupied with Garyn's memories. What kind of games was she playing with him, with all of them?

I knew when Clive got home. Fergus ran downstairs to wait by the elevator. Proving my husband always knew where I was, he correctly took the elevator to our bedroom, Fergus racing up the stairs a moment later.

Clive petted our pooch and then crawled onto the bed, lying down beside me. Much of the lingering pain disappeared. Clive could do that, create or take away pain with a thought. He kissed my forehead.

"I'm so sorry, darling." Resting his hand on my stomach, he added, "Is there anything I can do to help?"

You've already helped. It still hurts, but I might be able to sleep.

Good. He kissed my forehead again. *Can you tell me what happened?*

I began to and then thought better of it. His behavior had been so odd in her memories, I really believed she'd been using him as a stand-in puppet to play out scenes the way she wished they'd happened with whoever Clive's doppelganger was, but I needed his take. Maybe I was interpreting what I saw all wrong.

I shared the memories with him. My version wouldn't be exactly like hers, but I'd been paying close attention to him, so he was seeing what she remembered.

When I finished, he was lying on his back, staring up at the ceiling. Finally, he said, *I don't remember that. I have an excellent memory, but I don't remember those strange, cryptic conversations.* He shook his head. *At all.* He reached for my hand and squeezed. *She really did use me like a marionette, didn't she? She entranced me and then pulled the strings, making me say what she wanted to hear.* He turned his head to me. *Who do I look like and what does she want from me?*

I scooted over, wrapped an arm around him, resting my head on his chest. *Whatever he couldn't or wouldn't give her is my guess.*

He ran a hand up and down his face. *I told you what I remembered. Her in the road, at the door, falling on me when she turned me. I don't remember any of the rest, but now I want you to pry open her mind so I can find out how else she used me.* He closed his eyes, his hand clutching mine. *And yes, I realize how hypocritical that is, given what my kind do to humans in order to feed.*

I think she's nuts, like St. Germain-level nuts.

No doubt. We killed another forty-something of her people tonight and she's here, terrorizing you. Does she want me back as her puppet that badly? Enough to let all her people die? He made a sound of disgust in the back of his throat.

Two more planes landed tonight. Thirty-three more vamps. I had to use the wicche glass a lot tonight. The pain was unbelievable.

He kissed the top of my head. *I'm sorry, darling. I'm glad you had it, though.*

She's too strong. I'm going to need to take back the imbalance to keep her out of my head.

I felt him stiffen. *Martha went her whole life without pulling it back out. And you just did it a few months ago to challenge Abigail. Surely it can't be too full.*

Martha never had to battle the stuff we do, and she's the one who told me I had to balance the magic if I was going to be strong enough to handle my aunt.

No, Sam. You almost died last time. I don't want you to do that again. Clive.

No. You're not going to torture yourself because my maker is off her rocker. I'll deal with her.

Clive, you guys can't get close to her without her mesmerizing you.

I'll figure something out.

I tapped his chest. *I'll ask Thoth for advice. He might know nothing, as he's not associated with vamps, but it's worth a try. I mean, how often do we get to question gods?*

By all means, ask, but don't do anything that hurts you.

I make no promises.

Sam—

Shh. I'm so tired. Let's sleep, okay?

Grumbling, he stood, undressed, and then slid under the covers. He pulled me in close again and I was out almost immediately.

When I woke, Fergus had his head on the bed, staring at me. No wet nose today, just the stare. I reached for my phone and checked the time. "Oh, come on. I need more than five and a half hours of sleep. Go back to bed."

I closed my eyes and willed myself to sleep. It was no good. He was still there, wasn't he? I cracked one eye and saw two dark shiny ones staring back. Groaning, I sat up and slid out of bed. "Nag, nag, nag," I muttered, detouring to the bathroom.

As soon as I headed for the stairs, he raced ahead of me, like my own personal herald, his tail waving like a flag in the wind. I scooped his food out of the kibble bin, raining it into his bowl, and then refreshed his water before opening the back door. While he ate, I searched the fridge for my breakfast. If today proved to be anything like yesterday, I'd need to keep my strength up.

Eggs, smoked salmon, cheese, bell peppers, tomato, bacon. I spread them out on our beautiful new counters and started cooking breakfast. Fergus finished and went out to the little dog's room. I watched him go and then just gazed at the garden, letting my omelette firm.

I'd visited Benvair's mansion and Owen and George's new place. They were stunning. I loved visiting, but I didn't think I'd be comfortable in a mansion like that, not enough to think of it as home. The nocturne, another landmark estate in the city, had grown on me. I loved our bedrooms, the library, Clive's study, but taken as a whole, it was too much.

I'd grown up on the run with my mom, moving from one tiny apartment to the next. My small living space behind The Slaughtered Lamb was the nicest place I'd ever lived in up until that point in my life. It had also been the longest I'd ever stayed in one place. Our new house was fancy, but in a way that felt like home. I thanked my mostly lucky—though sometimes psychotic—stars to be living here with the man I loved and the dog I adored. Perhaps all the scary things that kept happening were the price I had to pay for living my dream. And my thoughts were back to balance.

After breakfast, I needed to head to The Viper's Nest Roadhouse & Café. Hopefully, Thoth was still there with some advice on balancing the payment for magic without risking my life.

Once cleaned, dressed, and bladed, I considered leaving Fergus with Clive but thought better of it. Fergus loved Thoth too much to deny him the visit. We took the elevator down to the garage. I let my buddy into the back seat before I slid into the front. I sent a quick text to Owen, letting him know I'd probably be late again. Jeez, I was becoming a serious slacker.

The ramp to the garage door was quite steep because the garage itself was huge. Clive loved cars a little too much. When we approached the garage door, it rose, but this time a white paper fluttered to the ground. What was—*Shiiitttt*. Trap or warning?

"Stay." I stepped out of the car, closed the door, and unsheathed my blades. Approaching the doorway, I looked everywhere but at the paper. If an ambush was brewing, I wanted to be ready.

The street was quiet. There was the sound of surf, the shush of cars on the main road nearby, a lady walking her poodle across the street. Fergus barked, because fuck that guy walking on his street.

As no one seemed to be around to jump me, I picked up an envelope with my name on it. "I swear, if this thing has anthrax in it, I'm going to be super pissed."

I got back in the car and drove out, making sure the door closed behind me. I couldn't even relax during daylight hours, as I still had members of the fae gunning for me. I stopped at the end of the driveway and opened the envelope. Fergus leaned over the seat to sniff and growl.

Tipping my head into his, I scratched under his chin. "I know. I don't like her either." I wasn't positive, but this felt like Garyn to me. "Perfect penmanship. What an asshole. And what is this? Wedding invitation grade parchment?" Mostly I was nervous, but it was also true that she sucked.

I slipped the letter out and unfolded it.

Samantha,

Would you join me for an aperitif this evening? We have much to discuss. I don't believe either of us want anyone else to die. I'll expect you at the penthouse shortly after the sun sets.

Cordially,

Garyn

I put the letter back in the envelope, tossed it onto the passenger seat, and drove to The Viper's Nest. Fergus sniffed at it occasionally, so I opened the windows in the back for him. We both needed to get the scent of that vampire out of our noses, and he could enjoy lolling out the window.

It was still early, so the parking lot was close to empty. Dang. Maybe Stheno and Thoth weren't here yet. The front door was locked, and the sign said it didn't open for almost two hours. I should have called.

Deciding I was here anyway, I knocked. "Stheno? It's Sam!" Fergus sat beside me as I waited. Distant footsteps. His ears went up. I patted him. "I heard it too."

A moment later, the door opened and Stheno squinted into the bright morning. "What?"

"Sorry to bug you, but is Thoth still in town?"

She waved us both in. "He's staying in the apartment upstairs."

"Oh, um…" I glanced up at the ceiling.

"If I heard you, so did he. He'll be down if he wants to talk with you. So,"—she gestured to the pastry display case—"anything?"

"Do you have any of Dave's meringue cookies left?" I went to the case to check.

"Hell no. Those are all mine." Stheno rubbed beneath her eye patch. "Do you want any coffee?"

"Can I have cocoa?" I sat on a bar stool, Fergus flopping down beside me. "Maybe a piece of that coconut cream pie, since you're too mean to share your cookies with me."

"Don't push me, kid. I'm tired. This working thing is bullshit." She went to her elaborate coffee maker and began the process for cocoa.

"I believe I'd like a piece of that pie as well, Stheno, and coffee for me." Thoth waved me over to the table we'd sat at before. "This will be more comfortable."

We both slid in, with Fergus slinking under the table and up onto Thoth's bench. I started to call him back but Thoth waved me off.

"He's fine where he is." He scratched Fergus between the ears. "You have a good one here."

"I know."

Stheno brought over a tray with two coffees, a cocoa, and three pieces of pie. "Scoot over, kid, and tell us what's got your knickers in a twist."

TWENTY-THREE

Devil's Food Pastries, a Division of Demon Delights, Inc

"Vampires," I said, taking a sip of cocoa. She'd even put whipped cream on top. "Mmm, thank you."

"Didn't I tell you not to marry a bloodsucker?" She took a bite of pie. "Your demon sure knows how to bake."

Snickering, I said, "Devil's Food Pastries."

Thoth forked up a bite. "I never thought I'd be ingesting something made by a demon."

I shrugged. "He's only half demon, and he's been upping his baking skills the last couple months. He's almost as good as my cousin."

"What seems to be the problem this morning?" Thoth took a sip of coffee and waited.

I explained what we'd been dealing with the last couple of days and then showed them the letter I found this morning. While I ate my pie, Stheno and Thoth read the note.

"Look at this bitch, inviting you to an apartment busting at the seams with bloodsuckers so you can have a cocktail and chat. Like her people haven't been actively trying to kill you." She rolled her eyes. "The nerve of this one."

"That's the point, I believe," Thoth said. "I would guess she's never been denied something she wants. Judging by the memories you saw—and I think you're interpreting them correctly—when people do or say something she doesn't like, she overpowers their will and makes them do as she wishes."

Stheno laughed. "She hasn't been getting her way since she came to this town." She eyed me. "Don't you dare come up with some stupid selfless reason for visiting her penthouse. I mean it." She glared at me with her one good eye.

I savored my last bite, took a sip of cocoa, and then gave her back my evil squinty eye. "I'm not a moron."

"I like the idea," Thoth said.

Stheno opened her mouth to argue, but he held up a hand. "I'm not saying she should walk into an enemy nocturne. The conversation, though, could be quite enlightening. Sam can keep Garyn out of her head. What happens when Garyn can't control the conversation?" He tapped a finger against his lips. "I'd enjoy being a fly on that wall."

Stheno shook her head but said, "Fine. Have her meet you here instead. We can keep an eye on you and Thoth gets to be a fly."

"I like that idea, but she's going to know that we know each other. They've been doing research on me." Which gave me a stomachache. My past was none of their business.

"Too fucking bad. She can't have home field advantage." She smacked her hand on the table, making the dishes rattle. "Damn, I wish I could have seen the local guys rush out of the dugouts swinging bats."

The corner of Thoth's mouth went up. "As do I."

"Where we meet isn't as important as my being able to withstand a direct onslaught. I wouldn't have survived last night if I hadn't had my wicche glass to siphon off the pain."

Thoth leaned forward. "Those are quite rare. I've only ever heard of them, never seen one."

I tugged the long chain from under my short-sleeve t-shirt, holding up the small, blown-glass ball. Crisscrossing filaments inside sparkled in the sunlight, throwing off rainbows as it twisted back and forth. "My great-aunt gave it to me. I'd needed to be at my strongest to face a sorcerer—"

"Her aunt," Stheno interjected.

Thoth's eyes widened.

"Apparently, I come from an old and very powerful wicche family on my mom's side, one with a nasty reputation for black magic and sorcery."

"Hm, that may be why you were drawn to this demon you befriended," Thoth said, taking another sip.

My relationship with Dave was complicated, and his reason for befriending me wasn't anything I wanted to think about at the moment. "Anyway, I had to be at my strongest, so my great-aunt Martha said I needed to balance the scales and take out the pain I'd already put into the wicche glass. Unfortunately, that meant taking all of her stored pain as well. I almost died, so I'm wary of doing it again, though it feels like I have to."

"May I?" Thoth held out his hand.

I lifted up in my seat and leaned over the table. When he touched the wicche glass, I felt an electric shock go through me.

He let go. "Forgive me. I should have realized it was tied to your magic. Please, put it back where it belongs. That's a priceless magical object you have there. Keep it hidden."

After dropping it back under my shirt, I said, "Any suggestions on extracting the pain without dying?"

He thought about it a moment. "The reason it was created was to protect the wicche who wore it. It then follows that there must be a way to convert the payment to something not painful."

"Convert how?" I got a fizzy, excited feeling. Maybe there really was a way to make this work without hurting myself.

He pointed to my hair. "Similar to how you stripped the pigment from your hair to divert the pain."

Stheno stood. "I've got to get ready to open."

We slid our empties to the end of the table, and she took them with her.

"Close your eyes and breathe deeply," he said. "Slow your

mind. Imagine the ocean waves spraying up against The Slaughtered Lamb windows. The wave recedes and another one hits."

I opened one eye. "How do you know that? You've never visited."

"Stheno told me about it. Close your eyes and visualize it."

I did as I was told, picturing my beautiful bookstore and bar.

"Good. Feel the tension draining out of your body. Think of something you could accept as a payment for your magic. We are made of magic. Suffering for who we inherently are is nonsensical. So, let's think of something uncomfortable, not painful." He thought a moment. "Which do you consider worse, being too hot or too cold?"

I remembered my time in Hell and said, "I'd rather be too cold."

"Fine. When you're ready, begin to pull out the contents of the wicche glass, but imagine snowy ice floes pouring out, an Alaskan river, the cold ocean water crashing into your windows. Don't allow it to hurt or freeze you. Take what you can accept and change what you can't."

Picturing the wicche glass deep in my chest, nestled in my magic, I imagined the swirly colors of the glass frosting over. Visualizing my magic like a long gold thread, I coiled it around the wicche glass and began to pull. Cold, clear water dripped down the thread, chilling me. Before I let the rest flood out, I imagined the summer sun warming the surface of the glass. Still cold, but not freezing, I pulled more from the wicche glass, feeling the cold travel down my arms and legs, up my torso, my head, down my hair. Wave after wave broke over me.

I heard Thoth say something, but I wasn't listening. I followed the cold as it worked its way through me. Before I knew it, the wicche glass was empty and I was wishing I was wearing one of my hoodies.

Opening my eyes, I found Thoth studying me. A fresh cup of cocoa was steaming on the table. I wrapped my hands around it, bringing it to my lips and drinking. Now it was heat that radiated down and out.

"Well?" Thoth asked.

Grinning, I shivered and took another sip of the hot cocoa. "It's empty, and that's a payment I can live with."

"Good. Now, how is your hard-shelled brain?"

I almost spit my cocoa. "It's holding up and my wolf and I are getting along."

Nodding, he tapped the table. "Will you meet her here?"

"I'm not sure yet. I want to think about it. My gut is saying no, but I don't know why. I'll let you both know, though, as soon as I figure it out."

Thoth leaned back in his seat. "From what I've learned, your instincts are good. Trust them."

"Thank you. I will." I got up and took my empty cup to the bar. "Come on, Fergus. I have to go to work." I waved to Stheno, who was plating another piece of pie for a customer. Oh! I dug in my pocket for a twenty-dollar bill and slipped it beneath my mug. "Thank you both!"

The drive home was thankfully uneventful, though Fergus did enjoy hanging out the window. Before I drove close enough to trip the garage door, I searched my mind for supernaturals who might be lying in wait. There were a couple of grass green fae blips in the area of the bar, but none here.

After I parked, we took the elevator to the bedroom so I could give Clive a kiss.

You smell like chocolate and coconut.

That's because I went to The Viper's Nest and had a slice of coconut cream pie and two cups of cocoa.

Sounds lovely.

It was. Also, Thoth helped me to redirect the payment from pain to the feel of chilly water. Consequently, the wicche glass is empty and after a few minutes in a warm car, my body temp is back to normal.

Wonderful news.

I felt a wave of relief from him.

You're a little more awake than normal. What gives?

He paused for a moment, and I felt his turmoil.

I've been trying to keep myself closer to the surface today. I wanted to hear it, feel it, if you were in pain and needed me.

I gave him another kiss. *Sleep now, love. I'm okay.*

Good. He sank down into deep vampire sleep.

"Come on, buddy. Let's go to work."

Fergus hopped up from his bed and tore down the stairs to the front door. Jogging after him, I checked my pockets for keys and a phone. Fergus still had his leash on, trailing behind him, so I grabbed the loop, checked my mind for fae and, finding none, opened the door.

We ran across the street, over the green, dodged tourists, and headed for the stairs. We paused a moment, let a group move ahead of us, and then went through the ward down to The Slaughtered Lamb.

Owen was behind the bar, Fyr tucking a fresh bar towel into the waist of his jeans. He must have been starting his shift. I took off Fergus' leash and hung it on the hook we'd installed for just this purpose.

I said hi to our early customers, most drinking tea and reading a book.

Owen came around to pet Fergus and check on me, kind man that he is. "Everything okay?" He meant because I was late again.

"Absolutely. I just wanted to talk with Stheno and Thoth. I needed some advice." I turned to Fyr. "Your other boss says hi, by the way."

"No she doesn't." He finger-combed his long blond hair back and then wrapped it into a messy bun, securing it with a band. He'd been working here for months and still the customers paused mid-sentence or page to watch this Thor-looking mountain of a dragon tie his hair back. It cracked me up every time. Owen gave me a look saying he saw it too.

"Okay. You're right. She didn't. But she was being super nice and got me pie and cocoa, so I think if she'd thought of it, she totally would have."

He shook his head, laughing. "Close enough."

"We received four boxes of books this morning," Owen said. "They're on a cart in the back."

"Yes. This day is getting better and better. Mind you, it's going to be a lot worse later, but I'm enjoying the better now."

As I passed through the kitchen, I remembered I needed to keep my wolf fed. Pie, though delicious, didn't do it for her. I checked the fridge and found a plate of fried chicken. Better and better! Dave must have started to make this when the vamps showed up to wreck our party. Speaking of which…

I ducked my head out the door into the bar. "We're closing before sundown until we get these warring vamps out of here."

The wicches and selkies looked at each other and then me. "Are we in danger?" Hepsiba, a crone wicche, asked.

"They're aimed at the local vamps and me. They don't seem interested in hurting any of you guys. I'm just trying to keep you out of the crosshairs, so I want everyone out and away from here before they wake up."

"But—" Liam looked at his selkie friend and then the wicches. "We don't want anything to happen to you, either."

Better and better. "That's part of why I was late today. I'm trying to protect myself and help my friends."

"Well," Hepsiba grumbled, "just make sure you don't die. We like this place."

TWENTY-FOUR

Conversations with the Mostly Dead

It was a lovely, quiet afternoon, like the ones I had a year ago. Owen and Fyr worked the bar while I processed and inventoried the new books. I helped a few customers find what they were looking for, but mostly I was adding titles to our software and reading book blurbs. Yes, I'd ordered the books based on the blurbs and reviews, but having it in my hand, reading the opening paragraphs, helped cement the book in my mind. Helping customers find books relied on my remembering the books.

About half past three, light footsteps danced down the stairs. Oh, good. Meri was here. I heard her greeting Owen and Fyr and then she came into the bookstore, tucking her backpack under the counter where I was working.

"Hi, Sam. Ooh, new books!" She reached for the cart parked behind me. "Are these ready to be shelved?"

"Yup. I organized them by section and then put them in alpha order, so it should be easier this time." I felt bad that last time, I'd left her piles of books I hadn't even separated into fiction and nonfiction. Owen and I each had our own way of organizing books and shelving, so I'd gotten into the habit of piling by size.

"Thank you, but I don't mind doing that." She shrugged a delicate shoulder. "I like organizing them on the counter, seeing everything I have before checking the shelves. Sometimes I need to shift the books before I can shelve. Then I look at where's the biggest need. I start with that section first, in case I can't get through all of them during my shift." Like Fyr, she pulled her long, wavy, white-blonde hair back and coiled it up in a clip. Dang. I had two of the most beautiful people in the world working for me. Weird.

"Oh," she said, pulling the cart over to the nearest bookshelves, "my dad thanks you for asking Fyr to drive me home yesterday. He knew a dragon would protect me, so he was able to relax."

"Yeah, about that—"

"Don't worry. I told him it was all my fault. I should have left before the vampires arrived. I just wanted to finish the display I was working on." Her gaze went to the back corner.

"Did you do something? I haven't been back there." I saved the record I was working on and went to the back of the shop.

She'd transformed the section with horticulture books into a garden. The bottom shelf now held a long shallow pot of sea glass green with flowering vines trained to climb the case. Small pots of the same cool color were dotted between books with violets and orchids. It was breathtaking.

Everywhere I looked, there was some new beautifully artistic element. "How did you do this? It's amazing."

Meri glowed. "Oh, good. I worried you'd think I was totally overstepping."

I gestured to the bar. "Have they seen it?"

She stuffed her hands in her hoodie. "I don't know."

"Fyr. Owen. Get in here."

They came on the run and I realized I should have rephrased that.

"Sorry! Not an emergency. I just wanted you to see what Meri did." I stepped out of the way so they'd get the full effect.

"Whoa," Owen said, leaning in to check out the details. "These pots won't drip onto the wood, right? These are brand new shelving units."

Meri shook her head. "No. I made the pots in my ceramics

class. There are no holes. I created a false bottom where water can accumulate without letting the roots rot. And I chose plants that I thought would work best for this environment. I can take care of them. You guys should probably just leave them alone."

Fyr chuckled, gesturing to the plants. "You have an affinity for growing things?"

She nodded, a flush in her cheeks.

"Beautiful," he said, "just like your front garden." Patting her shoulder, he turned and went back to the bar.

"It's really incredible, Meri," Owen said.

I studied the plants and the decorative tiles she'd added. "Now I want you to do a few of these around the bookstore."

Meri beamed. "I have ideas."

"Sam, you have something falling out of your back pocket," Owen said.

I patted my butt and found the invitation. Damn. I'd been distracted by this gorgeous bit of Faerie and forgot I still needed to figure out what to do. I pulled it out of my pocket and handed it to Owen.

"That was taped to our garage door," I explained.

"No. You're not going to that penthouse. You won't make it through the door before they're draining you dry."

"Oh, hey, I hadn't thought of that." Rolling my eyes, I smacked his shoulder. "Stheno offered The Viper's Nest for me to meet Garyn, but it doesn't feel right. By the time the vamps are up, Stheno's place is packed. It doesn't feel right for such a delicate, complicated conversation."

"You could meet at my aunt's, the Bubble Lounge," Meri volunteered.

I thought about it a moment. "I've never heard of the Bubble Lounge."

"I have," Owen said. "It's a mermaid nightclub, near Fisherman's Wharf, right?"

"Yes." Meri grinned. "My aunt Nerissa has owned it for years. I could ask if she'd be willing to provide a safe place for you to meet this Garyn lady."

Rubbing my hand over my stomach, I realized I was feeling relief. This felt right. "Yes, please. Could you ask her? Let her know this is a very dangerous vampire. I want her to understand what we're asking. And that we'll pay her to use her business for this."

"I will." She pulled her phone out and walked up the stairs.

We'd discovered that the top of the stairs, right before the ward, had the best phone reception and the most privacy.

"I don't like this," Owen said. "Even if Meri's aunt comes through, why do you need to meet with her? She wants Clive *and* you dead. Don't help her."

Leaning against a bookcase, I considered how to explain it. "Garyn's older than Clive. She's been turning people into vampires and collecting other vamps along the way for over a thousand years."

I took a minute to let Owen digest that info. The look on his face told me he had no idea just how old Clive was.

"She can mesmerize other vampires. The way they can alter the thoughts and memories of humans? She can do that to *them*. She has the devotion of thousands—probably more—vampires who she can call to her aid.

"Every day she's been in San Francisco, planes have arrived with more and more vampires. We've given over eighty of her people their final death, but she's not retreating. She keeps bringing in more. Last night, we had three groups of vampires walking our streets and feeding on our residents.

"Clive says her nocturne has always fed from live victims. They don't do the bagged blood thing. And there have been two humans drained of blood this week, the mark of a vampire bite left on their necks. Two that we know about."

I rubbed my forehead. "This whole thing is feeling more and more like a ruler across the knuckles for Clive. Like Garyn was pissed that Clive walked away and never looked back, so she's reprimanding him by putting him in the human police's crosshairs. The humans are inconsequential to her. It's the embarrassment and annoyance that Clive is dealing with that's the point."

"I think that disturbs me more than the war," Owen said, his face scrunched up in disgust. "She's a sociopath, isn't she? I mean, I get that—I won't say all—many vampires are cold and heartless, but she's using these poor humans as props in her made-up drama."

"I would have said she's really old and crazy with it, but I think she's always been like this. One of those people who believes themselves to be the only one who matters. Everyone else is a background player on her stage."

Owen let out a gust of air.

"Added to that, a lot of preparation is required for vampires to fly long distances, especially in summer when daylight lasts longer. We have no idea how many more are on their way or are waiting for the call asking them to join her.

"If this city is overrun with hundreds of vampires, what are we going to do? Clive said all the vamps he's fought so far have been experienced fighters. We're not dealing with newbie cannon fodder. Russell lost eight of his people last night. Granted, they killed thirty of Garyn's at the stadium, but that still means we're down eight vamps on our side."

"Can Clive call in vampires too?" Owen asked.

Fyr leaned against the doorway to the bookstore. Supernatural hearing meant we all heard everything. "The problem with that is even more bloodsuckers," he said. "The first rule of being who we are is we keep our existence secret from humans. Can you imagine hundreds of bloodsuckers brawling in the streets? Everybody has video cameras in their phones. How long before vampire videos start surfacing on the internet? How many humans are going to end up dead because a pissed-off bloodsucker threw a car at another bloodsucker, killing a family of four who were just driving down the street? No. Sam's right. We need to do whatever it takes to get these bloodsuckers out of here."

Meri walked back in. "My aunt says she'll do it. She mentioned seeing a group of vampires last night. She'd agree with you," she said to Fyr. "She wants them out of the city." Turning to me, she added, "She asked if you can come around seven-thirty. Sunset is at eight-thirteen tonight. She wants time to get people out before she closes the nightclub for a fake private party. She's worried about her customers getting hurt."

Fyr nodded.

I blew out a breath. I had to go tell Clive what was up, and he was not going to be happy. Patting Meri's shoulder, I said, "You are amazing. This display is incredible, and I really appreciate you finding me the perfect spot for tonight."

Looking embarrassed, she said, "No problem."

"Okay. I need to run home and take care of something. Meri, can you take the boxes I haven't processed yet and put them in the back?"

"I can do that," Owen said. "Meri still has more books to shelve."

"Perfect. Thank you, guys. I'll be back." Since Fergus was waiting at the bottom of the stairs for me, I grabbed his leash and clipped it on. "You're so smart," I said, scratching beneath his chin. "Did you hear me say *home*?"

My daily commute to work was about twenty seconds each way. When Fergus and I went through the ward, I took off at a run, my buddy galloping beside me. I let us in, reset the wards, and then jogged up the stairs to our bedroom. Fergus detoured to his water bowl and then followed me up.

Clive, looking gorgeous as always, was deep asleep in the dark room, window panels protecting my fangy beloved from the sun. Kicking off my running shoes, I crawled up on the bed and snuggled into his side.

Clive?

Nothing.

Oh, Cliiiive? I rubbed my hand over his abdomen.

Yes?

Oh, good. First, sorry to wake you again. Second, when I left last time I found an invitation taped to the garage door.

No!

No what, Mister Barky?

You know perfectly well no what and I don't bark.

Could have fooled me. A-ny-way, we've come up with a plan.

Sam.

Shh. I explained what the invitation said and why I felt I needed to go. He wasn't swayed. I added our moving the venue to the Bubble Lounge.

How do you know Meri's aunt isn't in league with Finvarra? That while you're preoccupied with vampires, the fae step in to steal you away?

Huh. Well, we know her dad is anti-king and they live in this realm, not Faerie, so... Yeah, okay, you're right. I don't know. But we have to do something, and my gut says this is the right choice.

Your gut.

Don't mock my gut. I have good instincts and—

You do, and I wasn't mocking. I was trying to accept that you were going to embark on another incredibly dangerous encounter because of my kind. I wish I were a better man, one who never pursued you, never pulled you into endless vampire intrigues, but I'm afraid I'm not a good man. Even knowing everything you've had to endure at the hands of vampires, I'd still do it all again. I love you far too much to be a better man.

I hugged him. *I don't think I could handle it if you were any better.*

He almost laughed, his arm wrapping around me. *This is like Canterbury all over again. I won't be able to be there to back you up. I'll have to sit on the sidelines and wait because I can't block the bitch.*

Isn't it cool that you know someone who can?

Sam.

I know. I'll be careful. I promise.

TWENTY-FIVE

Bubble Lounge
_____

I had to deliver my counter invitation to the penthouse before I headed to the Bubble Lounge. So, instead of running back to work, I went into the study and checked Clive's desk, hoping he owned fancy stationary like Garyn's. I needn't have worried. Posh was his middle name.

> Garyn,
> We do have a great deal to discuss, but I won't enter your penthouse. I like my blood right where it is, inside my own body. I'm willing to meet with you and only you at the Bubble Lounge. It is a fae-owned business and therefore neutral territory. If you agree, I'll meet you shortly after the sun sets.
> Already Second-guessing Myself,
> Sam

I dove into my closet and looked through the wardrobe Godfrey had built to find something appropriate for tonight. I wanted to appear competent and in control. I needed to find out what it would take to make her leave and didn't want to sabotage peace talks by wearing something that set her off. I needed to pick an outfit that was simple and understated. She didn't call attention to herself with bold colors or designs, so neither would I.

I found a silvery gray pair of wool crepe trousers, matching gray boots, and a light knit sea-glass green sweater. My wedding ring, Gloriana's pinky ring, Coco's protective choker, and a small set of matching stud earrings completed the look. I brushed my hair out and left it long.

Glancing in the mirror, I thought I'd hit the mostly understated mark. Coco's necklace was stunning—the one thing that stood out —but I didn't want to leave it at home. I needed all the mental protections I could get.

I considered my wallet, keys, and phone. Normally, I stuffed those things in pockets, but that didn't work with these clothes. Looking through the handbags I never used, I found a small leather bag with a long, thin strap. It was a soft blue gray and went well with the trousers and sweater. I slipped it over my head and wore it crossbody.

Checking the time, I decided I was good. I needed to hit the penthouse before heading down to the wharf. After strapping on my blades, I gave Fergus a good full-body scratch.

"You need to stay and protect Daddy, okay? Stay safe inside. Don't let anyone in. In fact…"

I went to the elevator, blew him a kiss, took it down to the garage, and then hit the override and lock buttons. It would require a code only Clive and I knew to get it moving again. On the off-chance vamps made it through the dragons' entrance to the folly, I didn't want them to find a passage from the folly to the garage. It'd only take one short elevator ride to bypass our wards. and our home would be overrun with vamps. Last time I checked, the dragon builders hadn't joined our home to the folly, but I wanted my guys to be safe.

It felt strange driving through Pacific Heights, the nocturne's neighborhood. I'd only lived here for a few months, and some of it had been awful—mostly the vamps who wanted me dead—but there was also a lot I'd loved. The houses, the views. I'd loved jogging from the nocturne to The Slaughtered Lamb every day.

This time, I parked a few doors down from the nocturne, across the street from the building Garyn was staying in. At ten stories high, it was the tallest building around, which meant the views from her penthouse must have been spectacular.

Once the street was clear, I crossed and walked up the brick drive. The building had its own private park, a stylized garden to the left. I strode under the ornate portico, then climbed the marble steps to a doorman who held one half of the double doors open for me. The lobby was all old-world elegance, with marble and dark wood antiques.

"Can I help you, miss?"

I turned back to the doorman. "Yes, thank you. I need to leave this note for Garyn, the woman in the penthouse."

He reached out to take the envelope from me, but I hesitated. This plan hinged on her seeing the note and knowing to come.

"I'm sorry, it's just really important that she gets this. Her plans for this evening have changed. I don't want her to accidentally go to the wrong venue. Could you make sure she gets it?"

"Of course, miss."

I handed him the envelope, along with a twenty-dollar bill. It was slick, if I do say so myself. I'd been watching Clive tip for a while. I knew how it was done.

Feeling like one hurdle had been cleared, I went back to the car and headed to the wharf. It was a clear, sunny day. Small puffs of white clouds drifted overhead. As I drove close to the water, the traffic got thicker. Lots of tourists were enjoying the perfect weather in San Francisco.

I'd already plugged in the Bubble Lounge's address, so I let my phone tell me where to go. The nightclub had its own parking lot with an attendant, no doubt to keep tourists from snagging parking spots from paying customers.

I pulled up and lowered the window. "I'm S—"

"We know who you are, ma'am," a distractingly handsome

man said. "You can drive down and park around the back of the club. Nerissa will be waiting for you." He waved me forward.

"Sounds great." It was so hard for me to not say *thank you* to the fae. Unfortunately for me, I did it all the freaking time. As nothing had happened yet, maybe that wasn't really a thing. I really hoped it wasn't. I didn't want to accidentally indebt myself to one of Finvarra's people.

The front of the building had a big neon sign that read *Bubble Lounge*. To the side of the lettering was a mermaid with long dark hair, winking a bright green eye. The sign had little circles flashing on and off, so it looked as though bubbles were keeping her afloat.

I drove around back and parked on the gravel beside a dumpster, close to the kitchen door. When I stepped out, I was met by a tall, willowy woman with light green eyes and jet-black hair that fell in waves down her back.

"Hello." I slammed the car door and locked it. "I'm Sam. Are you Meri's aunt?"

She held out a hand and we shook. "I'm Nerissa, and this is my club. It's good to finally meet you. Meri loves working at The Slaughtered Lamb."

"Oh, I'm glad. We certainly love having her with us. I'm actually surprised she doesn't work here."

Nerissa walked us through her large, gleaming kitchen, where a woman leaned against a prep counter, her arms crossed and brow furrowed. "Chef, I've heard your opinions, but this is *my* place and you'll do as *I* say. Take a break. I'm keeping the humans out until the bloodsucker has left."

"And you'll open us to attack from more like her just because you agreed to host this ridiculous meeting," she shouted, golden brown eyes sparking with anger.

Nerissa stopped and turned on her heels, staring down the chef. "I won't say this again. You do as I say, or you walk out that door and don't come back. Do. You. Understand?"

Jaw clenched, the woman gave one quick nod, and then stared out the back door to the water.

Nerissa walked us through the kitchen doors, down a hall, and into the lounge itself.

"Oh, my goodness! This is amazing." The walls had been painted as though we were deep underwater, the colors gradually lightening as they neared the ceiling. It wasn't cartoony. It looked more like a photo-realistic painting of the ocean. The floors were black, disappearing from notice. Above, though, was the most amazing thing I'd ever seen. Instead of the ceiling, we were looking up at a gigantic glass sculpture of an ocean wave.

The glass curved and twisted, like moving water, dark blue on the side coming off the back wall and moving through the color spectrum from indigo up to a pale green that matched my sweater. White bubbles appeared to glisten at the end of the wave, right over the opposite side of the lounge where a huge fish tank replaced the wall.

I walked beneath it the glass, craning my neck to see it from every angle. "How did you do this?" I shook my head. "How did you even get it in here?

Nerissa smiled, clearly enjoying my reaction. "I commissioned a wicche to make it for me. She is a gifted artist and an extremely powerful wicche." She pointed up. "You can't see it, but this wave is composed of many pieces. She had them brought up and then magicked them together."

I turned to Nerissa, stunned. "Is her name Arwyn?"

Nerissa watched me a moment, the good humor now lost. "Why do you ask?"

Grinning, I studied the glass, trying to find the lines where the sections met up. Nerissa was right. I couldn't see them. "Arwyn's my cousin. Her mother and mine were sisters."

"I thought you were a werewolf." Nerissa moved to a nearby table, gesturing for me to take the chair next to hers, so I did.

"Yes. I'm a Quinn wolf on my father's side, and a Corey wicche on my mother's." I didn't mean to be rude, but it was hard to focus on Nerissa when her nightclub was so magical.

"Quinn and Corey. Meri hadn't mentioned that." Nerissa brushed her long hair over her shoulder.

"I'm not sure she knows." I shrugged. "It's not a secret. It's just that I often have people after me, so my friends have learned to be tight-lipped about me. And I guess, since we're talking about this, it's important for me to know whether you support the queen or the king?"

"Why in the world would you need to know that?"

"If I'm about to get jumped by the fae, I'd like to be prepared."

Nerissa rubbed a finger over her red lower lip, thinking. Finally, she gestured toward the front of the club. "Go to the front door and tell me what you see."

It felt like I was walking on the ocean floor. I made it to the entry and looked at the doors, the benches on either side. I didn't get it. "What am I supposed to be—" I turned and froze. Gloriana's likeness was painted as a mermaid over the doorway into the club.

Nerissa stood nearby, waiting.

"Does she know you painted her as a mermaid?" I whispered. No idea why. It wasn't like Gloriana had me bugged. At least I hoped she didn't. That would be embarrassing.

Nerissa shook her head. "Our queen doesn't visit this realm."

Uh, yeah, she does, but I kept my mouth shut. I wasn't trying to tell tales on Gloriana. "That's good, although it's a beautiful likeness."

We walked back into the main room of the club, and I was blown away all over again. The fish tank wall had to be forty feet wide, fifteen feet high, and maybe five or six feet deep. The bottom had sand and what appeared to be living kelp, not plastic accessories. There were rocks and boulders teeming with life, multicolor sea anemones, sea urchins, and coral. Swimming in and out of the kelp were schools of fishes, some brightly colored, some silvery.

"This is extraordinary. I feel like I'm looking out my window in The Slaughtered Lamb. I keep bracing for a shark to swim by."

"No sharks. It's too small, and they get territorial. My cousins take shifts as the mermaid swimming in the tank, and I wouldn't want any of them bitten. I'd have to pay extra if they were. We do have an octopus, though. He usually stays over in this far corner. It's dark and he likes to hide."

While I was fixated on the tank, my wolf was paying attention to our surroundings. She heard the front door open and recognized scents. I turned to find Stheno and Thoth taking seats at a high top across the room, Owen and George crossing to a small table beside the tank, Fyr and Coco at a table near the entrance, and Dave and Maggie moving to one by the stage. In between, filling up more tables, were people I didn't know.

"These are some cousins who are helping us out tonight. Meri said you'd be paying for the use of this club, as well as all these actors." Nerissa gave me a look like she was daring me to argue.

"Of course. What were you thinking?" It was a good thing I'd married rich. Of course, I was here on vampire business, so it was only fair he picked up the tab.

"Let's wait until the end of the meeting. If this vampire causes damages, you'll be paying for that too."

"Absolutely."

TWENTY-SIX

Oh, Now We Got a Brawl Going

"Auntie, this is my boss." Meri came stomping out of the kitchen. Even spitting mad, she was radiant. "You can't blackmail her for more money. You said ten thousand." She looked at me, anger morphing into apology. "I'm sorry I didn't tell you. I really thought once she met you and understood what you needed to do, she wouldn't charge you anything." She turned to her aunt and hissed, "You're embarrassing me."

I patted Meri's shoulder. "No. Your aunt is right. I'm putting her business in danger. She needs to be compensated for that, as well as all these people who came to help."

Meri rolled her eyes. "Please. These guys never do anything. Now they're getting paid to do nothing."

The merpeople started screeching at each other in mermish, I assumed. The cousins did not appreciate Meri stepping on their easy, lucrative gig.

Nerissa ignored the fighting, looking over Meri's head at me. "You asked why she doesn't work here? This is why. Not to mention her father would never allow it. Human men are too dangerous. They'd take one look at this one and the stalking would begin. They already had to move her out of two schools. And it wasn't just the students who were a problem."

Nerissa barked something low and guttural. Everyone shut up. Meri's face was red from arguing with her cousins. She was so quiet and timid at work, it was a relief to see the real Meri. I worried the world was too harsh and scary for someone like her. I was glad to see she was a fighter.

Stheno had used the cover of Nerissa's barked command to whisper, "Twenty-five." Apparently, she thought twenty-five grand was the proper payment for what we were doing here. I glanced over and smiled to let her know I'd heard.

Nerissa turned to her niece. "What are you doing here? I told you not to come."

Meri looked like a gorgeous deer in headlights, gesturing weakly to me. "But it was my idea. And I'm the one who called to arrange it."

"That's all well and good," Nerissa said, her hand jerking angrily, pushing her long hair over her shoulder, "but how do you think your parents will respond to learning that you chose to walk into a club knowing a crazy bloodsucker was going to be here?"

I checked my watch. Sunset was soon and none of us had time to drive Meri home. "Do you have a back room or an office? Someplace safe for Meri to wait this meeting out?"

"But I want—" Meri began.

Nerissa gave one look and Meri shut up. A second later, she was stomping off the main floor of the club, down a side hall.

Once she was gone, Nerissa blew out a breath. "Jasmine, Delphine, Kai, start bringing food and drinks to these tables. We can't have a room full of people staring at each other. It's a nightclub. Marina, jump behind the bar and start making drinks."

"I can help," I said, "and so can Fyr, Owen, and Stheno." I waved them up. "We should make them look like cocktails, but they should probably be virgins."

"Screw that," Stheno muttered.

"You can make yourself whatever you want," I said as we rounded the bar. "I just thought it might be best if we kept our wits about us." I looked out at everyone sitting at tables. "We'll start making mocktails and putting them up on the bar. As we finish, you guys come up and grab one. We'll also make coffee, tea, and soda."

I turned to Nerissa. "Sorry. Do you mind?"

Shaking her head, she checked her watch. "Please do. We only have ten minutes until sundown." She glanced at the empty mermaid tank. "Nixie? Where are you?"

A woman with long red hair raised her hand.

"What are you doing out here? You're on mermaid duty tonight."

Nixie stood, staring at the empty tank and the table reserved for Garyn and me, directly beside the tank. "But—can't I just—I don't like bloodsuckers."

"Who does?" Nerissa pointed to a back room.

I loved one very much and liked a few others a great deal, but I got what she meant. I elbowed Fyr, whispering, "Bring Coco a soda so she doesn't need to come up here."

We all worked quickly, getting everyone in the lounge a drink. Nerissa had her grumpy chef bring out appetizers to a few of the tables.

My watch buzzed. "It's sunset. I don't know how long it will take her to read the note and come." I began walking to the table, my stomach jittering like mad. "Oh, and thank you to all the people not getting paid, who are just here to watch over me. I appreciate it so much."

"We love you, Sam," Owen called, George nodding.

"What the hell do you mean we're not getting paid?" Stheno grumbled. "That's bullshit."

Thoth patted her hand.

"You're welcome," Coco said.

"Wait," I said to Stheno, "If you and Fyr are here, who's covering your place?"

"Medusa."

At the name, every fae head turned to Stheno. They didn't know her. That was clear. They knew the name Medusa, though, and were suddenly looking far more uncomfortable than they had been a moment before.

"Won't she be able to tell there are no humans in here?" Owen asked. "George and Dave always know that stuff."

"As we don't have any eau de human, I'm not sure how we're supposed to fix that," Stheno said.

"Lost and found?" Coco suggested.

I popped up. "You're so smart! Yes, we need human clothes to drape over chair backs. Good one." I looked for Nerissa. "Where—"

"I have the lost and found box," Meri said, scrambling down the hall, carrying a tote box.

"Perfect." I lifted the lid and started sniffing garments. Sweaters, shawls, umbrellas, gloves, hats; they all still carried human scent. We passed them out and then I left the tote open, putting it under the black tablecloth of the empty table beside the one Garyn and I would sit at.

"This smells better to me. The rest of you with good noses, do you agree?" I looked to George, Fyr, and Coco. Dragons had an excellent sense of smell.

The dragons nodded, but so too did Stheno, Thoth, and some of the fae.

I stood again and shook out my arms. I was nervous as hell. "This vamp can control people mentally. I have no idea if she will have control over any of you, but if your head starts to hurt, go to the bathroom or the kitchen. Proximity counts with this one."

The fae looked at one another, clearly unhappy that their easy gig was turning out to be more dangerous than they'd thought.

Seeing movement out of the corner of my eye, I turned to see Nixie swimming beside me in the tank. I waved. She ignored me. Understandable. She didn't want to be here.

Nerissa turned the lights low, started the jazzy background music, and told everyone to start talking. It was too damn quiet for a nightclub.

We waited seven tense minutes before Nerissa touched her

earpiece. When she did, the chatter stopped. She nodded to us and then walked to the host podium to wait.

"Hey, that looks really good," Stheno said. "Can I have some?" When people turned, she lifted her eyebrows and stared back.

They got the message and began talking again.

Excellent hearing meant we all heard the car door slam and the front door open.

"Good evening. May I help you?"

"I'm meeting a woman named Sam Quinn."

Nerissa didn't answer right away. I heard a page turn and then she said, "Apparently, your party has arrived. Let me escort you to the table."

A moment later, Nerissa appeared around the corner into the main room, two leather-clad menus in her hand. Garyn was shorter than Nerissa, so it took a while to see her, though I scented vampire right away.

Nerissa moved around a small table, and I found Garyn staring through me, my head beginning to pound. Oh, good. We were starting already.

She wore a navy cocktail dress with three-quarter sleeves and a rounded neck. The skirt hit at her knee. She wore sensible heels, with small diamonds sparkling at her ears. Her golden-brown hair was loose, hanging in a perfectly straight bob to her shoulders.

Nerissa placed the menus on the table. "Your server will be right with you." She turned and walked back to the front of the club.

My head was throbbing, but I tried for a pleasant expression. "That's a lovely dress."

She looked me up and down, her smile sharp. "I hadn't realized the nightclub was so casual." She glanced at the other dressed-up patrons, before smoothing down the perfectly smoothed skirt. "Oh, good. I see at least one of us understands dress codes." She sniffed "I suppose I should be happy you're not wearing ripped jeans and a dog collar."

Everyone was doing a great job of holding up their fake

conversations, but I distinctly heard, "The fuck?" and knew it was Stheno.

"You and Clive." She furrowed her brow and shook her head. "How does that even happen?" She looked me up and down again. "It feels like a hideous mistake. Clive is handsome, successful, powerful, sophisticated." The look of distaste she gave me felt like a punch to the gut. "How do you keep yourself from feeling grossly inadequate at all times? He could have any woman he wanted and yet…"

The pressure in my head increased. "Listen, I know what you're trying to do—you're not exactly subtle—and it isn't going to work, so why don't we move on."

If looks could kill, I'd be dead on the spot.

She drummed one finger on the table. "If I were you, pup, I'd be very careful."

Slowly letting out a breath, I tried to shake off the jitters. Yes, she was a very old and powerful vampire, but I was a freaking necromancer. My wolf howled inside me. I found her blip and squeezed.

Blinking rapidly, she tapped her finger one last time and then it hung frozen in the air.

It hurt like hell, but I siphoned what I could into my white streak and choked down the rest. A moment later, the pain diminished significantly. How—

You can't be here! Damn, Clive. It was too dangerous for him to be this close to her.

I'm not. I'm on the roof of the building next door. Let me help.

With Clive helping with the pain, I squeezed harder. Leaning forward, I said, "And if I were you, I'd stop with the threats." I let one lethal claw slide out of my index finger, mirroring her and tapping the table with it.

Her eyes widened at the claw before she lifted her chin.

"By the way, thank you so much for those little presents you left us," I said.

She shook off the mental squeeze. "I have no idea what you're referring to." Movement in the mermaid tank caught her eye.

"I understand. It can be hard to remember things when you live so long. I mean, I totally get the phrase *older than dirt* now."

Sam.

Garyn's gaze snapped back to me. Unadulterated loathing was the best description for what I saw in her eyes.

"Maybe you've forgotten after so many centuries, but we don't kill humans and leave their dead bodies—bodies that still have vampire bite marks on them—lying around for the humans to find."

Her smile made my blood run cold. "Oh, no. Did Clive have to speak with the authorities about his little dead friend? How sad." She glanced down at her sapphire cocktail ring. "Perhaps if he'd remained in England with his own kind, those humans would still be alive."

"Isn't the first rule of vampire club that no one talks about vampire club? Remember? We're supposed to be a secret."

Shaking her head, she glanced around the nightclub. "I don't understand the gibberish coming out of your mouth."

"I can see how that would be a problem for you, the way the world is passing you by. Is that why you do it?" I tilted my head, all fake solicitude, studying her reactions. "Controlling people's thoughts and words, their reactions to you. Is that so you don't feel agitation and confusion?"

I shrugged. "My nona was very old when she passed," I lied, having never met my grandmother. "She was nowhere near as old as you, but she developed dementia and she experienced anger, confusion, and fear, just like you are. It's hard, isn't it? I understand. She fixated on things from her past too, just like you're doing now. You barely knew Clive, though. Is it just that he reminds you of someone else?"

When her eyes went vamp black, I looped my magic around her head and began squeezing again.

"What's the point?" I pressed. "These weird one-sided conversations you like to have, putting words in other people's mouths. Are you reliving something that happened a millennium ago or something you wished had happened?" Shaking my head, I glanced at the tank. "It's a kind of communication masturbation, don't you think?"

Damn it, Sam.

Red flickered in her eyes, so I tugged my magic harder. Her jaw clenched as her eyes flickered back and forth, blue, black, blue, black.

"Never knowing what anyone actually thinks," I went on. "Never knowing how they really feel. It's like playing dolls with people. Don't you ever get sick of having them all stare blindly at you while they say what you want to hear, do what you want them to do?"

Her fangs descended so I yanked on my magic as hard as I could. She was too strong. She was going to snap my hold any minute.

"I suppose what I don't understand is why you're still here. No one wants you here. Over eighty of your people have been given their true deaths and yet here you still are. Most people, once they've had their asses handed to them, would skulk off. Not you, though."

I leaned forward, my wolf lightening my eyes and growling in my head as I pulled with all my might. "All those yes-men you've surrounded yourself with have given you a false sense of your own superiority. My advice to you is to get the hell out of this city before you get hurt." I smiled, letting my teeth sharpen and lengthen.

It happened so fast, I didn't see so much as react. My wolf was at the fore, ready to take over. I felt a stabbing pain in my head and knew the control I'd had over her had snapped.

Her finger finally hit the table as she leapt over the top of it. I whipped out a hand, claws out, muscles bulked up. The claws on one hand tore through the side of her face while my other hand throttled her neck. My claws dug into her flesh as I lifted her off the ground and then slammed her head against the floor of the lounge.

The fae got up and moved out of the way.

Her hands flew up to break my arm, but I caught them, doing a knee drop on her stomach. I shoved my face into hers, eyes wolf gold, while squeezing her throat as hard as I could, her blood oozing over my fingers. "Get. Out."

I picked her up by her neck and slammed her head against the hard floor one more time. As soon as she hit, I let go and punched her in the jaw, breaking it. She shoved me off, backflipping to her feet. Opening her mouth on a wince, she snapped her jaw back into place. We circled one another, but I was still in her head, my wolf taking swipes at her mind.

TWENTY-SEVEN

Fight! Fight! Fight!

Garyn was shocked to have been taken down so quickly. I'd felt it. The problem was, she was gathering her strength and was about to kick my ass. If she overpowered me and reversed our positions, I'd be dead. I needed to keep her guessing. Surrounding herself with people who only thought and did what she wanted meant it took precious moments for her to figure out what was happening when it was out of her control.

Her cheek was already starting to heal, though she was smeared in blood. She flew at me and I pulled both my blades rather than retreating. Given how fast and strong vampires were, I'd rather she stayed a sword's length away from me. She grabbed the hand I had gripped around the axe hilt and yanked my arm out of its socket. As she was trying to rip it off completely, I considered the dislocation a win.

Painfully popping it back in, I spun out of her grip and sliced down with the sword, missing her neck and instead slashing across her shoulders. She was so freaking fast. She feinted left and then charged. I aimed my sword at her chest, but she knocked my arm out of the way. *Snap.* When she went for my neck, I dropped the sword I could no longer hold and started to flip her up with my elbow—yes, it was very painful—to bounce her off the ceiling, and then remembered the glass wave. Unfortunately, my hesitation gave her the opportunity to twist away and ram her head into my abdomen.

Breath gone, I struggled to get air. *Shit.* I could *not* pass out. Her eyes lit up in triumph when she reached for me again. I spun the other direction, slamming my good elbow into her cheekbone and then hammered my fist down on the top of her head.

I had just swung the axe to slice off her head when she knocked my legs out from under me. I heard a loud crack and went down. My brain was a black snarl of pain.

She fell on me, fangs glistening, lunging to rip my head off. Flattening my hands, claws up, I stabbed her neck and tore. Suddenly she was yanked off me.

Dave had her hanging in the air by her hair. She punched a hole through his stomach as he slammed a fireball into her face.

Screeching, hair on fire, she streaked from the lounge and out the hallway to the kitchen.

Dave dropped to his knees beside me, a hand over his gaping, bloody wound. Maggie screeched, pushing over chairs to get to him, but he disappeared through the floor before she made it. Keening, she fell in a heap on the exact spot he'd just disappeared. And then Dave was leaning over her, picking her up and cradling her against his chest.

"Shh. I'm okay now," he murmured. "Come on, baby. I'm fine." He walked her through the nightclub and into the entry.

"I'm calling Lilah right now," Owen said, staring incredulously after Dave.

Black spots crowded my vision. No. I would not pass out. Willing my vision to clear, I focused on Owen. "Dave can return from Hell at the same moment he leaves," I told him. "He was probably down there for a while healing before he returned at the moment he left." Thinking about Dave and Hell was helping to keep me distracted from the sickening pain hitting me in waves.

Clive appeared on my other side, pulling away as much pain as he could. He leaned down and kissed my forehead as his fingers flew over his phone screen. He held it to his ear. "We need you again. Sam has broken a leg." He glanced at Owen, who nodded. "One leg is broken but the second may be fractured as well." He listened a moment. "No. We're near Fisherman's Wharf at the Bubble Lounge."

"Thanks for that," Nerissa said to me, pointing to the glass wave hanging above us. "I saw you check yourself. It gave her the advantage, so I thank you for not trashing my business." She scanned the room. "You didn't even knock over a table."

Gritting my teeth, I responded, "You're welcome. Clive, we need to pay her for letting us meet here."

He got off the phone, barely glancing at Nerissa. "I'll take care of it. Dr. Underfoot will be here as soon as he can."

"Lilah's on her way too," Owen said.

Clive's hand hovered over my leg, not wanting to hurt me. "Where is it broken?" he asked Owen.

"Femur," George replied, kneeling on my other side.

I heard some mutters of concern and sympathy around me. Staring up at the glass wave gave me a focal point. I needed away from the pain. I'd let everyone else figure it out. I was done now.

George's gorgeous face blocked my view of the glass wave. "Hi there, beautiful." He placed one of his large, warm hands on the side of my face and neck.

I worried I was going to pass out or maybe vomit from the pain. I really hoped I didn't do either. I was pretty sure retching would cause everything to hurt more.

"Owen," George said in a slow, soft voice, "hand me your jacket. I think she's going into shock. Let's get her warmed up."

Owen knelt by his boyfriend, covering my torso gently with his jacket, while George had both hands on either side of my face. They were so big and warm, they helped me feel safe. Mostly, anyway. The psycho and her crew could come back at any moment.

"Should we have everyone clear out?" I asked. I didn't want my friends in the middle of a vampire bloodbath.

Clive shook his head. "We need to wait for Underfoot and Lilah." He looked up at the fae, as though noticing them for the first time. "You can all leave, if you wish. My wife can't be moved yet."

"What about that vampire?" Meri asked from somewhere behind me. "Is she dead?"

Clive shook his head again. "She leapt into the bay to put out the flames."

"Ow," I said.

Clive's focus shifted to me. "Where does it hurt?"

"Everywhere, but I meant *Ow* her, being set on fire." That had to be one of the worst ways to go.

"Darling, we want her dead. Let's not worry about hurting her." He motioned to someone behind me. "Can you get her some water?"

"Hey, look up." I wanted him to see the wave.

His eyes flicked up before pausing to tilt his head back and take it all in.

"Arwyn made it for Nerissa," I told him.

"Extraordinary. Truly." His gaze finally moved from the wave to the walls and then to the mermaid tank. "I've never been in here before." He addressed someone behind me. "Thank you for allowing us to use your lounge. I'll have a check delivered tomorrow."

"Will she be back with more of them?" Nerissa asked.

Clive stood, and I wrapped my bruised and bloodied hand around his ankle. I felt better when we were connected.

"She probably won't be, but her people most likely will. Are you warded against vampires?" Clive asked.

"I was. I had it altered this afternoon to allow Garyn in. The problem is, you're here. That means the ward isn't working correctly." Pushing out a harsh breath, she stalked away.

Clive crouched beside me again. "She's calling someone." *Can you see where they are?*

I wasn't sure. My head hurt so much, the idea of trying didn't make me happy. Closing my eyes, I breathed deeply and found the vampires, the one beside me and the others, thankfully, much farther away. Clive's blip looked a little different from the rest of the vamps, though. While all the rest of the vamps looked like dark, poisonous green blips in my head, Clive's was a shade lighter. Perhaps that was why he'd been able to pass through the ward. Or, more likely, I was seeing him differently because my head had been rattled.

Russell and his peeps are on Alcatraz. That's smart. Garyn's at the penthouse. They're all around her. Shit. Another plane must have arrived. Agh, why can't they all just stand still for a minute? There are... seventy-three now.

Seventy-three vampires who are out of their minds, wanting revenge for hurting their mother-goddess. And you said Russell lost eight of his people last night?

Yes.

There was noise at the front door. Dr. Underfoot. He had a slight hitch in his step. The limp was so mild, I'd never noticed it until I heard the almost imperceptible slide before every other step. My wolf was on it, noticing the little details I missed.

A moment later, the dwarf was standing where I could see him. "Hello, Mrs. Fitzwilliam. I'm sorry you've been hurt again. Let's see what I can do to help." He was a charming, soft-spoken man whose beard overtook most of his face and who I'd never seen in anything other than a three-piece tweed suit.

He took a stethoscope out of his bag and listened to my heart. "Nice and strong," he murmured.

Quick footsteps and then Lilah was standing on my other side, behind Clive. Surprising me, he moved closer and sat on the floor, lifting my head into his lap. He kept a hand on my forehead, dulling more of the pain.

Both Dr. Underfoot and Lilah ran their hands gently over my legs, Lilah keeping her hands a hair's breadth away. She then ran them over my torso, arms, and head, while Underfoot focused on the broken leg.

"Cracked ribs…the concussion is starting to heal…" she said.

"Broken femur," Underfoot added. "Miss Wong?"

"Yes," Lilah confirmed, "and a hairline crack in the radius or ulna. Sorry. I have a hard time telling them apart," she said.

"Understandable. You can begin the mending and then we'll get her in a cast." He moved to my feet, looking down at me. "I'm sorry, but we're going to need to take your pants off."

"Oh." I mean, sure, my scars were gone now but I was still in a room with a ton of people, unable to defend myself.

"Owen, can you find us some scissors?" Clive rubbed my shoulder. "That will work, won't it? We'll cut off that pant leg."

Thank you.

Owen knelt and very gently cut the thin fabric high on my thigh before clearing out of the way.

Underfoot slid off my shoe and then most of my pant leg. It hurt like hell. I felt Clive's hand flinch against my forehead and knew it must be bad. Low mutters broke out around the room.

"Miss Wong, when you've a chance…" Dr. Underfoot wrapped both his hands around my ankle. He then looked up to my right and left, signaling with a tilt of his head.

Dave and George dropped down to their knees beside me. I didn't like the look of this. When Lilah moved in next to George and held her hands over my leg, Underfoot finally looked me in the eye.

"Mrs. Fitz—"

"Just Sam, please."

He nodded. "Sam, I'm afraid when Garyn broke your leg, she pushed the bone out of alignment. Your own naturally fast healing is working against us right now. We need to realign the bone so it can mend properly. This is going to be quite painful. The men are here to hold you down so you don't hurt yourself."

"No." I looked up into Clive's eyes, mine filling with tears. "I'll be still. I promise. I don't want anyone holding me down."

He leaned down and kissed my forehead. He knew what I'd

been through and why I couldn't handle being held down like that.

"Dave, George, thank you, but we'll manage."

The men stood easily and moved away from the action.

"This is going to be more difficult without their help," Underfoot began.

"No," Clive said. "She'll be better like this."

Underfoot looked frustrated but said, "As you wish." He turned his attention to Lilah and said, "I'll pull so we can get the bones lined up. Can you use your magic to nudge it into place?"

Lilah nodded, sweat already forming on her brow from the healing magic she'd been performing.

Underfoot gripped my ankle hard. I closed my eyes, blew out a long, slow breath and then nodded. He yanked and rotated my leg to the right. Bone ground against bone. The pain was like an explosion of white in my head. Eyes screwed tight, I concentrated in my mind's eye on the glass wave, willing it to wash me out to sea, far away from the unbearable pain. After a few moments, I realized the strange high-pitched sounds I'd been hearing were actually my own whines.

Clive was leaning over me, his lips on my forehead. *I'm so sorry, love.*

Did I move?

Not a hair.

I just—I couldn't have two men hold me down, even if they're my friends.

I know, and so do they. Lilah is nodding. The bone seems to be back in its proper place. She's beginning the healing and Underfoot is readying some type of—

"I've never seen anyone stay still like that while I manipulated a broken bone. You have enviable control. I'm glad Clive and Lilah are here to deal with your pain because I need to rub a salve on your skin over the break and then I'm going to encase your thigh in an air cast. This should help keep it in place while you mend."

I gasped when he slid the cast under my leg, but I didn't move.

Once that was secured, he moved to my arm. In that weird way brains work, I'd forgotten I had more broken bones. My focus was on my leg. Once he moved up to my side, a million other hurts made themselves known.

"Stupid vampires," I muttered.

"I know, darling. We're the worst." He brushed his thumb along the side of my neck, somehow finding the one spot that didn't hurt.

Instead of focusing on the glass wave, I looked up into Clive's eyes and found love, safety, and home.

"And done," Dr. Underfoot said.

Surprised, I glanced down to see I had an air cast on my right arm as well. *You're very distracting.*

I know.

TWENTY-EIGHT

Bounced from the Bubble Lounge

"If she's all bandaged up, perhaps you would be so kind as to move on now," Nerissa said. "I'd like to keep my business intact and my building standing." She stood to the side of us, separate, arms crossed over her chest.

I tried to get up, but Clive pushed me back down.

"Don't." He kept a hand on my shoulder.

"But what are you going to do?" Meri asked. "You need to take Sam somewhere safe, but there's going to be a bunch of really angry vampires running around the city soon. Where's safe?"

"How many are there?" Owen asked.

"Seventy-three," Clive responded.

"Good Lord," Coco breathed.

"I think we should go to Alcatraz," I said. "Russell and his people are there. It's a way to get Garyn's vamps away from the general public and the Bubble Lounge—"

"Good. Do that," Nerissa said.

"Auntie," Meri hiss-whispered, clearly embarrassed.

I continued, pretending I hadn't heard, "I don't think they do tours at night. Maybe we—"

"No," Clive interrupted. "I'm taking you home. You have broken bones, Sam. You're not up for a fight."

"She's not," Dave said, "but we are."

Clive turned to Dave. "You'll help?"

"Fuck yeah," he said. "Setting a few dozen vampires on fire sounds good."

"We can help," Fyr said.

I looked over my shoulder and saw him standing with George, Coco, and Owen. "You guys are the best."

"You know," Stheno said, "Medusa and I rarely get to have fun anymore. I'll see if she wants to close The Viper's Nest and join us."

I tilted my head toward the table Stheno and Thoth were sitting at and found her staring back at me. She was only doing this for me, and I was so very grateful. "Thank you."

Looking back up at Clive, I said, "Fighting is only one of my skills."

"Let's keep it PG, sister," Stheno snarked.

Ignoring her, I said, "You can hide me somewhere safe on the island and I can help you guys fight."

"How?" Meri asked.

Clive turned and grinned. "Your boss is quite wily. She has her ways."

"I'll call my mom," Owen said. "I'm sure there are more wicches that'd be willing to fight."

"Help me up, please," I asked Clive.

"No."

I smacked the leg I was leaning on with my good hand. "It's not your decision."

Dave crouched beside me. "Couldn't you do what you do from home?"

I considered, appreciating that they wanted me out of harm's way. "I probably could. Garyn is very strong, though. She could turn all of our vamps into hers. I feel like I need to be there to block her, distract her. Alcatraz has got to be haunted. I could use that to my advantage. I can't explain why. I just know I need to be there."

"I agree. She does," Thoth said, and that seemed to settle the matter.

Clive looked between Dr. Underfoot and Lilah. "Can Sam be moved?"

Dr. Underfoot looked uncomfortable. "Within reason. She's injured, but circumstances being what they are, if she's moved carefully, she should be okay." He turned to Lilah. "Miss Wong, do you agree?"

She nodded. "The mending has begun but she needs to be kept in a protected place. It won't take much to rebreak the bones."

Clive moved, gently placing my head on the floor. He stood and looked around the lounge. "I don't suppose anyone has a gurney we could borrow?"

"Maybe we could just get me up." Anything was better than lying on the floor while everyone discussed what to do with me.

Clive picked me up by the waist, trying to avoid the broken ribs, and stood me on my good leg. He did his best to hold me upright without accidentally making contact with my leg, arm, or ribs. Owen grabbed my blades and resheathed them for me.

"What you need," Stheno said, "is a boat. How are you planning to get to Alcatraz?"

"The nocturne owns one," Clive said, "but I would assume they used it to get out there."

"Maybe you all could have this discussion outside," Nerissa suggested.

Now that I was standing and could see what was going on, I realized almost all the fae had left. Nerissa, Meri, and Kai, the guy who was helping us distribute appetizers earlier, were still here, but everyone else, including Nixie in the tank, was gone.

"I could—" Meri began but everyone else in the room shouted, "No!"

"If it'll get you out any faster, you can borrow my boat—for an additional fee," Nerissa said. "Kai, you drive them out and then bring my boat back."

I could tell Clive was reluctant to rely on the fae, but we needed to get out of here and onto the Rock. "Sounds good. Thank you." I glanced around. "Okay. Whoever's coming, let's go."

Lilah started to walk toward the back hall and both Owen and I said, "Wait."

"No. You're too tired." Owen went to his sister and steered her toward the front door. "You're a healer, not a fighter, and you've already worn yourself out healing Sam."

"Thank you, Lilah, but Owen's right," I said. She was looking wan and no doubt needed sleep after working on all my injuries.

I wasn't sure who would come and purposely didn't look at anyone as Clive took most of my weight heading out the hall, through the kitchen, and past my car still parked by the dumpster.

Kai led the way down to a slip where a white sailboat gleamed in the moonlight. Clive was able to get us aboard the boat without jostling me too much, which was quite a feat. We stepped down into a teak seating area.

Clive put me in the corner, thinking it the more stable option. Sitting wasn't easy, though, as everything hurt. The boat bobbed and swayed as people got on. Clive sat beside me, keeping an arm around me so I didn't reinjure myself.

I looked up as the boat drew away from the dock and found everyone still with us, minus the fae and Lilah. Stheno, Thoth, George, Owen, Coco, Fyr, Dave, and Maggie. I was surprised, though, to see Dr. Underfoot sitting beside me.

"That is a most excellent axe you have, Mrs. Fitzwilliam."

"Sam," I said.

"Sam," he corrected himself. "May I see it?"

"Of course." I gingerly leaned forward and withdrew it from the sheath on my back, then handed it to Dr. Underfoot.

He studied the markings, the handle, and finally sniffed it. He was about to test the blade's edge by cutting his callused thumb when I stopped him.

"I'm sorry, but you can't do that. Algar enchanted it. It's deadly to the fae." And to me if I attacked a peaceful member of the fae, but I didn't want to broadcast that.

"Algar," he repeated. "I recognize these markings. I know whose axe this was and yet it's changed its allegiance to you, so you must have bested him. I was curious, though. It glows—to my eyes—as though it's been touched by the queen herself. If Algar gifted you with this protection, it was at the behest of the queen and therefore holds her light."

He handed it back to me. "Do you know why the queen has taken a special interest in you?"

Clive was on the phone with Russell, explaining what had been happening and that we were on our way to them.

Shaking my head, I resheathed the axe and started to shrug, setting off too many hurts. "I don't. I had to visit Faerie to deliver a message last year. Maybe she's just wondering about the rando who stumbled into her home."

He *hmm*ed, clearly not convinced, and then said, "Perhaps."

I looked at my left foot, propped on the bench in only a sock. "Hopefully, I won't have to walk on pointy things."

"You'll be carried, love," Clive said. "Godfrey and Audrey are currently scouring the prison for a safe place to tuck you away from the battle. You'll be on the island. You can do what you do without being in the middle of a brawl."

Owen leaned back in his seat. "We're close. We should be there in a couple of minutes."

"We need somewhere safe for Owen to be as well," George said.

"Maybe up high so I can see what's going on and who to spell." Owen patted George's thigh. It was a *Don't worry; I'll be okay*, and an *I can handle this* all in one pat.

The look George gave in return clearly said, *You're not allowed to get hurt.*

Kai sailed around the back side of Alcatraz to the tour boat dock. Everyone got out, Clive and me being last as he was trying his best to hold me in a way that didn't knock anything that hurt. We were met with a large sign stating this was a United States Penitentiary. Around it, though, was graffiti left from the 1969

Native American occupation. Spray-painted were phrases like *Indians Welcome* and *Indian Land*.

We climbed a steep hill beside a large four-story building that looked like a barracks. I assumed it had been used by the civilians who worked on Alcatraz. The prison was up the steep slope, past some hollowed-out ruins, on top of the Rock.

Russell waited for us beside the lighthouse. "My lady," he said, tipping his head, "I'm sorry to hear about your injuries."

"Thanks. By the way, great job last night. That was a hell of a fight." A few of his people were ranged around him and they nodded, acknowledging the comment.

"Unfortunately, eight of our people were given their final deaths, but they went honorably, in battle against an aggressor." He half turned to his men before turning back to me. "We're told you took on Garyn herself and sent her racing back to her penthouse."

"The first part is true. Dave's fireball is what sent her racing out into the bay to douse the flames, though." I glanced around for Godfrey or Audrey. "Have they found me a place yet?"

Russell nodded. "They're trying to make it a little easier for you, given your injuries."

George and Owen walked back to us, with Fyr and Coco right behind. "We've found the three highest vantage points on the island for Coco, Fyr, and myself," George said, pointing. "The lighthouse, the water tower, and a smokestack. We can hit the ground with dragon's breath from those heights, but we need to know who our enemies are. Can you have all your people come here so we can memorize their scents?"

"Good," Clive said, nodding.

Russell didn't say anything, but apparently as Clive had been able to do, Russell could communicate with his nocturne mind-to-mind. A few moments later, twenty-something vampires assembled in a semicircle around us.

"Spread out. These three need your scents so there are no mistakes when Garyn's people arrive," Russell said, and his people immediately arranged themselves in a single line, an arm's length away from one another.

George, Coco, and Fyr walked down the line, sniffing, processing, and moving on. When they were almost done, Godfrey and Audrey returned, stepping into place at the end of the line.

Coco and Fyr took off, running toward the other side of the island. A few moments later, there were two bright flashes and then huge dragons were flying low over Alcatraz, one black with red eyes like George, the other a dark green with orange eyes. They each circled a few times before one landed on the water tower and the other on the smokestack. George grabbed Owen's hand and they went in the lighthouse.

"Hello, Missus," Godfrey said. "Audrey and I found a place that we think will work for you."

"Where?" Clive asked.

"The basement of the prison," Audrey replied. "In the kitchen."

"There are rooms within rooms," Godfrey broke in. "We heard you were hurt again—you should probably rethink your life choices, by the way—"

"I've been telling her that for a while," Stheno shouted from somewhere, her voice slicing through the roaring of the surf, though I couldn't see her or Thoth. "Oh, and once this gets started and I lift my eyepatch, no one look at me."

Clive must have picked up on my confusion. He pointed to the prison. Stheno and Thoth were apparently on the far side, out of sight.

"I think we made a fairly comfortable seat for you," Godfrey continued.

"Thank you," Clive said. "Let's get her down there and then we'll call Garyn." He gestured for Godfrey to go first and then held me as gently as he could while taking all of my weight.

I heard a noise and looked up. A naked George leapt out of the top of the lighthouse, burst into flame, and shifted into his dragon form. Like his sister, he had a black scaly body with bright red eyes. He circled the island, as the other dragons had, and then came back to sit on the lighthouse. When he landed, pieces of the roof fell to the ground.

"Will that building hold him?"

"If not, he'll move," Clive said. "The dragons are the safest ones on this island."

We followed Godfrey through the prison door. A chill ran through me as we stepped inside. It had concrete floors and a center walkway. On both sides of us were three stories of small cells with bars across the front. Halfway down, we passed one cell with an open door, which I assumed was for the tour. A dim red light glowed in the distance. As we got closer and no longer had bars in the way, I saw it was an exit sign, again, no doubt for the tour.

"We want cell block D," Godfrey told us.

Shivering, setting off hurts, I realized I was getting really cold. I closed my eyes and tapped into my necromancy, afraid I was in a lot of trouble. When I opened them, I discovered that Alcatraz was lousy with ghosts. Some had faded to indistinct hovering specters. Others were fully-formed, sentient beings, watching us, more than a few following.

We have some jailhouse ghosties shadowing us.

Can they hurt you?

No. I should be okay. It's just creepy.

Godfrey led us around a corner into a new cell block. All the doors to the cells were open. A couple of new transparent people slouched around the bars and drifted toward me. We passed a spiral metal staircase. If this place hadn't been freaking me out, that would have been cool.

Behind a half wall were stairs down to the lower level. When my dead fan club started to follow us down the stairs, I held out a hand, pushing them back. They paused but looked far too interested to let a shove stop them.

TWENTY-NINE

Captain Sam

I didn't think this section of the prison was on the tour because it was decidedly dustier and dirtier down here. Sections of the walls had been broken through and we could see the foundations of what looked like an earlier building.

Vampires were silent beings. Although I could barely hear their footsteps in the layers of settled dust, I saw the shoeprints.

Godfrey eventually led us past green and white tiled walls with long metal prep tables, and a couple of huge, cauldron-like pots, probably for making mush for the whole prison population.

He took us past the open work areas to an oversized closet that had *Flour Room* stenciled faintly beside the door. When he opened the door, dust plumed up into the air.

"Over here," Godfrey said. He walked to the far end, past shelves, to a narrow alcove, out of sight of the door. "We think this is where they used to stack the institutional-sized bags of flour. This should be a good spot for you. Out of the action. Your back and sides are protected by these cinderblock walls. Threats should only come at you head-on."

"I like the chair," I said. It was a stark white leather seat on a thick pole with a wide base.

"Eh, what the Master doesn't know won't hurt him," Godfrey said with a grin.

"Tell me you didn't rip the captain's chair out of the nocturne's yacht." I had to admit, though, I'd been worried I'd be sitting on the filthy floor.

He put his index finger to his lips and then gestured to the chair.

"Will it tip over with me in it?"

Godfrey pointed to the base. "Audrey and I drove the bolts into the concrete. That chair isn't going anywhere."

Clive carried me into the small space and then placed me in the chair. It was taller than a regular chair, but not too bad. I hated having my stocking foot on the floor, though.

Clive took fabric out of his pocket—my cut-off pant leg—folded it, and placed it on the floor beneath my heel. "Better?"

I nodded and he gave me a kiss.

"Good. Stay here. Stay safe. We'll be back before you know it." Clive started to leave but I grabbed his hand while reaching for Godfrey's.

"You guys need to stay safe too, okay? It's going to be almost four-to-one and you need to win. I mean it."

"We promise, Missus. Don't forget, we've got dragons, a gorgon, a wicche, and a demon on our side. We're golden." Godfrey bent over my hand and kissed it before rushing off.

Clive stayed a moment. "You have your blades?"

Nodding, I said, "I do."

He gave me another kiss. "I don't like leaving you down here. I'd rather you stayed with Owen."

"Godfrey and Audrey picked a good place. For what I do, I need peace and quiet. Expect me to pop into your head a lot, so I know what's going on."

"I welcome it."

"You should go. I'll be okay." I hoped.

"See that you are." He gave me another quick kiss and was gone.

Trying not to dwell on my current predicament—sitting in the dark, ghost-filled basement of a prison—I tapped my necromancy and looked for the vampires. There were two green clots of vampires in San Francisco, one on this island and one in Pacific Heights at the penthouse.

I started counting at the penthouse. Oh, no.

There are more now. Two more planes must have arrived while we were at the Bubble Lounge. There are now ninety-seven vamps in that penthouse.

Lovely. I'll pass it on. Russell is calling her now.

Zeroing in on Garyn's blip, I didn't bother trying to hide my presence. I was pretty sure she'd be too distracted to notice me. I pushed my way through, dropping into a raging mind. The pain was unbearable, but she had to keep her focus on maintaining control of the ninety-six vamps in her penthouse. She was terrified they'd leave her if her control wavered.

"It's Russell on the phone, my lady. He asks to speak with you." Reginald leaned over, waiting for Garyn's response.

I heard her voice, though she didn't speak out loud. She must have been doing the Master vampire mind-to-mind thing. *What does he want?*

"My lady requests to know the nature of your call," Reginald relayed.

"Tell your lady that she and all of her people will die tonight. This is my city. As she has chosen not to leave it peacefully, she will die in it painfully."

All the vamps in the room turned to Garyn, some gazing adoringly but most angered that Russell would speak to their lady so. Could they have just left the city and lived another few centuries? Of course. Russell taunted her, though, guaranteeing they'd focus on punishing him, which kept our human population safe.

Garyn laughed. She commanded the superior forces. They would annihilate the pompous Master and his anemic nocturne. *We accept his challenge. Where shall we hand them their true deaths?*

Reginald relayed her message.

"We await you on Alcatraz," Russell sneered before disconnecting.

"My lady," Reginald began, "we will make you proud. They will regret they ever raised a hand against you and yours."

See that you do.

Reginald called all the vamps to the formal living room to lay out their battle plan. The men were furious and vibrating with the need to exact revenge. Garyn's second was having a difficult time keeping so many vampires, many of whom were Masters themselves, focused on him and his plan.

From what I could see from Garyn's perspective through the open bedroom door, quite a few of the men were talking in low whispers to those around them, ignoring Reginald.

Instead of healing her burn, she focused her energy on maintaining a perfect image in the eyes of her people. If she'd addressed the ninety-six vampires herself, they would have listened and done her bidding. She couldn't relinquish control, though, couldn't split her focus and trust that they'd follow her if she wasn't influencing their thoughts. And so, she waited in the next room, watching Reginald flounder and her power structure fracture.

Her pain was overwhelming, but she didn't care. The devotion of those men meant everything to her and she wouldn't let it go.

A memory glowed brightly right beside me, so I stepped in.

A mother and daughter are walking down a narrow path in the woods. Each wears a long, belted green woolen gown over a white smock. The child's long golden-brown hair is loose, hanging to her waist. The mother wears a large piece of cloth draped over her head and around her neck in a wimple.

Encroaching branches tear at the girl's hair and gown. She considers falling back to walk behind her mother and avoid the branches, but she prefers to be in front. The mother regularly touches something in the folds of her gown. The daughter knows it's the last of their coins. She's been down this path with her mother before. She's going to give what little they have left to the wise woman in the woods.

Garyn, the child, doesn't like the woods or the wise woman. She doesn't much care for her mother, come to that. Her father is the one she adores. Her mother's just the pathetic woman her father left.

Finally, after leaping over a brook, they come to the wise woman's cabin. Garyn never goes in. Her mother has secret things to discuss, so Garyn is left out in the shadowy woods on her own. She doesn't know why her mother doesn't let her into the warmth of the cabin. It isn't as though Garyn doesn't know what's going on.

Her mother is back to buy another spell. She wants Garyn's father to return, to take care of them. Her father, though, is smart, leaving his wife behind. She's dumb and ugly. Garyn, though, is beautiful. Her father has often told her so. She's sure her father hates her mother as much as Garyn does.

Garyn knew, when her father didn't return from the hunt, that he'd left her mother. Good for him. He was supposed to take her with him, though. She doesn't know what her mother said or did, but she knows her mother is the reason her father hasn't returned to retrieve her.

He'll be back soon. He loves her too much to leave her. When he returns to claim her, she'll be happy and they'll both leave Mother behind. She smiles, ignoring the branches grabbing at her. Soon she'll be far away from her sad mother and back with her handsome father. Soon.

The wise woman and her daughter are in the dooryard. They're picking leaves and berries from the plants crowded together in a shaft of sunlight breaking through the dense trees. They both have long black hair and green eyes. The daughter's are a bright, vibrant shade, though she has dark circles under them, as though she hasn't slept in some time. The wise woman stands, tucking handfuls of greenery into the pockets of the apron tied around her waist.

"Come, Chloe, let's go in." The woman glances at Garyn, smiling cautiously.

Garyn's mother eyes Chloe and hesitates. "What I have to speak of is private. Perhaps the girls might occupy themselves while we conduct our business."

The wise woman looks uncomfortable with the suggestion but turns to her daughter, eyebrows raised. The child straightens her shoulders and nods.

"Good. You could show her the sacred pond." The wise woman runs her hand down her daughter's hair.

Garyn's mother barely turns her head to say "be good" before stepping into the dark cabin.

Once the women go in and the door is closed, the girls stare at one another. Chloe is smaller and younger than Garyn, though she wears an expression of world weariness.

"Come on, then," Chloe says, leading the way through the forest.

Garyn's hair and face are scratched painfully by the branches she bats out of her way. She notices that Chloe doesn't have the same problem and grows more resentful.

When the path finally opens, there is a beautiful pond surrounded by lush green grass and two large boulders for sitting. A patch of sunlight sparkles on the water as dragonflies zigzag over the surface.

Garyn stands close to Chloe. "Why is it sacred?"

Chloe leaps over smaller rocks, moving to the far side of the pond and sitting in a shaft of soft light. "It's not. We just call it that."

Garyn slowly makes her way around the pond. "How many years have you?"

"Seven in the spring. And yourself?" While Chloe speaks, she stares into the water.

Garyn sits beside her. "One and ten."

Again, Garyn is too close, so Chloe leans away from her.

"Do you bathe here?" Garyn asks.

Chloe shakes her head. "Nay. We bathe in the stream."

Garyn reaches out to touch the girl's thin leather foot coverings. They have embroidered flowers on them, and Garyn wants them desperately. Chloe slides her foot under her skirt and then stands abruptly to pick a flower and sit again farther off.

"Why do take yourself away from me?" Garyn asks.

Chloe stares at Garyn in a way that makes her feel exposed. The little girl turns back to the pond and the dragonflies. "I'd rather not say."

Garyn sits with that a moment but doesn't like it. Her father never *said why he was leaving either, though she assumes it was because of her mother, the ugly old hag. "Is it her?"*

Chloe's brow furrows and then clears. "Nay. Your mam is lovely, just sad."

Garyn throws a small rock into the pond, disturbing the surface. "She's not."

Chloe glances over and away. "Not?"

"Not lovely," Garyn spits out.

Chloe shrugs one delicate shoulder, watching the dragonflies again.

They sit in uncomfortable silence before Garyn blurts, "Why won't you look at me?"

Chloe turns back to her, wary. "You've a darkness surrounding you. I don't like it."

"No I don't," Garyn insists.

Again, Chloe shrugs, studying the small wildflowers by the pond's edge.

"I don't." Garyn crosses her arms, glaring at the little girl.

"As you say," Chloe responds before standing and walking around the edge of the pond again.

Garyn rises, stalking after the little girl. "Take it back."

Chloe startles, not realizing the other girl is so close. Cringing away, her foot slips and her arms pinwheel. Before she falls in, Garyn grabs her arm. When her hand touches Chloe, though, the young girl's eyes roll back into her head as she falls to the ground, convulsing violently.

THIRTY

She's a Charmer, All Right

G aryn drags the little girl away from the water's edge before dropping her arm. She's not surrounded by darkness and her mother isn't lovely. Garyn halfheartedly kicks the little girl in the side. "Liar. You don't know anything."

She walks to the boulder and sits. She knows she should call for help but doesn't want to. If the girl is so smart, she can wake herself.

After what should be a concerning amount of time, the girl bolts upright in a panic. Garyn is distracted from a daydream about her father returning and begging her forgiveness, which she eventually grants.

The little girl's eyes are wide as she scoots farther away from Garyn.

"What?" Garyn asks. She isn't happy about being interrupted. That's her favorite part, when her father apologizes, promising to get her gifts while they leave her mother for good.

"You…" Chloe swallows. Eyes like saucers, she gets up on trembling legs and then clutches her side where Garyn's foot connected.

Garyn looks up, unconcerned, searching for the blue of the sky through the branches. Sighing, she gives up the ruse of nonchalance and focuses again on the little girl. "What about me?" As much as Garyn doesn't want to ask, she is curious as to why the wise woman's daughter seems so scared.

"Nothing," Chloe says. "I want to go home now."

Garyn is closer to the path back to the cottage. She steps in Chloe's way and jabs a finger in the little girl's chest. "Say it."

Chloe moves back, not wanting to be too close. Her eyes flutter and she says, "Blood. Rivers of blood. Dead bodies stacked like firewood. Family and friends fade and die, but you go on, always reaching for what you can never hold. Lifetimes in the future, you see a light-haired man with storm-grey eyes who reminds you of someone you lost. You want to keep him close, but he walks away, just like the first one. He doesn't care about you. He leaves and you rage. Far in the future, in another world, he finds his love, his mate, a woman with claws who will finally end you, who will scatter your dust in the wind."

Garyn doesn't believe it, not any of it. The wise woman's daughter is playing tricks, pretending she has the sight. Garyn lashes out, shoving the little girl over, causing her to hit her head on a rock.

Garyn runs back up the path to the cottage, branches tearing at her. She pounds on the door; her face and hands smudged in blood. When the door opens, she takes one look at her mother and bursts into tearless sobbing, pointing back along the path. "She's evil. The things she said." She whispers, "She's bedeviled."

The wise woman runs out of the cabin and up the path.

Garyn's mother looks between her daughter and the back of the woman as she disappears into the woods. "What did you do?"

"It wasn't me," she says, outrage replacing faux fear. "It's her. She's crazy. Demon touched." Garyn waits for her mother's shock, her protection.

Instead, her mother sighs deeply and with a small shake of her head steps back into the cabin, taking the small fabric pouch from the table. She begins to walk out, pauses, and then turns to leave her coins.

"I should have left you at home to finish your chores." Grabbing Garyn's arm, she pulls her along the narrow path back to the village. "If you hurt that little girl... I don't know what to do with you."

Garyn yanks her arm away and walks behind her mother, content to consider what the girl said. Her mother will fade and die. Good. She hopes it's soon. Maybe her father will return then and take her away. She skips over the warnings of blood and death, focusing on the light-haired man with gray eyes, just like her father.

The memory went black and I was back in Garyn's mind, looking though her eyes at the vamps in the living room. The meeting had broken down into threats and accusations. Garyn got herself up, her burned head still causing overwhelming pain. Focusing on maintaining her image in their eyes, she stepped into the doorway. The voices went silent as they all turned to her.

"I needed you and you came. You came to protect and defend me. I thank you all." She moved into the room. "They hurt me tonight." A low rumble of anger sounded in the palatial room. "Will you be my warriors?"

There was a bark of "War!"

"Yes. It *is* war and you will win it for me, won't you?"

More angry roars fill the room, echoing off the walls and ceiling.

"You will go there, and you will destroy them. You will be my army and you will decimate their ranks for me, won't you? All that will remain is their dust floating on the bay."

More shouts.

Garyn bowed her head, as though overcome by the show of loyalty. Lifting her head, eyes fierce, she said, "Go, my knights. Kill them all!"

They ran through the balcony doors and leapt over the railing. Landing silently in the courtyard ten stories below, they raced down the street in the direction of the bay, like a dark bat flying low over the city.

I almost spoke to Clive before remembering I couldn't, not until I left Garyn's mind. Honestly, though, there was no point. They knew Russell had taunted her and they knew her vamps would fight, not retreat. I wouldn't be telling him anything new.

When a memory lit up beside me, I stepped in.

A man who looks enough like Clive to be an uncle or a brother is saddling his horse. "I'll return before you notice I've left."

"I've noticed," a younger Garyn says. "Now you must stay."

Laughing he swings onto the horse and looks at the doorway of the cabin, where her mother stands. Lifting a hand in farewell, he turns the horse toward the road, and it trots away. Garyn runs after him and waits until even the speck of him has disappeared.

The memory darkened, but another a short distance away lit up.

Clive, working in the fields past sundown, leads the oxen off for food, water, and rest. Adult, undead Garyn is standing in the trees, silently watching him. She knows he's not her father—he's been gone for hundreds of years—but the resemblance is uncanny, so she stays to watch, trying to remember if that was how her father moved, how he took care of animals.

Clive looks over his shoulders, exactly where she's standing, but it's dark and he's human, unable to discern her shape in the dense under-brush. Clearly exhausted, he walks to the cabin steps and then stops. Shoulders drooping, he turns from his empty home and heads toward the main road and the tavern in the nearby village. Garyn, keeping to the shadows, follows.

When the memory darkened this time, I left Garyn completely. *Clive?*

Hello, darling. Look who's here. He turned his head and through his eyes, I saw Kai had brought Nerissa's boat back. Disembarking were Owen's parents, Benvair and Alec, Medusa, Grim with a few dwarfs I didn't know, and a certain very large gangster with slicked-back hair and a pinstriped suit.

The giant gangster sprinted up the slope, looking in every direction. "I GUARD!"

Under the roar of the waves, I distinctly heard Godfrey's laugh. *Fangorn!* The queen had sent her soldier to me. *I've missed him!*

Strangely, so have I.

Please make sure Owen's parents don't get hurt.

Already on it, darling. They're going to the lighthouse, where George will watch over all three of them.

The vamps will be appearing shortly. They just left the penthouse—

Clive shouted, "They're on the way! Prepare!"

"Are they coming by boat?" Stheno shouted over the roar of the surf.

Let me check. I felt the chill of ghosts moving into the flour room with me, but I ignored them to drop into Reginald's mind, to see what he was seeing. Water, that's what he was seeing. *They're swimming.*

"Swimming," Clive shouted in response.

"I'm the front line. No one look at me," Stheno said. The earlier shouting had been for Owen and his parents' benefit. As they weren't going to be in a position to accidentally be hit by Stheno's gaze and turned to stone, she didn't bother to raise her voice. All the supernaturals could hear a whisper across the island.

"I'll hang out on the far side," Medusa said. "Some might circle around back."

Not sure if this is helpful, but I've just been in a couple of Garyn's memories. She has serious daddy issues. He left her and her mom. She blames Mom. Dad looks like he could be a member of your family. That's why she's fixated on you. When she was human, she ran into a Cassandra wicche, like Arwyn, but six years old. She told her she'd live for ages, there'd be lots of blood, and—important for the two of us—that the light-haired man with gray eyes would take to mate a woman with claws who would deliver her final death.

You don't say?

I do.

Stay where you are. Stay safe. And I'll deal with meting out final deaths, all right?

That's the plan. I checked back in with Reginald. *They can see Alcatraz. They'll be on the rocks any second.*

Clive stood near the prison, looking out over the dark water. "Stheno, move back. They're fast."

Thank you.

I don't want any of our friends getting hurt either, love.

A few of Russell's vamps walked past Clive, swinging baseball bats, and I smiled in the dark, ghost-laden flour room, deep underground.

Dropping back into Reginald's mind, I checked to see what was happening. The vamps in the lead had made it to the rocks. Stheno stood above them, her high beam sweeping back and forth. I was so used to averting my eyes, I tried to close them before I remembered I was in Reginald's mind and therefore couldn't. Quite a few vamps were turned into statues, forever frozen climbing the rocks.

Stheno retreated quickly just as a huge shadow flew overhead, breathing a jet of fire over the rocks, giving final death to the vamps who had avoided Stheno's gaze. Reginald, like dozens of other vampires, bobbed in the water, recalculating their plan of attack.

I heard Reginald's thoughts, a mix of terrified and tangled ideas. A gorgon and a dragon? How had they not known that there was a gorgon and a dragon here? He didn't have a connection with his lady's people. Only she could communicate and coordinate this battle, but she wasn't here. He feared it would turn out like the baseball stadium battle. Every man had fought on his own. There was no general directing troops, so they'd been beaten badly.

"Spread out," he said and then swam to the far side of the island.

THIRTY-ONE

Sam Could Really Use Some Aspirin

Tracking the vampire blips in my head, I watched them fan out around Alcatraz. I popped into Russell's head, as he could communicate with his people. *Sorry to bust in, but they're swimming around the island. Some are coming ashore on the northeast side. Two just climbed the rocks on the west side, closer to the dock.*

Good. Thank you.

One of the vamp blips on the west side disappeared. Damn, Russell's people were fast. I left his mind and jumped into Godfrey's. He was on the northeast tip of the island. Four of Garyn's vamps swarmed up the rocks, but before he could move, Coco let loose her dragon's breath. Three turned to dust but the fourth dove back under the waves to avoid the flames.

Nice!

Hello, Missus. Yes, I'd like dragons on my side in every battle.

He turned at the quiet sound of a foot tread. Four dwarfs ran by, their axes bloody.

And dwarfs.

I felt a vamp nearby. *Behind you!*

Godfrey spun and attacked the vampire that was just about to take his head. I withdrew from his mind, afraid I was going to get someone killed by distracting them.

Back in my own mind, I heard a shoe scrape. My eyes flew open to see a hulking figure looming over me. My hands flew to my blades before I recognized the scent. "Fangorn! You came back."

He grunted in acknowledgement.

"Is the queen okay with you coming here?" As soon as the words were out of my mouth, I wanted to take them back. Fangorn would never go against his queen or leave her in danger.

"Algar guard queen. She safe."

"Perfect. I need to concentrate here and pass on information to the people fighting on our side. Could you guard me from out there a little?" Having a fae soldier breathing down my neck was unnerving.

Another quick grunt and he moved out of my narrow alcove.

The dark shadow of his head returned a moment later. "Fergus?"

"Sorry. He's at home." I think Fangorn loved my dog almost as much as I did.

Another grunt, this one lower, and then his head was out of my space.

The transparent ghosts of the prisoners watched me avidly and it was super creepy. "Fangorn?"

His head came back around the corner.

"Can you see ghosts?" If he could get rid of them, I could breathe a little easier. Yes, I was a necromancer, but having a bunch of see-through men leering at me was getting old real fast.

Fangorn shook his head.

"Okay. Never mind."

Fangorn moved away silently and I was stuck with an audience of long-dead criminals. Yeah, this wasn't at all unnerving.

Hey, scary ghost guys? How about if you make yourselves useful and let me know if you see anybody sneaking up on me? I had no idea if their intel could be trusted, but when all but one left, seemingly happy to have a task, I breathed a little easier. Unfortunately, the one left behind was the creepiest of the bunch. He stood in the corner, staring, his eyes dark voids, his face frozen in a rictus of pain.

I checked in with the blips. Many of her people were keeping to the water, no doubt trying to gauge who they were fighting before they came up the rocks.

Two on your back!

I know, love. It's called luring them in. Oh, look here. He turned his head so I could see three vamps glowing in the dark.

"Hey, asshole!" Stheno shouted.

One vamp looked and was turned to stone. The other two averted their eyes and therefore didn't see the burst of flame that took them both out.

Owen and his parents are spelling Garyn's people to glow in the dark, which we're finding both helpful and amusing.

They're closing in on you.

Don't worry, darling. I'm ready.

I slipped out of Clive's mind, again, not wanting to sidetrack him when he was about to get jumped. And that gave me an idea. If anyone needed distracting, it was Garyn's crew.

Checking in on Reginald, I found him still in the water. I let loose a howl in his head and stuck around long enough to watch him spin in the waves, trying to find the source, before I slipped out.

There were two vamps that appeared to be right on top of George. I dropped into one of them. I wasn't going for secretive; confusion and fear were the point. They were scaling the back of the lighthouse. For a moment, I worried about Owen and his parents, but I needn't have.

The vamp looked up, focusing on the windowless openings near the top and the heartbeats inside. What he seemed to be missing was the huge black form with bright red eyes staring down at him. *Oh, shit!* The vamp looked up at my words, seeing the dragon. He had barely a moment, not enough time to let go and drop, before George opened his mouth, incinerating them.

Not this again. Woozy, stomach dropping, head exploding, I

was definitely going to hurl before the night was over. I had to work on the timing of my exits so I wasn't in the vamp's mind when he was given his true death. Holding my stomach with my good hand, I tried to soothe it. I was just about to jump into another blip when I blinked in the dark and realized that creepy-corner-dwelling guy was now halfway across the small room, just a few feet from me.

Sweat gathered at the base of my spine. There was something about this guy that raised my hackles. My wolf was pacing and snarling. She didn't like him either. Giving him one last look and a push back into the corner, I dove into a swimming vamp's mind.

Treading water, he was studying Alcatraz, looking for a section that wasn't being defended, a spot to come ashore. He heard an engine and looked over his shoulder. A Coast Guard boat was on its way. *Shitshitshit.*

A let my wolf howl in his head and then pulled out. Of course, people were going to see flames shooting over here. Grabbing my phone, I dialed Owen. It took a few rings for him to answer.

"Sam?" he whispered.

"Yeah. Look to the east. Do you see that boat coming straight at us? That's the Coast Guard. Can you and your parents spell them? I don't know. Make them think we're shooting a movie here or something. *And* that we have all the permits." Hopefully, that'd work.

"On it." The phone went dead.

I dropped into Clive's mind, but he was fighting two vamps, so I got out quickly. I checked the island for blips again. Two vamps were sneaking up behind Stheno.

Dropping into Russell's mind, I shouted, "Stheno, behind you!"

Russell echoed me and the two blips disappeared.

Two more vamps were sneaking around the side of the prison, coming up behind Medusa. I almost shouted at Russell again before I realized they had three dwarfs on their tail. Dropping into the mind of one of the vamps, I saw Medusa straight ahead, her long curls blowing in every direction, stone vamps littering the land before her.

A throat cleared. Both vamps stopped and spun. Shocked and confused by the presence of dwarfs, my host vamp was barely able to register the fact that three fierce, bearded dwarfs were sprinting toward him. One dwarf bent over and another ran, vaulted off the back of the first one, and flew at my guy, eyes wild, a bloody axe over his head. The third dwarf leapt off the first guy, diving at the second vamp. Learning my lesson, I withdrew just as the axe blade touched my vamp's neck.

I felt breath in my face. "I'm fine, Fangorn. Move back." Something cold and wet touched my cheek. Eyes flying open, I found creepy guy right up on me, licking my face as a hand slid around my neck. Unwanted images from his life flickered in my head.

The shadow of Fangorn's head tipped into my space.

Using my good hand, I tried to shove the creepy ghost off but couldn't move him. *Asshole.* In my mind's eye, I saw him dragging a baton across the bars in the middle of the night, waking the prisoners. He often stopped, using a cattle prod to zap the ones who'd slept through the racket. A sadistic guard, that was who I had glued to me. No wonder all the prisoners took off when I asked them to keep watch.

His memories were playing in my head, turning my stomach. He loved working the night shift, after all the inmates were locked in. He could do whatever he wanted to them. He had a sterling record on the job. No one would believe a criminal over him. He wore a scowl on the outside, but inside he was giddy as hell, exacting justice as he saw fit.

Fangorn grunted. It was his inquisitive grunt.

My claws slid out as I tore at the ghost guard's hand around my throat. He was strong and it hurt, but he wasn't powerful enough to kill me. Lightheaded, sure, but not dead. The problem was my sword was on the broken arm side of my body.

Gasping, I pushed out, "Grab. Sword."

Fangorn leaned closer and unsheathed it for me. I knew this

was a ghost, not a demon, but given how he'd spent his life, he was pretty damn close to a demon. I motioned with my casted arm where to stab, and Fangorn did.

A high-pitched wail almost broke my eardrum. "Hold him. Don't move," I told Fangorn. The guard was pinned to the wall. I laid my good hand on his head, touched the sword with my bad hand, and pushed hard in my mind, calling up the spell I'd found in an old grimoire a while ago. I began to recite it from memory.

On my third time chanting the spell, dark shadowy figures flew up from beneath the floor and carried the guard away while he screamed and clawed at me. I felt no remorse. He was evil and that was where he belonged.

Blowing out a breath, I shook my head and wished I had some aspirin. "Great job. He's gone now. Can you resheathe the sword?"

Fangorn grunted in assent and returned my sword to my hip. When he moved back out of the way, I saw all the ghosts were back, eyes wide, staring at the floor. Glancing back and forth to each other, a few smiled.

"You guys are on duty, remember?"

THIRTY-TWO

It's the Fricking Dream Team

Our side was horribly outnumbered, but the lack of coordination amongst Garyn's crew was giving us an advantage. Well, that and the dragons. I popped into a water-logged vamp and told him to turn around, which he did. Good little vamp. The Coast Guard ship was gone.

I left him and checked back in with Clive. He wasn't actively fighting anyone, so *Hello, handsome.*

Oh, good. You haven't checked in recently and I was getting concerned.

I started to check in a little while ago, but you were fighting two guys and I didn't want to distract you.

I felt you come and go. It let me know you were all right.

Hey, did I already tell you Alcatraz is lousy with ghosts?

Not surprising. As I recall, it was a fort before it became a prison. Wait. Here they come. Watch this.

Clive was staring out into the water. A moment later, a dragon flew by, low over the waves, breathing fire on the vamps still in the water. Most ducked under before the flames hit them, but the dragon caught a few. Not three seconds later, another dragon flew even lower, its talons out, skimming over the water. It caught two vampires tight in its claws, ripping them in half, their dust raining down on the bay.

Damn. Kinda makes you wonder what it was like when dragons ruled the earth.

I'd guess quite brutal, but I'm very happy to have them on our side.

I checked the blips again. There were fewer in the water. The dragons seemed to be forcing them ashore. *One's coming up behind you!*

I know, love. He's one of ours.

Not him. The other one.

Clive spun and launched himself at one of Garyn's, coming at Clive from between a bush and the side wall of the prison. Clive slammed the vamp's head into the stone wall, stunning him, before ripping his head off.

I think that was Stephen, Garyn's third.

Good. What about her second, Reginald? Is he still among the living?

Last time I checked, he was in the water.

Can you check again? If we can dismantle her power structure, it'll be easier to pick them off.

Be right back.

I found Reginald's blip. He was still among the living-ish. He'd made it ashore between Medusa and Fyr, who were attacking in opposite directions. Four other vamps raced up the rocks with him. They moved into a section of tall grass, aiming for bushes along the back side of the prison.

Low light glinted off the sharpened edges of axes. First one vamp went down. Then two. Then three. Their legs had been hacked off. The dwarfs popped up and slammed their axes down, right where the vamps' heads would be. Reginald and the fifth vamp skirted the high grass and death by dismemberment.

An ungodly shriek caused both vamps to turn. The last thing they saw was Maggie standing beside Medusa, their clothes and hair torn by the wind, Medusa's glowing eyes.

I pulled out quickly and only felt a little sick. *He's gone now. The dwarves got three and then Maggie and Medusa got Reginald and another guy.*

Excellent. What I wouldn't have given to have all these people working together—on my side—in every battle. Were it not for you, they wouldn't be here.

Were it not for me, Garyn wouldn't be here.

He chuckled. *There's that.*

I saw a fireball out of the corner of his eye.

Was that Dave?

Yes. He's been patrolling the rocks, fireballing anyone coming out of the ocean. Dave had a huge grin on his face.

At least he's having a good time.

It isn't often, in this civilized modern world, that we get to be truly who we are. Like Dave, I believe our other friends are finding a certain satisfaction in laying waste.

Who doesn't love to lay waste?

Who indeed? Clive turned his head so I could watch the dragons fly by again. *I believe the first one breathing fire is Alec and the second is Benvair. That takes real skill and coordination to pluck vampires out of the water and shred them before they're able to break her claws.*

She's a badass.

Would you check to see how many of them are left and if Garyn is still at the penthouse?

You betcha. Back in a minute.

Back in the flour room, I noticed a transparent guy pointing out the door. I searched for what was nearby and found a green blip walking through the kitchen, on his way to my hiding place. I dropped into his head to turn him around but was taken off guard by blocky white teeth glowing in the dark. A hulking figure in a 1920s gangster's pinstriped suit stepped forward. He had a club in one hand and a broadsword in the other. His arms moved so fast I couldn't prepare. The club bashed in the vamp's head before the sword cut through his neck.

Stomach dropping, heart stopping, head exploding. Damn it! Not again. I couldn't pass out. I was sitting on the edge of the captain's chair, so my cast-wrapped leg wasn't sticking straight out. If I lost consciousness, I'd hit the ground and probably rebreak my leg.

I smacked my face a few times. Fangorn poked his head in again, giving me an inquisitive grunt.

"I'm okay. I was in that vampire's mind when you killed him. If I don't leave their minds before they die, it makes me sick."

He fiddled with a pouch at his waist. The gangster disguise was a glamour he wore in the human realm. Under the spell, he was his usual self: huge and scary-looking, with bulging muscles under a tunic and breeches, a pouch at his waist and a broadsword on his back.

He took out what looked like a seed pod, crushed it between his massive fingers, and held it under my nose. I took a whiff and light exploded in my head. Holding on to the armrest, I blew out a breath and steadied myself, feeling better than I had in a while.

"That helped."

Grunt.

"Was that the first vamp that had come down here?" I was surprised they hadn't sniffed me out before now.

Deep grunt with a head shake. "Five bloodsuckers."

Oh, crap. "I'm really glad you're here to guard me, Fangorn. This was the first one I noticed. I'd have been dead four times before he showed up."

He bashed his fist against his chest. "I guard!"

Nodding, I said, "You do, and I'm very lucky to have you guarding me."

He gave a quick exhalation and nod and then he moved back to his on-duty position. It was scary to think about how dead I'd be if he hadn't walked off the boat to guard me. I lifted Gloriana's ring to my lips. "I'm very grateful." The ring warmed in response.

Okay. Back to work. I checked all the cold green blips. A few winked out as I was counting. *We're at about thirty-three vamps left, including Russell's guys. Nine are still in the water.*

Good. And Garyn?

Haven't checked yet. We had a vamp down h—

I'm on my way.

Stop! No need. I have Fangorn. He's taken out five vamps so far. Give me a minute to check on Garyn.

There was only one vampire in San Francisco not on Alcatraz, and that was Garyn. Her defenses weren't what they used to be, so I pushed through and found myself in a chaotic mind. They'd all left her, just like she knew they would.

She stopped at an ornate mirror over the fireplace. Her face was red and horribly scarred, half of her hair missing. The healing had begun, though. New skin stretched over her left cheekbone. She had turned her head as Dave hit her with the fireball, so it was the left side of her head that had been the most damaged.

Pacing back and forth in the formal living room, she couldn't hold a thought. They slipped through her fingers, falling in a jumble on the carpet. She was trying her best to pick them up, but they kept slithering away. She needed to go to Alcatraz and lead her men. She needed to stay put until she'd healed. She needed to focus her energy on keeping her men loyal to her. She needed to use all her strength to heal.

She needed to kill that damn werewolf, and this would all stop. She'd have beaten the prophesy. With the woman gone, she could bring Clive back under her wing. She'd have a family: her many times great-grandnephew. They'd be a team. If he didn't fall into line, though, she'd have to kill him. He would stand by her, though. She knew he would. That first night she'd come to the local nocturne, he'd hung on her every word. It could be like that forever. She should go and kill the wolf. No, later. After she'd healed more.

Stopping, she stared at herself in the mirror. Anger consumed her. She punched a fist through the mirror and the wall behind it. Shaking her hand, blood droplets flew. She stared fixedly at a droplet, sparkling on a shard of mirror.

Blood. Rivers of blood. Dead bodies stacked like firewood. Family and friends fade and die, but you go on, always reaching for what you can never hold. Lifetimes in the future, you see a light-haired man with storm-grey eyes who reminds you of someone you lost. You want to keep him close, but he walks away, just like the first one. He doesn't care about you. He leaves and you scream. Far in the future, in another world, he finds his love, his mate, a woman with claws who will finally end you, who will scatter your dust in the wind.

Garyn slammed her fist down on the fireplace mantle, reducing the marble to rubble. Her phone buzzed in her pocket. She took it out and read a text from one of her men. *We need you.*

"And I need you to take care of this problem for me," she stormed, pacing around the living room. "We had them outnumbered ten to one and still you let me down." She swatted a vase off a small table. "If you loved me, you'd fight for me. You'd sacrifice yourselves for me!" She looked at herself in what was left of the broken mirror. "I. Want. Her. Dead!"

Garyn stalked across the living room, out to the balcony, and leapt over the railing, headed for Alcatraz and that bitch wolf.

I pulled out of Garyn's crazed mind and popped back into Clive's. He had a vampire's body in a vice grip under his arm, while his free hand was wrapped around his jaw, ripping his head from his body.

Back to your ol' tricks again, huh?

It's a classic for a reason, darling.

Try not to inhale the dust. That has to be toxic.

I'm trying, but it isn't easy.

Is everyone okay?

Mostly. Russell says he's lost two of his people. I fear our ranks would have been decimated without all our friends here to help.

You know how St. Germain was super old, even by vampire standards, and was going crazy with it?

Yes. Hang on a minute. Clive moved back, standing right inside the door of the penitentiary. A vamp padded in silently, unaware his death was seconds away. As soon as he passed, Clive leapt on his back, driving him onto the concrete, both hands around his neck. One yank and Clive was kneeling in dust. He stood, brushing his trouser legs. *I don't think these clothes can be salvaged. Corpse dust has permeated the weave.*

Lucky for you, you have a huge closet filled with more of the same.

He slipped out the door and back to the spot he was standing in before. *That is lucky, isn't it.*

Are you guys playing a zone defense?

Man-to-man certainly wouldn't work. We were outnumbered over four to one and most of them were content to be soggy.

We both know they stayed in the water because they were rethinking offering up their true deaths for that lunatic who made them. Which reminds me; the lunatic has finally settled on killing me as her next act, thinking you'll fall in line as soon as I'm gone. She's on her way now. Let me check where…

I found Garyn halfway across the bay. I dropped in to see if she was swimming or had stolen a boat. Nope. She'd gone for the most disturbing option. She was walking across the floor of the bay toward Alcatraz Island. Psycho.

THIRTY-THREE

Heartless

S he's walking under the bay. She should be here in a minute or two.

Tell Russell. He needs to pull his people back from her before we end up fighting each other.

On it!

Locating Russell, I dropped in. *Quick update: Garyn will be on the island in a minute or two. Clive recommends pulling your vamps back so they don't fall under her spell again.*

He told his people to move to the far side of the island, near the dragons, because Garyn was coming. *Thank you, and done.*

I wish we knew if her mind control worked on dragons and dwarfs.

Let's hope not. We'll never survive if the dragons turn against us.

True. Good luck, and you stay away from her too, okay?

Yes, my lady.

Dropping back in with Clive, I watched Garyn rise out of the teeming ocean. A dragon swooped down from the top of the prison, fire shooting across the rocks, but Garyn became a blur, streaking up the slope and out of the path of the dragon's breath. I'd never seen anyone other than Clive move that fast. Crazed or not, the woman had skills.

I couldn't track where she went.

Into the prison.

Avoiding dragons.

Coming for you.

I'll alert Fangorn.

"Fangorn?" I whispered—which was stupid, as I'm sure she heard our heartbeats a mile away.

He leaned into my space.

"Vampire coming. Crazy fast and deadly. And just plain crazy."

He grunted and moved back to block the door.

Using my left hand, I wiggled the handle until I was able to get my sword out. It felt a little weird. Normally, I held my sword in my right hand and my axe in the left, but my right arm was broken, so adjustments needed to be made.

Closing my eyes, I checked the vamps on the island. There were none left in the water and only twenty-four left on the rock. Make that twenty-three. Wait. How many of Garyn's were left? I almost started to check but decided I had more pressing problems. I trusted Russell's vamps and our friends to take care of the last of Garyn's people. The biggest of the more pressing problems were the two vamps streaking through the prison, Clive chasing Garyn.

Balancing the sword on the armrest so it stuck straight out, I closed my eyes and popped into Garyn's mind. I wanted to distract and enrage her so she couldn't use her Jedi mind tricks on Clive and the other vamps. Since I'd seen the image of her father in her memories, I shared it with her now. Screeching echoed in her head. That seemed to do it.

A bright memory throbbed right beside me. I worried about leaving myself defenseless in in her memories, but also worried I'd miss important information if I didn't, so I stepped in.

Garyn is walking through dense underbrush, through a deep, thick forest. She's following a path only she seems to know, as there's no trail, no markers, and yet her steps are sure. And silent.

Her mind is tangled with thoughts of blood, of her father, and of that wise woman's daughter who had foretold this all those years ago. Garyn smiles, remembering that the girl drowned in the sacred pond not too many years later. The little busybody probably told the wrong person something they didn't want to hear.

Garyn slows her steps as she approaches a clearing. A snug cabin sits at the edge of the trees, with fields on the far side. A farmer, then. Garyn tracked him for years and believes she's finally found him. In Canterbury, of all places.

Light from a fire glows through the cracks in the shutters over the window casings. She looks through and sees a clean, warm home. A woman sits in a chair by the fire, a babe at her breast. Garyn looks past that, uninterested. She moves to another window where there is a thin gap between the shutter and the sill. She wants to see the whole of the front room. The furnishings are sparse, but what they have looks to be well cared for.

A man is sitting on the floor, his back to the window. His light hair glows in the firelight. It's hard to see past his broad shoulders to see what he's doing, but then the man falls on his back laughing, with a small boy climbing all over him. She can see him now. She knows that face, that laugh.

He'd left her and traveled halfway across England to start a new family. Garyn watches, sorrow and anger battling inside her. Perhaps he wanted a boy. Mother couldn't give him a son and so he went to find one. She always knew her mother was to blame.

Her father throws his arms around his son, kissing the top of his head, and Garyn begins to seethe.

She stares at his new wife. She bears a resemblance to her mother. Why would he do that? Why would he leave them and travel so far only to marry another woman who could have been her mother's sister?

He sits up, his son in his lap. Garyn can't remember ever being held on his lap like that. His wife puts the babe in his arms, moving to the pot simmering over the fire. While she stirs, he kisses the babe's head and rocks her in the crook of his arm, softly singing.

The longer Garyn watches, the more incensed she becomes. And then suddenly she's stalking to the front door. She rips it off its hinges and flings it into the yard. The wife screams. Garyn's father stands, passing the babe back to his wife and pushing his son behind his legs.

When he reaches for his axe, Garyn shakes her finger at him. She knows her eyes have gone vamp black and enjoys that the little giggling boy is now crying behind his mother's skirts.

She points at her father and beckons him out the door. She waits in the yard for him to follow. She doesn't care about them. She wants answers from him. A moment later, he stands silhouetted in the doorframe, the axe in his hand.

"What do you want?" he demands.

Garyn laughs. "I want you to be as good of a father to me as you are to those two brats. Or will you be leaving them soon too?"

His head tilts to the side as he squints into the dark. "Garyn?"

"Oh, you do remember me."

He steps down into the yard. "Is it really you?"

"In the flesh."

His wife pushes open a shutter to keep an eye on him, and Garyn wants to slit her throat.

Shaking his head, he steps closer. "How are you here? How did you know where to find me?"

"Were you hiding?" She stands with her hands on her hips, disgust lining her face.

"Was I—Of course not. I'm just surprised. Look at you. You look just like your mother." He moves closer, trying to get a better look.

"No. I. Don't. I'm nothing like her. I look like you. We even have the same hair."

In truth, they don't. Her father's hair is a sun-ripened gold. Hers is a golden brown, not as dark as her mother's, but not her father's either. Neither does she have her father's gray eyes. Hers, like her mother's, are a pale, watery blue.

"Yes. Of course. I just—I can't believe you're here." He glances around the yard, ignoring the heavy door she's ripped off the cabin. "Have you a horse that needs watering?"

"Why did you leave me?" The black bleeds out of her eyes as they speak, though he doesn't seem to notice. Perhaps the yard is too dark for human eyes to discern the change.

Under the anger in her voice, there is hurt, and he hears it. He begins to lift his hands and discovers he's holding an axe. He stares at it a moment, clearly trying to remember why he picked up an axe. He walks to the open door and leans it against the wall of the cabin. When he turns back, he finds Garyn much closer than before. He stares at her in the light from the doorway.

"You grew up so beautiful."

"Grew up without you," she accuses.

"Yes." He lets out a gust of breath. "You're right to be angry. I was young and stupid." He shakes his head again. "I loved your mother, but it was all so much more difficult than I thought it would be. You were always so angry. I knew it had to be my fault, that I was failing you as a father. What I did is a stain of shame I'll never wash clean. But know, when I left, I planned to return. I was only going to be gone a few days."

He runs a hand through his hair in the exact way Clive does when he's frustrated. How odd to see someone else duplicate the mannerism.

"I was tracking a wild boar. If I could get him, we'd have meat over the winter. I didn't want to lose him, so I went farther than I'd intended, thinking I'd catch him the following day and the following day. I was a week's journey from home when I finally came upon him. Or, I should say, he came upon me. He found me sleeping under a tree before sunrise. He trampled and gored me." He lifts his shirt, showing Garyn the huge scar on his side.

"I thought I was going to die. Eventually, a farmer found me and brought me to his cabin. He treated me as best he could. I got the fever and my wounds festered. I didn't think I'd survive. When I was in my right mind, I worried about you two staying safe without me. When I was not in my right mind, I sweated and groaned and slept.

"It took many weeks for the wounds to heal and for my mind to work properly. By then, I worried if I'd ever fully recover. My breath was short. I tired after only walking a few yards. I couldn't help with the harvest. If I went back, I'd be a burden on you both. If I'd died, your mother could remarry. Find herself a good strong man to work our fields."

"You look hardy enough," Garyn said.

"Aye. It took near five years to feel like myself. By then, I assumed your mother had remarried. I didn't want to ruin her life, so I stayed away. I thought about you two every day. I'm so sorry to have caused you pain."

"You look to have landed on your feet with your new family." She looks up to see his wife holding both children, staring out the window. "Aren't they precious?"

Her father doesn't hear the sarcasm. "They are. I don't know why God granted me a second chance, but I thank Him daily for the blessings." He glances over his shoulder.

Garyn sees the look of love he sends them, and it infuriates her.

"Would you like to meet them? They're my world." When he turns back, he finds Garyn standing directly in front of him, her eyes vamp black.

"And you were mine." She punches through his ribcage, captures his heart in her talon-like fingers, and rips it from his body.

The wife screams. The little boy stares with eyes too big for his face.

Garyn drops the heart in the dirt beside her father. "Now they can learn what it's like growing up without you."

THIRTY-FOUR

I Want to Go

I pulled myself out of the memory. Garyn was still racing through the prison, snaking up one cell block and down another, like she was searching for something. It couldn't have been me because she was on an upper floor. Fangorn and I had heartbeats. Vampires could zero in on that stuff. It was innate for them once they'd been turned. So, if she wasn't trying to find me, what was she looking for?

She finally stopped in front of a cell, halfway down the block. Clive was on her heels, but when she stopped, he lurched to one too. The black drained from his eyes and his expression went slack. *Damn it!* She'd snared him again.

Smiling, she pointed at the barred door to the cell. He went to it, gripped the bars, and pulled. Muscles straining, metal screeching, he yanked the door off and set it aside.

She watched, appreciating that he was doing her bidding again.

I sent him an image of us at our wedding and got no reaction from him. Damn her!

She strode into the cell and slammed her fist on the concrete floor. The top layer cracked. She called Clive in with her and then they both smashed the floors together. Once. Twice. Three times and then the center of the cell collapsed into the floor below.

Garyn jumped through the hole and stood in the rubble, dust floating in the dark. Glancing around, she looked into a shadowy corner and saw a light color behind the silhouette of a person. Finally, she'd found the bitch.

My stomach knotted and flipped. That was me, sort of sitting in my captain's chair, eyes closed, seeing the world from Garyn's perspective. Huge chunks of concrete had fallen into the flour room. Garyn glanced to the side. Though it didn't seem to register for her, I saw the bottom of a leather boot between chunks of rock. She'd knocked out Fangorn.

Resisting the urge to leave Garyn's mind, I played the end of her own memory for her, the way her father had gazed at her with such wonder and love right before she punched a hole through his chest, her hand forever stained with his blood. Clutching her head, she growled.

I hit her with the wise woman's daughter and her prophesy. Garyn's growl turned into more of a moan. I showed her going back to that same cabin near the woods and finding Clive, her stalking him and then turning him. She'd lost focus on killing me and was instead fixated on the memories running through her mind.

Her people were gone. Her obsessions—with her father, the prophesy, Clive, me—had led to her calling almost two hundred of her people to their final deaths. As Chloe had prophesied, Garyn's long life had created rivers of blood and dead bodies stacked like firewood.

I shared with her my memories of all the ways her people had been given their final deaths on this rock and with each one, she became more and more unhinged. I knew she was going to snap and when she did, she'd attack.

Pulling one of my aunt's spells out of my arsenal, I let my magic gambol down my broken arm, watching it pool in my hand, false fire glowing in the Stygian darkness.

"You don't love Clive. Why do you cling so tightly to him? If you weren't such a heinous bitch, I'd feel sorry for you. You've driven everyone away while desperate to make them love you. They don't, you know. If you didn't mesmerize them, they'd *all* have left you. It's pathetic, don't you think? I mean, even your mother and father didn't like you. You disturbed them. Dad left and Mom got stuck with you. Poor woman."

Garyn growled again, speech seeming to have abandoned her as well.

My wolf paced inside me, desperate to be in on the kill.

"Clive just happens to have inherited the Fitzwilliam looks. He isn't your father. He can't give you some kind of twisted paternal love. That ship sailed over a millennium ago when you ripped your own father's beating heart from his body. You're done, Garyn. The world has moved on. It's time to for you to return to dust."

My wolf let loose an earth-shattering howl in Garyn's head. The black drained from the vampire's eyes.

With part of my mind, I lifted the sword, aiming for her heart; with the other part, I showed her Stephen's death and Reginald's, showed her what dwarfs, dragons, gorgons, wicches, a demon, a banshee, and many well-trained vampires could do, even when outnumbered.

The scream she let loose caused more rubble to fall, but I was ready when she pounced. In one thought, one motion, I pulled completely out of her mind and stabbed the sword through her heart as I smashed my aunt's spell into the unmarred side of her face. It was the spell that shatters minds, that makes it feel as though it's raining glass. When I pulled my hand back, her head rolled off her body. It stopped directly in front of my chair before turning to dust.

Confused as to why her head had fallen off, I stood on my good leg and leaned out. Had Fangorn come to?

"Darling, what did I say about not moving or exerting yourself?" Clive took me in his arms and held me as close and as gently as he could.

"You broke her hold."

"I did. I assume you had something to do with that." He kissed my head.

"I was doing my best to bombard her with upsetting memories. I needed to give myself a moment to plan before she attacked."

There was a groan and Clive propped me back on the edge of my chair before shifting rocks to uncover Fangorn. I turned on my phone's flashlight and pointed it at the ground. I knew Fangorn's night vision was as good as Clive's and mine, but I hoped a little light might help him orient himself when he came to.

Clive moved a few more rocks, then Fangorn surged to his feet on a roar, sword drawn.

"Everything's okay!" I shouted. That was all we needed, to make it through the battle and then die by friendly fire.

Ignoring Clive, who had moved out of sword range, Fangorn came to my cubby to check on me. Looking me up and down, he grunted and turned, apparently satisfied that I hadn't been hurt. He kicked through the pile of corpse dust, a low snarl in the back of his throat.

"Yep. We totally agree, but she's dead now, thank goodness. Clive, can we go up? Are all of her vamps dead?"

"You tell us." He lifted me off the chair and held me close, my forehead against his jaw.

Closing my eyes, I touched each blip on the island and found only Russell's vamps. Before I told him we were clear, I looked farther afield and found something.

"Four of her people are back at the airport."

"Isn't that interesting?" Holding me with one arm, he pulled out his phone, carrying me over the rocks and out of the flour room. Fangorn led the way through the tunnels.

"Russell, how did we fare?" He paused to listen while Russell gave him the rundown. Two of his vamps had been given their true death. One of the dwarfs had a serious injury, but Underfoot was on it. Other than that, everyone else was fine and looking to celebrate.

"Sam just checked. She says four of Garyn's vampires are at the airport." He paused. "Your call. You're Master of the City. Do we wipe them out or let them go?"

"Kill them," Fangorn grumbled.

"I must admit, I'm inclined to agree with our fae friend. They may have been under her influence, but that should have broken when they came to the island. They were far enough away from her to stop and contemplate," Clive said.

"Probably why so many of them tried to stay in the water," I volunteered.

"I don't like punishing people for being manipulated by others," Russell said through the phone.

"Fuck that noise," Stheno could be heard shouting. With supernaturals, there were no private conversations.

"But," Benvair said, "these may be people who came to their senses once they were away from her and left, not wanting to be part of her occupation. If you kill people trying to do the right thing, you may incite other nocturnes to attack this city."

The dragons must have shifted back while we were dealing with Garyn down here.

I patted Clive with my good hand. *Let me check.*

I felt Clive walking us up the stairs, but my mind was in the cabin of a small private jet. *All of them arrived earlier tonight. Three of them were ready to fight until they saw what they were up against. They never came ashore on Alcatraz. They swam away and made for the airport.*

The fourth one—Theo—isn't like the others. He never wanted to come. He hates Garyn, hates that she can control him. It isn't until he is away from her that he realizes what she's done. He can't fight her in the moment.

Clive relayed what I told him, without telling anyone it came from me. For those that didn't know what I could do, it just expanded Clive's reputation, which was fine with me.

"We'll go take care of the three," Russell said.

Clive hung up and pocketed the phone. *Thank you, darling.*

You've helped Russell make the right decision. "I would have killed all four," he added aloud.

Fangorn grunted in agreement.

"But Theo doesn't deserve a final death because he couldn't shake off Garyn's influence. Neither could any of us," Clive said.

"Except Audrey," I clarified.

"Yes. Except Audrey. And isn't that fascinating."

When we came out of the prison, we found everyone standing in a loose group. Noticeably missing were Russell and Audrey. Godfrey was near the door. I smacked his shoulder with my good hand.

"Yes, Missus." He hadn't turned around.

"How'd you know it was me?" I wondered.

"You mean aside from your scent, your heartbeat, and your voice as you were walking through the prison?"

"Yeah, aside from all that." Duh. I needed a nap.

He turned, grinning. "Lucky guess."

"Knew it."

Clive chuffed out a laugh and kissed my cheek. He took in the crowd and then looked at Godfrey. "Is there a plan?"

"I have plans to consume a case of wine with my new friend Maggie," Medusa said.

"On behalf of the San Francisco nocturne," Godfrey began, his voice pitched louder for the Wong family, "we'd like to thank you for coming to this city's aid. You were all quite extraordinary. I've been in many battles in my long life, but none compared to this one. Had we not lost two of our own and badly injured one of our friends"—he nodded to the dwarfs—"I'd say this was the most fun I've had in quite some time."

Most of the supernaturals glanced at each other, chuckling. Clearly, they agreed.

"Russell and Audrey have gone to take care of the last of Garyn's people," Godfrey continued. "Good fortune to all who survived the war!"

A cheer went up. I hugged Clive tighter with my good arm.

"You're all invited to the Viper's Nest. Drinks are on Russell," Stheno said.

Godfrey nodded. "We'd be honored to pick up the bill."

"If we can all fit into the nocturne's boat, we can take it to the Viper's Nest pier," I said.

"Oh," Owen began, "I think my parents—"

Lydia, Owen's mom, patted his arm. "Your father and I want to go, dear."

"Okay. Forget I said anything." Owen and George shared a grin.

I just noticed that Mr. and Mrs. Wong were dressed in black from head to toe, including black knit caps. They looked like they were going cat burgling.

How are you feeling? Shall we go home?

No way. Like the Wongs, I want to go. It isn't every day you get to be part of—even as an observer—a battle with vampires, dragons, gorgons, dwarfs, wicches, a fae soldier, a demon, and a banshee. I mean, come on!

Good point, and you did considerably more than observe. We'd have lost far more of our people without your help. He kissed my temple.

Which is how we ended up sitting in the Viper's Nest at one in the morning. We had the joint to ourselves, and it was a blast. I sat in the booth closest to the bar so I could prop my leg up on the seat. Clive had called Lilah to see if she could check on me and give me another treatment. She'd told me with femur breaks, it could take a human four to six months to heal. With her treatments and my naturally quick healing, it'd probably take a couple of weeks. I think what bothered me the most was not being able to run for that long. My wolf was whining in my head, and I didn't blame her.

"Here you are, love." Clive slid a soda and a slice of lemon meringue pie in front of me. "Do you mind if—"

Thoth patted Clive on the back. "I'll keep your wife company while you talk with your friends."

"Sam?" Clive lifted his eyebrows.

"He's right. Go ahead. I have pie and excellent company. I'm good."

He nodded and left, going to speak with Russell, Audrey, and a strange vamp I had to assume was Theo, the fourth vamp trying to escape at the airport.

Thoth put his teacup down and slid into the booth across from me. "And how are you really feeling?"

"I'm okay." I held out the first bite of pie to him, but he politely waved it away.

"I've had far too many baked goods since I arrived. Thank you, though." He studied me a moment. "You do look a little better than you did on Alcatraz."

"I *was* feeling decidedly grumpy before. My head and leg were killing me, and I was so tired. After Lilah's healing session and Clive siphoning off the pain, I'm feeling much better. Plus, pie."

"Good." He took a sip of tea and then glanced around the room at all of our friends, chatting and laughing. "I don't know if you're aware—young and sheltered as you've been—but this is unprecedented. All of these people working together, not grudgingly, not by threat, but choosing to support one another and fight side by side." He shook his head. "This doesn't happen."

Stheno walked over, a huge glass of wine in her hand. She tapped Thoth's shoulder, asking him to slide down. Once he had, she sat beside him. "It's true. Medusa and I are almost as old as this guy, and I've never been in a battle like tonight's. I was surrounded by allies— all deadly in their own right— working together to take out a far larger army."

She grinned. "There's nothing quite like killing at will to make your blood tingle."

Thoth shook his head and patted her knee. "You'll survive without it."

"Clearly." She took a sip of wine. "It's just not as fun."

"Psycho." I took another bite of pie.

"Probably." She scanned the room. "Fyr!"

He turned from his conversation with Coco and Maggie.

"Yeah?"

"We need music," Stheno said.

He nodded, went behind the bar, and hit a button.

"Okay," Medusa sang, "now we got a party." She grabbed a hot vampire whose name I didn't know and pulled him into the center of the floor to dance. A few others joined them, Dave and Maggie, Owen and George, Coco and Fyr, Godfrey and Benvair...

"What happened to that large fae man who was guarding you?" Thoth asked.

"Fangorn? He went back to Faerie. He's one of the queen's guards. He was kind enough to come when he knew I needed help."

"So, Faerie is interested too," he murmured.

"Hey, where were you during the battle? I never saw you." We both knew how I jumped from head to head to *see* people, so I didn't have to say it out loud.

"Dr. Underfoot and I were on the prison roof observing the battle. It made us both wish we could join in."

Underfoot, along with Grim and his two buddies, was sitting at the end of the bar. A large tankard of mead waited in front of each as they talked in low voices, one occasionally reenacting a particularly violent killing.

It should probably have made me uneasy, the way so many gloried in the killing, but it didn't. We were all predators who had together defeated our foe. We hadn't died on the field of battle and were therefore celebrating. We had been victorious, and to the victors go the spoils. Like pie.

Clive moved away from Russell, pulling a phone from his pocket and stepping outside.

Lydia, Owen's mother, placed a teacup in front of me. "Drink this, dear. It's far better for you than that." She picked up my half-empty glass of soda and walked it back to the bar.

"Thank you," I called.

Darling?

Yes. I watched Clive walk back into the roadhouse.

That was Sebastian on the phone.

Who's Sebastian?

Hmm, let me explain something first. Vampires are very independent, though we do organize ourselves into nocturnes. Originally, this was so we could coordinate ourselves, pooling resources and information.

And probably so you didn't feel so alone or monstrous.

Yes. There was that as well. We were no longer a part of our families or villages. Nocturnes gave us the semblance of community.

I see.

When there are new Masters, they often have to figure out a great deal in a short period of time. Some haven't lived long enough to know the complicated histories of all their people, and some were trained by Masters who were batshit crazy—to borrow one of your phrases. It can be overwhelming and confusing dealing with all the problems your own people bring to you, not to mention the humans surrounding you, and the outside vampires who trespass.

It's a lot.

It is. We have a Guild of thirteen vampires from around the world. They serve as advisors. Masters are encouraged to create bonds with other Masters, so they have someone to consult.

Like the ones that keep calling you.

Exactly. But sometimes that isn't practical. Occasionally, the local Masters of the City are wicches or werewolves. Sometimes the other vampires in your region or state refuse to cooperate.

Vampires can be such dicks.

We can. So, if you have questions or problems and can't lean on another Master, there is a Counselor you can petition for aid. It doesn't happen often. Most vampires prefer to keep their own counsel, but that person exists.

Nice.

In theory. If the Counselor for your area is good, then yes, they can be quite helpful. If they're not, they often cause more problems than they solve.

Oh.

Eli, the North American Counselor, has been quite problematic for centuries. *That phone call was to let me know that Eli has been given his true death and a Counselor position has opened. My name has been added to a short list of possible contenders. Sebastian wanted to know if I was interested.*

If you got the job, you'd be the Master of North America?

I'd be more like the advisor to the North American Masters.

Huh. So, if you decide to do this—and I can feel that you want to— what does that mean?

I'd have to go through interviews and tests, background checks and who knows what. I've been adrift since passing the reins to Russell, so you're right. I do want to say yes, but we need to discuss it further once we're home.

Would we have to move? I really didn't want to leave San Francisco, our friends, and The Slaughtered Lamb.

No. We would need to meet with Sebastian and the Guild to discuss it, though. If we decide I should join, it would mean very occasionally going to different parts of North America to meet with Masters and help them navigate their issues. Most of that can be done over the phone, but I will need to travel. One of the problems with Eli was he refused to travel. Or answer his phone, come to that. I believe much of what I'll be doing in the beginning is cleaning up centuries-long messes.

Fun for you. Do I get to tag along or will they flip out about a werewolf?

If they want my help, they better respect my wife. I'd love to have you travel with me whenever you can.

So, we'll talk about it later but, just so I know, what are the next steps?

A trip to Budapest to meet with Sebastian and the Guild.

Budapest, huh? That's rather close to Transylvania.

It is.

Do we need to worry about more crazy ancient vampires?

Darling, the Guild is filled with nothing but. If you're wondering about one particular vampire, though, yes, he'll be there.

My heart raced. *Who?*

Vlad, of course.

Acknowledgments

Thank you to my family and friends for helping me to find the time and the quiet so I could write this book. If you have elderly parents, you probably know how hard it is to take care of them while trying to be present with your spouse and children, not to mention keep up with your work. Let's just say I've been drowning and so many kind, loving people have been throwing me lifelines. Thank you! You know who you are and I'm so very grateful.

Thank you to Peter Senftleben, my extraordinary editor. You have the enviable knack of getting to the heart of the story and then helping me to see my own work through a different lens. Thank you to Susan Helene Gottfried, my exceptional proofreader who always knows exactly where the commas go (unlike myself).

Thank you to the remarkable team at NYLA! You've made every step of publishing a little easier with your wit, compassion, and expertise. Thank you to my incomparable agent Sarah Younger, the fabulous Natanya Wheeler, and the incredible Cheryl Pientka for working together to make my dream of writing and publishing a reality.

Dear Reader,

Thank you for reading *The Viper's Nest Roadhouse & Café*. If you enjoyed Sam and Clive's sixth adventure together, please consider leaving a review or chatting about it with your book-loving friends. Good word of mouth means everything when you're a writer!

Love,
  Seana

Want more books from Seana?

If you'd like to be the first to learn what's new with Sam and Clive (and Arwyn and Declan and Owen and Dave and Stheno...), please sign up for my newsletter *Tales from the Book Nerd*. It's filled with writing news, deleted scenes, giveaways, book recommendations, first looks at covers, short stories, and my favorite cocktail and book pairings.

I hope you enjoyed Sam and Clive's latest adventure. A new Sam Quinn book The Bloody Ruin Asylum & Taproom will be arriving in the fall of 2024, so stay tuned for more Sam & Clive.

Have you picked up my other series yet? It's set in the same world as Sam Quinn, though in Monterey, California. Bewicched: The Sea Wicche Chronicles is the first in the series.

Read on for an excerpt of BEWICCHED: The Sea Wicche Chronicles

They Weren't Kidding When They Called Me, Well, a Wicche

U rsula, a villain who did not deserve to be considered one, was my favorite. She was a working woman, offering a service, and was vilified for it. The payment was obvious. The whiners knew the score. They just thought they were special, that they could get magic without paying for it. That's not how magic works. You always have to pay. Plus, octopuses were incredible, so I refused to support fairytales disparaging them.

Little Mermaid aside, I was calling my Monterey seaside art gallery and tea bar The Sea Wicche because I, Arwyn Cassandra Corey, was a sea wicche, or at least I really wanted to be. The wicche part was true enough.

It was a perfect day, with clear blue skies and a cold salty wind on the California coast. I went out the back door of my studio to the deck that ran along the ocean side of a small, abandoned cannery I was having renovated. The deck gave a little with each step. Strangely enough, weathered, rotting wood was a bit of a safety hazard. I loved this place, though, even with the standing water and the rusted machinery.

I used to break in and run around here when I was little. Mom worried I'd hurt myself, but Gran said she'd seen in a dream it would be mine and to leave the poor child alone. In wicche families, the older you are, the more powerful. No one messes with the crones. I was, consequently, looking forward to getting old. The crones do not give a fuck. They've seen and done it all and have lost the ability to be polite about it. They'll tell you what they think to your face, because what are you going to do about it? That's right. Nothing.

I couldn't wait. Anyway, Grandmother said the cannery was mine, so it was mine. Even at seven, it was all mine. It sat on tall pylons that were mostly submerged at high tide. Now, though, at low tide, the barnacles, oysters, coral, and algae were visible. There were even a couple of gorgeous orange starfish that had made my pylons their home.

I sat on the edge and leaned over, holding on to the weather-warped wood with my ever-present gloves. The two starfish were still there. One was clinging to a portion of the support pole that was covered in a carpet of purple and green algae. I needed photos. Tourists snapped them up, especially this close to the Monterey Bay Aquarium.

Tipping back, I rolled over onto my stomach and took my phone out of my back pocket. Dangling over the deck edge, I framed the shot and took it. Perfect. Yes, my DSLR camera would be better, but the light was magical now. The colors were so vibrant, they'd pop out of the frame. If I ran back in for my camera, the light could change and I'd lose the shot. I'd made that mistake too many times. I had a phone with the best digital camera on the market and I could tweak the image once I got it on my laptop.

I wear special gloves all the time, not just when touching rotting wood. They are a thin, soft bamboo fabric with connective threads on the fingers so I can still use my smartphone. Touch is a problem for me; clairvoyance is not for the faint of heart. I see too much, hear too much. You try shaking someone's hand and hearing that he thinks you're a money-grubbing fake taking advantage of his mother, that you're bilking her out of her last dime, and he wished you'd drop dead. All of that the moment his hand touched yours.

Or, even better, how about finally getting a kiss senior year from the guy you've had a crush on since sixth grade, only to learn that he really wished your boobs were bigger and he hoped Rachel heard about his kissing you because he was trying to make her jealous. Oh, and he actually thought you were a weirdo, but a boob was a boob, so…

Yeah, dating sucked ass when touch meant picking up every stray thought and emotion. For a while, I self-medicated with booze. If it weren't for alcohol, I'd still be a virgin. That wasn't a sustainable plan, though. I hated drunk Arwyn and hated even more the predators who moved on me when they saw I was wasted enough to dull the voices. So, new sober me wears gloves and has sworn off dating and sex. It's a modern world. There are electronic alternatives that don't close their eyes and think about someone else.

I took a few more shots as long as I was hanging here, none as perfect as that first one, though. A text popped up on my screen and I flicked it away. It was my mom again, reminding me that Gran expected me at dinner tonight. They'd been trying to get me to join the Council since I was in my teens—maiden, mother, and crone.

The Council oversaw all disputes, heard pleas for help, granted magical aid, usually for a fee. Now that I was back from England— and my chess set was finally in the hands of the werewolf book nerd it was intended for—they were pushing hard for me to join. It wasn't that I wouldn't help when they needed me. I didn't want to be tied to the regularity. I had my work and really did not care about the day-to-day petty bullshit. If they needed me to power a spell, fine. The rest of it, not so much. Mom and Gran knew the toll it took on me, knew I lived through the worst horrors the people petitioning us carried with them, but they didn't experience it, so it was easy to forget the price I paid for my magic. I hadn't had a full night's rest in ever. The nightmares haunted me as though they were my memories.

So, gloves, isolation, and my ocean buddies. There was movement in the water below. A tentacle almost broke the surface. Yes, my octopus friend was still hanging out below the cannery. "Hello, Cecil! I hope you have a lovely, watery day!" The way he moved was mesmerizing to watch. So much so, it took me too long to realize what was happening. Damn it! I was going to end up in the ocean.

Throwing the phone over my shoulder, I gave it a magical push to get it to the deck and then hoped for the best. Lights went off in my head and my vision went dark. Snarling. I heard that first. Often the sounds and scents came to me before the images. Growling and the scent of the forest. Two yellow eyes, huge, staring into me, before the scene formed. Large wolves circling one another, one jet black, the other gray and tan.

They circled one another and then the gray lunged. The black met him, clashing tooth and claw. Blood flew as they shook off the pain, circled, and charged. It was vicious and violent. I didn't want to watch, didn't want new nightmares. The gray one, bloodied and limping, cringed away when the black one howled, but then the black wolf was set upon by others as they drove him into the dirt...

My body tipped as I watched the wolves tear each other apart.

Damn it, I knew it. I was about to drown, watching wolves kill each other.

YELLOW EYES STARED INTO MINE, WAITING.

I WASN'T IN THE WATER, WASN'T WET. WHAT I WAS, THOUGH, WAS hanging in the air. A very tall, very strong man was holding me a foot off the deck, a hand gripped around the back of my neck. I stared into warm brown eyes and shouted, "What the fuck? Put me down!"

He dropped me like I was on fire. Thankfully, my balance was pretty good and I kept my feet under me.

He cleared his throat and pointed toward the water. "You were sliding in." He handed me my phone.

"Thanks," I said, "for picking up my phone and grabbing me before I went in. I'm an epileptic." Not really. I just needed a cover for my habit of hitting the ground. "This is private property, though. You shouldn't be here." I shaded my eyes. Oh, my. He had to be six and a half feet tall, a perfect muscular specimen, with dark hair starting to curl around his ears and a full dark beard. He wore faded jeans, sturdy work boots, and a t-shirt topped with a flannel. I might not be able to touch, but I could look.

"Sorry. I'm on the construction crew. Stan asked me to stop by to take measurements on the deck." He stared at me as though he was pretty sure I was insane but was too polite to say it.

Ha, joke's on him. People have been calling me nuts my whole life. It didn't even register anymore.

"So you're okay?" He had a deep growly voice that I liked. "You threw your phone at me and then just flopped over the edge, like dead weight dropping into the ocean."

I checked out my phone. "Seizure. I'm fine now." No scratches on the screen. Score! "Go ahead," I said, gesturing to the rotting deck. "Do your thing." I started back into my studio and stopped. "Why are you working today? It is Sunday, right?" I checked my phone for the date.

"I wasn't doing anything, so I figured I might as well get started." He shrugged one beefy shoulder. "Plus, I need the work." He pulled a measuring tape off his belt. "Do you want the deck any different, or am I replacing this one exactly?" He took a receipt and a pencil from his shirt pocket, starting to take notes.

"You can do it without dropping planks into the ocean or pounding on the pylons so hard you disturb the ecosystem, right?"

"Ecosystem?" He walked to the edge and leaned over, peering down. "Is that what you were looking at?"

"My starfish Charlie got a new friend." I peered over the edge and saw the guy's arm move, like he was ready to grab me if it looked like I was about to go in. "The friend kind of looks like a... Herbert." I slid the phone back in my pocket, brushing the dirt from my gloves. I owned many pairs, all washable.

"Herbert and Charlie, huh? Which one is which?" His balance was amazing. He'd been leaning out past the edge of the deck for a while and not a bobble or tremor in sight.

Wicches can see auras. We can tap a part of our brains that allows us to see a person's aura, essentially to see what kind of person we're dealing with. The brighter and shinier the aura, the more trustworthy the person. The smokier the aura, the more we needed to watch our backs. Yes, I was a strong wicche who could take care of myself, but six and a half feet of muscle on a psycho was probably something I should prepare for.

Letting my vision relax, I sized up this guy who wanted to work here while I was alone in my studio. Huh. No aura. Well, hell, that's why I had the vision. Fingers twitching at my side, I readied a spell, just in case. "Werewolf?"

Poor guy looked like he'd been smacked in the face with a shovel. "What?"

"It's okay." I pointed at myself. "Wicche."

"I know, but how did you?"

"You know?" I'd never laid eyes on this guy before. How did he know?

He tapped his nose. "You have a scent."

I felt my face flame. I showered this morning, didn't I? *Shit.* When I got involved in a project, I lost track of time and personal hygiene.

Chuckling, he clarified, "Wicches as a group, not you in particular. You smell like plaster and paint. And the ocean."

"Oh." Well, that was okay then. Not all werewolves were psycho killers. In fact, very few of them were. Still, I let the spell dance between my fingers in case I'd read the situation wrong.

He wrote something on the paper in his hand. "What kind of railing do you want?"

"None."

He raised one eyebrow. "You'll need some pretty good insurance to cover all the lawsuits from people falling off this thing."

"The plaster and paint you're smelling are from the tentacles I'm building. They'll be thirty feet tall and come up from below the water, curving this way and that to keep people from falling in. It'll look like a sea monster is pulling us into the ocean."

His eyes flicked from the ocean to the edge of the deck. "Nice." After pausing a moment, he asked, "What about kids? The curves will leave holes, the perfect size for little heads."

I stopped the automatic denial and thought about the design I had in mind. I waved him in the back door of my studio. It took up about a third of the cannery building and was the first section remodeled. I needed a place to work. The shop could wait.

I stopped him before he stepped over the threshold, though, my hand on his chest. "Wait. What's your name?"

He stared down at my hand until I moved it. "Declan."

"Declan what?" I'd be texting all the cousins first chance I got to see if anyone knew anything about this guy. I hadn't had that vision about bloodthirsty werewolves for no reason.

"What's it to you?"

"Maybe you're a serial killer." I doubted it, but it was possible.

He stared at me, his intense brown eyes making my stomach flutter. "You're the wicche," he said, leaning in. "Am I a serial killer?"

Damn, he was potent. Instead of answering, I just waved him in. I was pretty sure he was safe. Being a werewolf, I couldn't read him easily, but I had a spell at the ready if he gave me trouble.

"You know, I'd like to know your last name too?" A second man's voice made me jump.

Who the hell was that? I ducked my head through the open door and found another muscular guy on my doorstep. Unfortunately, I'd met this one before. He was Logan, the Alpha of the local pack. Six-four, tawny hair, tanned skin, blue eyes, he was the golden child of Monterey. Women flocked to him, and he'd never met one he hadn't liked.

"Arwyn." His gaze traveled from my out-of-control curls down to my paint-spattered sneakers. "Good to see you again, although I can't say much for your company."

My cousin Selena had dated Logan in high school when he was the star athlete on every team. She was head over heels, but he was working his way through the female student body, so it didn't last long. She said he wasn't a jerk about it. He was just a guy who loved women and couldn't rest until he'd bedded all of them. Everyone needed a hobby, I supposed.

When he turned to Declan, the physical change was extraordinary. Relaxed and flirtatious morphed into clenched jaw, puffed chest, hands fisted. "You know the rules. You can't come into my territory without meeting with me and getting my approval. I'm Alpha." Logan crossed his arms over his chest and glared at Declan, his eyes going wolf gold.

Declan didn't flinch, didn't seem the least bit concerned. "I'm not in *your* territory. Pack grounds are in Big Sur. I live and work in Monterey. Eve is the Master of Monterey."

Logan growled, "Bloodsuckers don't rule us. You want to stay here, you meet with me."

"Gentlemen," I interrupted, "I have reason to believe this won't end well. What do you say you just shake hands and walk away? In fact," I added, glancing back in my studio, "I can offer you both a freshly baked fudge brownie with a layer of caramel in the middle. Can you smell them?" Being werewolves, they'd never back down from a fight, but it was worth a try.

Declan studied me a moment, lifting his head to scent the air, and then grinned. "I'm in." He stuck out his hand and waited.

I did *not* expect that.

Logan smacked Declan's hand away.

Yep, totally expected that.

Declan blew out a breath and leaned against the doorframe. "Where and when?"

"Pack grounds. Full moon. And since I had to track you down, you'll join our hunt instead of meeting me in my office. You think you can handle that?" Logan sneered.

Declan's expression was priceless, like he was dealing with a toddler having a tantrum. "I'm sure I'll be fine. Thanks for your concern, though."

I had to bite my lip not to laugh. Laughing at a pissed-off Alpha was a good way to lose a hand.

"We'll see what happens when you're on pack lands and whether or not I let you stick around." When Logan grinned, for just a moment, his teeth seemed too long, too sharp, but it could have been a trick of the light.

And then his eyes were back on me and all the aggression was gone. "You Corey girls sure do have the biggest, prettiest blue eyes."

"Green," I corrected.

"Right. So, I've been meaning to ask you, there's a new Mexican restaurant in town I'd like to take you to. What do you say?"

"Well, I'll have to think about that, won't I?"

"You do just that. And I'll see you again real soon." With a warm grin, he sauntered off.

I stuffed my hands in my overall pockets. Logan had been doing his damnedest to seduce me since I was fifteen. When I turned back to Declan to discuss railings, though, he wasn't watching the threatening Alpha leaving. He was watching me.

BEWICCHED: THE SEA WICCHE CHRONICLES IS OUT NOW!

What else has Seana written? Well, I'll tell you...

The Slaughtered Lamb Bookstore & Bar
Sam Quinn, Book 1

Welcome to The Slaughtered Lamb Bookstore and Bar. I'm Sam Quinn, the werewolf book nerd in charge. I run my business by one simple rule: Everyone needs a good book and a stiff drink, be they vampire, wicche, demon, or fae. No wolves, though. Ever. I have my reasons.

I serve the supernatural community of San Francisco. We've been having some problems lately. Okay, I'm the one with the problems. The broken body of a female werewolf washed up on my doorstep. What makes sweat pool at the base of my spine, though, is realizing the scars she bears are identical to the ones I conceal. After hiding for years, I've been found.

A protection I've been relying on is gone. While my wolf traits are strengthening steadily, the loss also left my mind vulnerable to attack. Someone is ensnaring me in horrifying visions intended to kill. Clive, the sexy vampire Master of the City, has figured out how to pull me out, designating himself my personal bodyguard.

He's grumpy about it, but that kiss is telling a different story. A change is taking place. It has to. The bookish bartender must become the fledgling badass.

I'm a survivor. I'll fight fang and claw to protect myself and the ones I love. And let's face it, they have it coming.

The Dead Don't Drink at Lafitte's
Sam Quinn, Book 2

I'm Sam Quinn, the werewolf book nerd owner of the Slaughtered Lamb Bookstore and Bar. Things have been busy lately. While the near-constant attempts on my life have ceased, I now have a vampire gentleman caller. I've been living with Clive and the rest of his vampires for a few weeks while the Slaughtered Lamb is being rebuilt. It's going about as well as you'd expect.

My mother was a wicche and long dormant abilities are starting to make themselves known. If I'd had a choice, necromancy wouldn't have been my top pick, but it's coming in handy. A ghost warns me someone is coming to kill Clive. When I rush back to the nocturne, I find vamps from New Orleans readying an attack. One of the benefits of vampires looking down on werewolves is no one expects much of me. They don't expect it right up until I take their heads.

Now, Clive and I are setting out for New Orleans to take the fight back to the source. Vampires are masters of the long game. Revenge plots are often decades, if not centuries, in the making. We came expecting one enemy but quickly learn we have darker forces scheming against us. Good thing I'm the secret weapon they never see coming.

The Wicche Glass Tavern
Sam Quinn, Book 3

I'm Sam Quinn, the werewolf book nerd owner of the Slaughtered Lamb Bookstore and Bar. Clive, my vampire gentleman caller, has asked me to marry him. His nocturne is less than celebratory. Unfortunately, for them and the sexy vamp doing her best to seduce him, his cold, dead heart beats only for me.

As much as my love life feels like a minefield, it has to take a backseat to a far more pressing problem. The time has come. I need to deal with my aunt, the woman who's been trying to kill me for as long as I can remember. She's learned a new trick. She's figured out how to weaponize my friends against me. To have any hope of surviving, I have to learn to use my necromantic gifts. I need a teacher. We find one hiding among the fae, which is a completely different problem. I need to determine what I'm capable of in a hurry because my aunt doesn't care how many are hurt or killed as long as she gets what she wants. Sadly for me, what she wants is my name on a headstone.

I'm gathering my friends—werewolves, vampires, wicches, gorgons, a Fury, a half-demon, an elf, and a couple of dragon shifters—into a kind of Fellowship of the Sam. It's going to be one hell of a battle. Hopefully, San Francisco will still be standing when the dust clears.

The Hob & Hound Pub
Sam Quinn, Book 4

I'm Sam Quinn, the newly married werewolf book nerd owner of the Slaughtered Lamb Bookstore and Bar. Clive and I are on our honeymoon. Paris is lovely, though the mummy in the Louvre inching toward me is a bit off-putting. Although Clive doesn't sense anything, I can't shake the feeling I'm being watched.

Even after we cross the English Channel to begin our search for Aldith—the woman who's been plotting against Clive since the beginning—the prickling unease persists. Clive and I are separated, rather forcefully, and I'm left to find my way alone in a foreign country, evading not only Aldith's large web of hench-vamps, but vicious fae creatures disloyal to their queen. Gloriana says there's a poison in the human realm that's seeping into Faerie, and I may have found the source.

I knew this was going to be a working vacation, but battling vampires on one front and the fae on another is a lot, especially in a country steeped in magic. As a side note, I need to get word to Benvair. I think I've found the dragon she's looking for.

Gloriana is threatening to set her warriors against the human realm, but I may have a way to placate her. Aldith is a different story. There's no reasoning with rabid vengeance. She'll need to be put out of our misery permanently if Clive and I have any hope of a long, happy life together. Heck, I'd settle for a few quiet weeks.

Biergarten of the Damned
Sam Quinn, Book 5

I'm Sam, the werewolf book nerd owner of The Slaughtered Lamb Bookstore & Bar. I've always thought of Dave, my red-skinned, shark-eyed, half-demon cook, as a kind of foul-mouthed uncle, one occasionally given to bouts of uncontrolled anger.

Something's going on, though. He's acting strangely, hiding things. When I asked what was wrong, he blew me off and told me to quit bugging him. That's normal enough. What's not is his missing work. Ever. Other demons are appearing in the bar, looking for him. I'm getting worried, and his banshee girlfriend Maggie isn't answering my calls.

Demons terrify me. I do NOT want to go into any demon bars looking for Dave, but he's my family, sort of. I need to try to help, whether he wants me to or not. When I finally learn the truth, though... I'm not sure I can ever look at him again, let alone have him work for me. Are there limits to forgiveness? I think there might be.

The Viper's Nest Roadhouse & Café
Sam Quinn, Book 6

I'm Sam, the werewolf book nerd owner of The Slaughtered Lamb Bookstore & Bar. Clive, Fergus, and I are moving into our new home, the business is going well, and our folly is taking shape. The problem? Clive's maker Garyn is coming to San Francisco for a visit, and this reunion has been a thousand years in the making. Back then, Garyn was rather put out when Clive accepted the dark kiss and then took off to avenge his sister's murder. She was looking for a new family. He was looking for lethal skills. And so, Garyn has had plenty of time to align her forces. When her allies begin stepping out of the shadows, Clive's foundation will be shaken.

Stheno and her sisters are adding to their rather impressive portfolio of businesses around the world by acquiring The Viper's Nest Roadhouse & Café. Medusa found the place when she was visiting San Francisco. A dive bar filled with hot tattooed bikers? Yes, please!

Clive and I will need neutral territory for our meeting with Garyn, and a biker bar (& café, Stheno insisted) should fit the bill. I'd assumed my necromancy would give us an advantage. I hadn't anticipated, though, just how powerful Garyn and her allies were. When the fangs descend and the heads start rolling, it's going to take every friend we have and a nocturne full of vamps at our backs to even the playing field. Wish us luck. We're going to need it.

The Bloody Ruin Asylum & Taproom
  Sam Quinn, Book 7

I'm Sam, the werewolf book nerd owner of The Slaughtered Lamb Bookstore & Bar. My husband, Master vampire Clive, has been asked to go to Budapest to interview for a position in the Guild, a council of thirteen vampires who ~~rule and~~ advise the world's Masters. The competition for the recently vacated spot is fierce. I worry about Clive, as it quickly becomes apparent that the last person to hold the position didn't leave voluntarily.

Ever the supportive wife, I'm tagging along. I researched Budapest and had a long itinerary of things to do. That is, I did. When we arrive, we find out that the Guild headquarters is in the ruins of an abandoned insane asylum. Awesome. If there's one thing I love, it's being hounded by mentally unstable Hungarian ghosts.

Let's just say this isn't the romantic getaway I'd been hoping for. With Clive in top secret meetings and a bunch of creepy Renfields skulking around corners, nowhere is safe. I want to help Clive because I know he really wants the job, but the other Guild members are ancient and scary powerful. Between you and me, I thought Vlad would be taller.

Wish us luck! We're going to need it.

Bewicched: The Sea Wicche Chronicles
Sea Wicche, Book 1

We here at The Sea Wicche cater to your art-collecting, muffin-eating, tea-drinking, and potion-peddling needs. Palmistry and Tarot sessions are available upon request and by appointment. Our store hours vary and rely completely on Arwyn—the owner—getting her butt out of bed.

I'm Arwyn Cassandra Corey, the sea wicche, or the wicche who lives by the sea. It requires a lot more work than I'd anticipated to remodel an abandoned cannery and turn it into an art gallery & tea bar. It's coming along, though, especially with the help of a new werewolf who's joined the construction crew. He does beautiful work. His sexy, growly, bearded presence is very hard to ignore, but I'm trying. I'm not sure how such a laid-back guy got the local Alpha and his pack threatening to hunt him down and tear him apart, but we all have our secrets. And because I don't want to know his—or yours for that matter—I wear these gloves. Clairvoyance makes the simplest things the absolute worst. Trust me. Or don't. Totally up to you.

Did I mention my mother and grandmother are pressuring me to assume my rightful place on the Corey Council? That's a kind of governing triad for our ancient magical family, one that has more than its fair share of black magic practitioners. And yes, before you ask, people have killed to be on the council—one psychotic sorceress aunt stands out—but I have no interest in the power or politics that come with the position. I'd rather stick to my art and, in the words of my favorite sea wicche, help poor unfortunate souls. (Good luck trying to get that song out of your head now)

Wicche Hunt: The Sea Wicche Chronicles
Sea Wicche, Book 2

I'm Arwyn Cassandra Corey, the Sea Wicche of Monterey. Want a psychic reading? Sure. I can do that. In the market for art? I have all your painting, photography, glass blowing, and ceramic needs covered in my newly remodeled art gallery by the sea. Need help solving a grisly cold case? Unfortunately, I can probably help with that too.

After more than a decade of being nagged, guilted, and threatened, I've finally joined the Corey Council and am working with my mother and grandmother to hunt down a twisted sorcerer. We know who she is. Now we need to find and stop her before more are murdered.

The evil the sorcerer and her demon are doing is seeping into the community. Violent crimes have been increasing and as a result Detectives Hernández and Osso have brought me another horrifying case. I'll do what I can, because of course I will. What are a few more nightmares to a woman who barely sleeps?

Declan Quinn, the wicked hot werewolf rebuilding my deck, is preparing for a dominance battle with the local Alpha. A couple of wolves have already left their pack to follow Declan, recognizing him as the true Alpha. Declan needs to watch his back as the full moon approaches. The current Alpha will do whatever it takes to hold on to power, including breaking pack law and enlisting the help of a local vampire.

And if Wilbur, my selkie friend is right, I might just be meeting my dad soon. Perhaps he'll have some advice for this wicche hunt. I'm going to need all the help I can get.

About Seana Kelly

Seana Kelly lives in the San Francisco Bay Area with her husband, two daughters, two dogs, and one fish. She recently retired from her career as a high school teacher-librarian to pursue her lifelong dream of writing full-time. She's an avid reader and re-reader who misses her favorite characters when it's been too long between visits.

She's a *USA Today* bestselling author and a two-time Golden Heart® Award finalist. She is represented by the delightful and effervescent Sarah E. Younger of the Nancy Yost Literary Agency.

You can follow Seana on Twitter/X for tweets about books and dogs or on Instagram for beautiful pictures of books and dogs (kidding). She also loves collecting photos of characters and settings for the books she writes. As she's a huge reader of young adult and adult books, expect lots of recommendations as well.

Website: www.seanakelly.com

Newsletter: https://geni.us/t0Y5cBA

X x.com/SeanaKellyRW

instagram.com/seanakellyrw

facebook.com/Seana-Kelly-1553527948245885

bookbub.com/authors/seana-kelly

pinterest.com/seanakelly326